(Pronounced "way-CHU-gay")

A Novel

Gregg Bartley

Dedicated to the Original Peoples of North

America. They deserved much better.

There are many different events in a person's life that are liable to bend and twist that person into someone else, somebody different from what he would have been otherwise. It might be something as trivial as getting a flat tire on a rainy night, which at first glance might seem to be notable only in the amount of discomfort the experience inflicts. However, under just the right circumstances, that same event might result in being rescued by a pretty girl who'll eventually become his wife. Bingo, there's a life-changing event, all gift-wrapped for you, and you had absolutely no idea it was coming. Another example might be as soul shattering as being a Petty Officer 3rd Class aboard the *U.S.S. West Virginia* moored in Pearl Harbor at exactly the wrong time in that majestic ship's life: December 7th, 1941.

It is a truism that the type of events I am referring to never occur in a vacuum. One life-altering event invariably sends the recipient down an entirely new path, one which would have not existed except for the first event. That is the meaning of "life-altering," after all. Given that, I suppose one's entire life can be viewed as a continuous chain of life altering events, each one of them affecting the next and then the next, on and on, at which point my analogy breaks down completely. The point I am trying to make and doing a piss-poor job of it is, if I hadn't been an unwilling participant in the Japanese sneak attack on the U.S. Pacific Fleet at Pearl Harbor, none of the rest of what I am about to relate would have happened.

Even from my retrospective perch of old age, I am still not certain how to talk about what happened in those three months I spent in the Cascade Mountains of Washington. Much of it remains an enigma to me. Age and illness have made my memories of those events even more suspect.

The one thing I *did* discover, and I have no other way to say this, is there is no such thing as "absolute reality." All people bring with them their own unique life experiences, and those experiences are going to influence how those events get interpreted. That is what is stored into a person's memory, his *interpretation* of an event — not an absolute recording of the event itself. It follows, then, when two people have very different life experiences, they will likely not interpret an event — especially a very unusual or frightening event — in the same way. For instance, a deeply religious person may understand an unusual event as a sign of Divine Providence: God's intervention in the physical world. A person who is not particularly religious, on the other hand, will interpret that same event as just something fairly uncommon and put it down as coincidence to have experienced it. Their different understandings of the same event were assembled from their personal experiences, their own "realities." This clash of differing realities can often lead to increased stress due to an inability to satisfactorily resolve the conflict, and stress has been known to do some mighty strange things to a person's head. People operating under stress for extended periods of time, just to state one example, might start seeing things that aren't actually there.

This, along with my increasingly suspect memory, is why I cannot categorically say that my narrative reflects "what happened." This story, by definition, includes my own interpretation of those events.

But I have gotten sidetracked by my need to explain myself. I should return to the first link in the chain of life-altering events, the Japanese attack of the U.S. Pacific Fleet at Pearl Harbor.

Looking back, I now realize that I was one of the lucky ones. I happened to be topside at the beginning of the attack and was able to make my escape into the burning water as the Japanese torpedoes and bombs made staying aboard a death wish. My physical recovery, once the doctors in charge of my case decided that a recovery would indeed occur, was a protracted and very painful seven months spent being shuffled around a number of hospitals that mostly looked and smelled exactly the same such that I am no longer able to distinguish which memory belongs to which hospital. The last of these wards for the critically injured was the U.S. Naval Hospital in Oakland, California. My recovery — such as it was — left me with several areas of thick scar tissue of mottled scarlet and pink skin that to this day looks like it has been melted and then congealed. The largest of these run from my right calf up past my hip and then another one that goes around my shoulder area, up the side of my neck and terminates around my right ear. These were more than just cosmetic injuries, as my right leg and wrist are still only partially functional.

All those days, weeks and months blurring into each other left me unable to discern not only where I was but also when I was. By the skill of the doctors involved and whatever Devine Providence that I have doggedly refused to believe in, I emerged alive and able to walk — slowly at first — without a cane, which is more than I could say for tens of thousands of other men that continued to fight in the huge conflagration that was in the process of engulfing the globe.

Needless to say, there wasn't any question of being able to rejoin my crew. I was given a Purple Heart, a Medical Discharge, some back pay and a small pension going forward. With that, as soon as it was feasible, I was summarily released back into the 'real world.' In addition to the pay I was due, I had a little cash of my own sitting in my bank account back home. Not much — it would last me a few months if I was careful about it — but it seemed obvious to me that I was going to need a source of income sometime in the near future.

During my time convalescing in various military hospitals, I had a lot of time to think about what I was eventually going to do with myself. I knew that I was never going back to the little town of Kalama in Cowlitz County, Washington. Even in the best of times, there weren't many jobs to be had in a town of just a tad over a thousand people. Besides, I truly despised the town of my birth. As an old railroad and logging outpost sitting on the north bank of the Columbia River, I suppose it was the same as a lot of other small towns in the area. It's just that I had too many very bad memories associated with that particular place. Too many ghosts of the past lived there. I doubted I could ever feel at peace.

My mother was deceased and the old man, a big burly alcoholic Irishman with red hair and a mean streak that flared up whenever he had been drinking, managed to kill himself a couple of months before I joined up with the Navy. He craved his booze too much to give it up even when he was on the job in one of the town's remaining sawmills. Working around sharp blades moving at a high rate of speed is a lethal combination for the inattentive or inebriated. He bled to death rather unceremoniously on the shop floor before any medical help could even be called, not that it would have gotten there in time anyway. He was the primary reason I sold the house and joined the Navy as soon as I hit eighteen. Yeah, he was dead but I couldn't stay there in the family house where my mother had died and my father had taken out his drunken rage on his family. Angry drunks usually have a lot of grievances stored up that they like to take out on their families, usually in the dead of night when I was fast asleep and not able to fend off a surprise beating because of some imagined insult to his 'honor.' Or maybe he just felt like beating the crap out of someone and he found me a handy victim, helplessly lying there in the next room. There's nothing like being cold-cocked at three in the morning.

My mom had escaped his wrath some months earlier, but only after suffering a slow, agonizing death from cancer. Once she received her diagnosis, it appeared that she had just given up on living. Her life with her husband was certainly no bed of roses even when he wasn't potted to the gills. Her job at a local restaurant wore her down, and when she came home it was only to more work and an angry drunk. She wouldn't go to any of the large hospitals in places like Portland or Seattle. 'God's will' or something, I don't know. Like I said, I am not a believer so I couldn't tell you what kind of thought process she might have come up with where the Creator of the Universe purposely gave her a deadly disease that almost always results in a protracted and humiliating death. At least she didn't have to put up with Dad's abuse after that.

After his accident, there was the question of what I should do with our house in town. I didn't want it. I contacted old Alan Simms, one of Kalama's only real estate agents, and told him to put the house up, as is, for whatever money he could get for it, which wasn't going to be much. When it sold, I had enough to pay off the family's debts and stick the remainder in the bank downtown. I was then out the door as fast as I could manage, off to see the world courtesy of the United States Navy. After some basic training, I found myself in Newport, Rhode Island and then, after two years there, in Honolulu, Hawaii at the Pearl Harbor Naval Shipyard. And we all know what happened there.

This was the situation I found myself in the spring of 1944, a 23-year-old kid with a mediocre high school education, very little in the way of resources and some major physical and emotional handicaps that would do little to convince any employers of my potential. However, after the initial shock of the attack on Pearl and America's entry into the war in both the Pacific and Europe, suddenly there were many openings in companies that would soon begin the deadly serious work of supplying armaments to the U.S. military. I had an elderly aunt, Dad's only sister, who lived near Greenlake just north of Seattle. Seattle had Boeing, and Boeing made airplanes for America. America needed airplanes to drop bombs on Germany. Making airplanes required workers, a lot of them.

I hadn't talked with Aunt Irene very many times in my life, maybe three or four times when she came down to Kalama to visit us. However, considering I was all that remained of that branch of her family tree, I thought that perhaps she would have a spare room I could use while I searched for a job in Seattle, starting with Boeing. My thinking was that they must have a job for a wounded veteran where the compassion and patriotism should be running high. That was my plan that resulted in me jotting off a quick telegram to her one afternoon and then hopping a train north to Seattle the next morning.

* * * *

Aunt Irene was the elder sister of my father. Irene's appearance could modestly be described as 'matronly.' Many years later, I realized she bore a passing resemblance to Aunt Bea on *The Andy Griffith Show*. Her Irish disposition, however, was more in line with my father's. She could cuss a blue streak if the mood struck her. That might have been one reason she never married. She likely put off most of her potential suitors after giving them a sample of her sharp tongue and acerbic wit. "I just speak my mind, plain and simple," I remembered her saying on more than one occasion.

Irene knew I had been injured at Pearl and had been discharged. I told her as much in my telegram. I took it as a small blessing when a man wears normal clothing, almost his entire body is covered. Dressed in a long sleeved shirt, my only visible scars were on the back of my right hand and on the right side of my neck and my ear. When Aunt Irene opened the door of her small house to greet me, I could see her gaze immediately fasten on my right ear. I thought I caught a small shiver of disgust, but I suppose that could have just been my imagination.

After I tossed my suitcase and small valise onto the bed in her spare room, we settled down in her parlor for 'a little talk.' I made it plain to her I had no desire to force myself on her any more than necessary. She had her life, her bridge club with 'the girls' and her pleasant Sunday mornings after church having a civilized tea. She let me know, in her direct Irish manner, I could use her spare bedroom until I got myself set up with a job and a place of my own. Not directly stated but definitely inferred was that such would be the extent of her support of a family member she barely knew, and the sooner that happened, the better it would be for the both of us.

The next morning, I made my way down to the offices at the big Boeing factory about twelve miles south of Seattle. At that point, American industry was still in the process of changing over to wartime production. Boeing had been producing the heavy B-17 bomber for several years prior, but after war had been declared all the way around, production was going to have to ramp up very quickly. There were definitely some employment opportunities, as many of the men who had been employed had quit to join up and go fight the Krauts and the Japs, and Rosie the Riveter had yet to become a major force in the wartime industrial effort.

I assured the man behind the desk in the personnel office that, other than not being able to kneel or bend over without some effort, I was perfectly capable of helping them in their effort to win the war and couldn't they help out a wounded veteran? Given my experience with mechanical and electrical components in the Navy, their answer was a qualified 'yes.' I was given a job on the production line installing aircraft components of all types. The shift started at 7:30 a.m., making it difficult for me to get from Greenlake, north of Seattle, to the Boeing plant south of the city. Extra buses had been put on well-traveled routes in order to accommodate all the new workers streaming into town, but that still meant I was getting up at around 5:30 in the morning to make it to work on time. I was able to gradually wake up while on the bus, but I was usually still bleary-eyed and dog-tired by the time I punched in.

The job itself wasn't bad. Everyone was working for a cause as well as a paycheck. The fact there was any work at all after the Depression was a real cause for celebration for most of the people working there. I met several people that had been out of work for several years. The general attitude around the plant seemed positive and energetic.

The work was tougher than what I had become used to in the Navy, but that was in Hawaii during peacetime. I certainly wasn't going to complain. After months of inactivity lying in hospital beds interspersed with painful sessions of physical rehabilitation, I began to feel alive again for the first time since that horrible day. I was making money and, if things kept going the way they were, I was going to be able to have enough cash to establish myself somewhere and remove myself out from under any aunt's ever-watchful eyes.

I should have known this wasn't going to last. Life rarely deals out consecutive winning hands to any one person and certainly not to me. I had become accustomed to catching the raw end of the stick throughout most of my life. Still, when my manager called me into his office one day during morning break, it took me by surprise. I wiped my dirty hands on the greasy rag I kept in the back pocket and followed him to his little office squirreled away underneath some metal walkways.

When we were seated, he looked down at his desk and shuffled some papers. He looked distinctly uncomfortable.

"So, Sean. How's it going out there? You doing okay?"

I was instantly on my guard. Busy managers rarely call busy workers away from their position just to ask how things are going. There was more to come and he would likely get to the point very quickly.

"Yeah, it's... It's going good. Really good. I'm glad I am able to be able to contribute to the war effort after, you know..." I held up the back of my right hand, just in case it had slipped his mind that I was a veteran and had spent months in the hospital after the sneak attack on Pearl.

"Good. That's really good, Sean." He was using my name too many times. My suspicion jumped up a couple more notches. "I, uh, I noticed you punched in late this morning. Can you tell me about that?"

"Oh, that!" I felt a little surge of relief. "Well, the bus was late again. You know how those things go." I shrugged my shoulders in a way that I hoped conveyed my resignation at being at the mercy of things that were totally out of my control.

"Yes, I suppose so. I thought that I had read somewhere that the bus company was doing a very good job at keeping the buses on schedule." He looked down at his desk and shuffled the papers again. He was an officious little man with a bald area on the top of his head that he tried to cover up with the little hair he had remaining. I got the distinct impression he didn't want to be here any more than I did. "This isn't the first time you have been late. You were late three times last week. Maybe you ought to try to catch an earlier bus if the one you are taking now keeps getting here late. We really are trying to run a tight ship here, Sean." There was my name again. I didn't like when people kept calling me by my name in situations that really didn't seem to require it. "Our production schedules are going to go through the roof here in the next few weeks and we really can't have people who don't pull their weight. It's not fair to the rest of the team and could really jeopardize our production here. You have a responsibility to the company and to the people who work here." He coughed and looked up at me expectantly.

He sounded a lot like my Ensign back on the *West Virginia*, who had a talent with vague catchwords like 'teamwork' and 'responsibility' which he deployed when he felt like bashing sailors he didn't think were doing their jobs. I tried to keep the annoyance out of my voice. "Yes, sir. I realize that. I agree with you. It won't happen again. Sir."

I hoped he was done. He had fulfilled his duty by handing me a reprimand and I had done my duty by accepting it with a promise to do better. But he shuffled his papers again and cleared his throat.

"That's good, that's good. There's one other thing that I need to bring up, Sean. It seems that, uh, several of your co-workers have reported that you have come back to your place on the line after lunch smelling like liquor. You aren't drinking on the job, are you? Because that is one thing that we absolutely cannot tolerate here, drinking. You understand that, don't you?"

I became aware of a tinge of red around the periphery of my vision. I clamped my jaw shut before anything could escape. My co-workers were running to the boss and telling on me? *What is this, elementary school?* My inner voice raged. *Running to the teachers, telling on people?*

"Sir. I do not know anything about that. Whoever said that must be mistaken. Me and my buddies in the Navy, we would go have a few after hours when we weren't on duty, but I have not had a single drink since I have gotten out of the hospital. Sir." Without realizing it, I had shifted back to my military persona during his questioning, squaring my shoulders and gazing rigidly ahead somewhere over and behind the officer's right shoulder. I knew my last statement regarding 'a single drink' was correct only in a very literal sense. It would not stand up to further questioning. I fervently hoped that he wouldn't pursue the subject.

"Right. Right. They must have been mistaken. But look here, Sean. You need to consider a few things. You are here to help the company do a very important job. You should know this better than anyone." He nodded his head toward the area of my right arm. "If you can't do the job, we need to find someone who will. You can see that, can't you?" I noticed beads of sweat forming along the brow of his florid face.

"Yes, sir. I can see that." I took in his obvious discomfort with a small measure of satisfaction. "If that is all, may I go now? Break time is over and I would like to get back to my post."

"Ah, yes. Yes. You may go. Just remember what I said, Sean. Responsibility!" He seemed relieved that I was leaving his office. "I'm glad we had this talk."

I resisted the urge to slam his door on my way out and stormed back to my place on the production line, underneath one of the big bomber's huge wings. *Look, everyone has got to have some relief!* I thought angrily to myself. *Seven months flat on my back in the hospital recovering from second degree burns after watching my buddies on my ship die in the explosions and fire and those that survived ended up trapped under the waterline after the ship went down is enough to drive anyone buggy!* I was also experiencing vivid, nasty nightmares almost every night that would jerk me awake in a panic. It was usually over an hour before I could calm myself enough where I was able get back to sleep. Sometimes, five-thirty rolled around before any further sleep did. Having a drink now and then seemed like a perfectly reasonable reaction to my situation.

I kicked at one of the fat tires of the plane's landing gear. "Dammit!" I said to no one in particular.

A lean, unshaven face poked out of the open hatch in the bottom of the fuselage. I seemed to remember the guy's name was Darnold or something stupid like that. "Something the matter, Sean? Did'jer girlfriend say 'no' again last night?" I heard him snigger loudly as he pulled himself back inside the belly of the airplane.

"Screw you, jerkoff," I muttered to myself. He was probably one of the ones that took extreme pleasure in ratting out others to the boss. There wasn't any use in giving him any more reasons to indulge himself. I yanked my tool belt around my waist and grabbed my clipboard of paperwork before heading back up to electrical panel behind the cockpit.

*   *   *   *

As it turned out, that was my last full week of work working on airplanes. It was obvious to me that my manager, along with several of my co-workers, really had it in for me regardless of any question of guilt or innocence. I was let go the following Wednesday. What made it all worse — although getting fired from a good job is never very good to begin with — is that the immediate circumstances weren't anything I could have fixed. The bus I had boarded that morning overheated after being stuck in traffic thanks to an accident on the Aurora Bridge, one of the few ways of getting across the canal that separates the city of Seattle from the suburbs to the north. The bus company took their time in sending a replacement bus to rescue the stuck passengers and get us on our way. I was over an hour late getting to work. By that time, it was too late. My manager accused me of 'taking advantage of his good will' and showing 'complete and utter disrespect toward him and my responsibility,' on and on. He had a good head of steam built up at that point, so any attempt at an explanation I tried to give wasn't going to cool his tirade. Even worse, instead of calling me into his office as he had done the previous week, he confronted me right there at my workstation underneath the big bomber's wings. With my erstwhile co-workers standing in a semi-circle around the two of us, I could feel my face grow hot while my boss waved his handful of paper in my face. My humiliation grew as I saw the smirks and grins on the spectator's faces. They were obviously enjoying the show at my expense. I would have shoved the little twerp aside and stalked out except for the fact I had to go to the payroll office to sign some papers and collect my pay. There, I was made to turn in my security badge and was escorted off the premises.

As I waited outside the high fence topped with barbed wire for the next bus heading north, I seethed about the injustice of being let go. Me, a veteran injured in the line of duty, fired. It wasn't until I was actually on the bus that I wondered what I was going to do now and how I was going to tell my aunt.

*   *   *   *

As it turned out, I didn't have a lot of time to consider my future, immediate or otherwise. As I made my way up the steps of my aunt's house, I saw her face poke out from behind the white lace curtains. When I entered, Irene was standing there, hands on her hips, waiting on me.

"Sean, why are you home?" She looked over at the cuckoo clock hanging on the wall. I hated that damn clock. The incessant 'TICK-TOCK' sound it made was audible through the entire house. It drove me a bit nuts. "It's only noon. Are you sick?" Her expression made it clear to me that she did not consider this a reasonable explanation.

"Hi, Aunt Irene. No. I'm not sick. I... I was fired. Look, it..."

She didn't get me an opportunity to explain. "Fired? FIRED? Sean Gallagher, you look at me! What did you to get yourself fired? You tell me right now!" Her eyes were like knives.

11

"Look, it wasn't my fault, really! There was an accident on the bridge and the bus overheated! I was an hour late, but my boss didn't give me a chance to explain! He never liked me anyway. He was just looking for an excuse to get rid of me. I..."

Again, she interrupted. "He fired you just because you were late one time? I seriously doubt that, Sean. It didn't have anything to do with your drinking, did it?"

I always found it uncanny how people are sometimes able to hit just the exact spot that you would rather not have to talk about. "What? No! Of course not! Yes, I admit that I was late a few other times..."

"And how many 'other times' was that, Sean? How many? No, don't tell me. And don't tell me that it wasn't about your drinking. I know you keep a bottle in your room and that you sometimes come in at night smelling like a distillery! Don't tell *me* it wasn't about drinking! You're just like your father! He was a drunk and that's where you are heading if you don't change your ways!"

I stood there, helpless in the face of her blazing anger. I had no idea that she knew about Dad. She might have talked with my mother on the few occasions when Irene came down to Kalama to visit. It was apparent that she was not going to let me say much of anything in my defense.

"Here's the facts, Sean. I didn't mind you staying in my home until you got yourself set up. It's the least thing I could do, seeing as you're family and a war veteran. But I don't have a lot of patience with drunks. I'll give you just one week, you understand? One week! And if you aren't sober and have a good job, you are out of my house. You have disrupted my life enough as it is! I don't owe you anything more!"

With that, I watched her grab her coat and stormed out the front door. I sighed to myself as I threw myself into the overstuffed lounging chair. I imagined that there could be no one in the world with worse luck than I had. Bad luck seemed to be woven into my genes. *One week,* I thought miserably to myself. *That's not very long! What the hell am I going to do now?*

I leaned as far back in the lounger as I could and closed my eyes in order to more completely wallow in my misery. It felt as if the entire world — which included the Japanese Empire with their torpedo bombers — was conspiring against me. I could physically feel the clacking noise from the clock penetrate my skull like a sledgehammer. When I finally opened my eyes, I looked around the room where I focused on the morning's newspaper lying in sections on the round table next to my chair. With very little enthusiasm, I rummaged around the paper until I came to the *Help Wanted* section. My expectations were less than zero at that point, but it was obvious I needed to start somewhere.

2

The train from downtown Seattle to Skykomish took over three hours. I was barely aware of the magnificent scenery as the train rushed northward along the eastern shore of Puget Sound and then turned east to head toward the Cascade Mountains. I was still upset about the scene in Aunt Irene's living room. I was also very depressed about losing my job. With time to reflect on the situation, I had to admit that a lot of the blame had to land squarely on my shoulders.

I realized I could have found work around Seattle somewhere, but I didn't fancy slaving away behind a lunch counter or sweeping out someone's store as the night janitor. After the humiliation dealt out by my manager, surrounded by the leering faces of the line workers, coupled with the crushing judgment dealt out by my only living family member, I decided that I had my fill of Seattle. I needed to get out. I was not a city boy, in any case, and did not care to become one. However, returning to Kalama was out of the question.

I held up the folded newspaper that I had in my lap to view the "Help Wanted" ad that I had circled in red and read it for the twentieth time.

> HANDYMAN/GARDENER WANTED:
> Full time work on small farm outside town limits of Skykomish. Room and board supplied. Seven days a week. Able to do all types of tasks, including drive an auto. Apply Martha Cahill residence.

I had never heard of Skykomish before this. I had to get a state map to find out that it was on the way to the summit of the Cascade Mountains over Stevens Pass. It looked to be a very small place, much smaller than Kalama, which is saying something. However, it did have the advantage of being on the rail line of the Great

Northern, so getting there — aside from the length of the ride and the unforgiving lack of padding in the coach cushions — wasn't going to be a problem.

It seemed to me a full-time, live-in job up in the mountains of the Cascades would be a godsend. After seven months recovering in the hospital and the embarrassment of the last week, all I wanted to do was to get away from people. I had my fill of judgmental people with their snide remarks and accusing looks. In my heated and confused state of mind, I had forgotten one very large truth that should have been self-evident — but for some reason wasn't. No matter where you go, you can't hide from yourself. Running away accomplishes very little except for a chance of scenery.

As the train slowed on its approach into Skykomish, I could see that the town itself was indeed very small, oriented parallel to the rail line. The main street was dominated by the large, cube-shaped structure of the Skykomish Hotel. As we lurched to a final stop, I grabbed my suitcase and valise from the overhead rack and made my way into the town that I hoped would become my new home.

The hotel was just across the tracks from the small train station. While I was checking in, the clerk launched into what I took to be his normal spiel for tourists. The hotel was purported to be haunted, of course. Back in the 1920s, a hooker was murdered by a jealous boyfriend or something to that effect. Her ghost went by the moniker of the Blue Lady. After handing over several dollars, I told the clerk that I looked forward to seeing her. On my way out of the lobby, I stopped to scan several framed, yellowing newspaper pages that hung on the wall. They turned out to be stories about the hotel. They described in breathless language that, in its heyday, the hotel had hosted such luminaries as Teddy Roosevelt and Clark Gable. I wondered idly if Gable had run into the Blue Lady and what he might have said to her.

After a quick clean-up in my room, I ventured back to the front desk for directions. The day was getting late already, around one o'clock, and it was going to be a walk of several miles to Mrs. Cahill's farm. I didn't expect I would be able to whistle up a taxi in this backwater burg. If I didn't get the job, I was hoping Mrs. Cahill would find room in her heart to at least give me a ride back into town.

The dirt road to her farm turned off the main highway a few hundred feet above the town. As I walked, I began to really take notice of my surroundings. It was nothing short of spectacular. Huge granite mountains dominated the vistas. Towering trees, mostly Douglas firs and pine, with some cedar and hemlock throw in for variety, loomed over me. 'Scenery' suddenly became a completely inadequate description. In its place, the word 'grandeur' snuck its way into my thoughts. Hawaii certainly had been magnificent, although in a much different way than what I was now experiencing. Besides, all my memories of Hawaii were now contaminated with razor sharp images of burning ships, exploding torpedoes, falling bombs and sailors trying to escape what had become a flaming hell. I didn't want to think about Hawaii anymore. This was majestic stuff. I had never really seen anything like this, even back home in Cowlitz County.

As I walked, I felt as if a weight were being lifted from my shoulders. The air was clean and smelled of trees and running water. I begin to actually look forward to living out in the mountains and truly experiencing nature, rather than just hiding out in it. I began to believe that this might work out after all. However, I knew that much would depend on the reception I would get from Mrs. Cahill. My conversation with the desk clerk at the hotel had boosted my spirits in regard to getting the job. He confirmed to me that she had been looking for someone for the last six months and that the job, as far as he knew, was still open. There weren't a lot of people interested in working at an old house several miles from town. The only people living there were Mrs. Cahill, a widow from the time of the Great War — soon to become known as The First World War — and her live-in Indian maid who came into town once a week for their supplies. She apparently always paid in cash, although where the money came from, he was could not say. There were rumors of the Cahill family owning some oil wells back in the 1930s in Oklahoma, but given the notorious unreliability of whispered rumors in small towns, he could not vouch for the veracity of that little tidbit of information.

Such were my thoughts as I hiked slowly up the road toward my destination. I slowly became aware that my right hip was beginning to pain me rather badly and that my limp was getting more and more pronounced as I went. Without warning, the reality of my injuries came rushing back to me. No one would knowingly laugh at a wounded veteran, of course, but the pitying looks and awkward questions that I had received during my time in Seattle burned in my stomach like a puddle of molten lead. It had hurt and I didn't want to experience it again. I realized I was very worried about the reception I was going to receive from my prospective employer. Would she recoil in disgust at the pink scar tissue visible on the side of my neck and ear? Would she believe that I could do the job after she found out that I had difficulty bending over and kneeling, simple actions that would no doubt play a major part of being a handyman and gardener? I began to get that familiar feeling in the gut. I hated pity. I hated being embarrassed. I hated being different.

As I got closer and closer to my destination, my discomfort grew into the cold certainty of the coming rejection and humiliation. What would I do then? I was without any immediate prospects and the pool of cash that I had on hand was getting smaller by the day. I couldn't stand too many more failures without somehow coming up with a steady paycheck. What was I going to do then? I couldn't face the prospect of taking the train back down the mountains to Seattle, but there weren't too many other ideas that presented themselves. To make matters worse, I was getting very hungry. Belatedly, I realized that I should have eaten something before I had set out from town. The only bright spot I could see in the entire coming debacle was if I couldn't beg a ride back into town, at least the walk was downhill.

After stumping along the uneven dirt road a few more minutes, I could make out the top of the house peeking over the treetops. *This must be the place,* I reasoned. There weren't likely to be many small, white, two-story houses with a porch swing on the covered porch out here in the mountains. To the right of the house was a small patch of furrowed ground that was obviously the garden I would be expected to tend. At first glance, I could see several rows of stunted corn plants and, in front of the corn, what looked to be potato, squash and zucchini plants. On the other side of the house was a small running creek, really not more than a brook. Looming over the house was a grand vista of several craggy mountains, their shadowy crevices still exhibiting traces of snow even though this was still August. A number of hens of various colors seemed to have free run of the front yard. I could see several eggs peeking out from underneath the overgrown bushes by the side of the stairs.

Other than the fact that it was the only one out in this hidden valley — which carried the less-than-imaginative name of Deer Valley — the house itself did nothing much to make an impression. It certainly wasn't as majestic as its surroundings. I later learned it had been built in 1890 by a businessman from back east somewhere who had aspirations of becoming a timber baron. His financial backing, however, didn't match the grandeur of his dreams. The house, like most houses built in those years outside city limits, appeared to be very small from the outside. The white paint on the siding looked like it had been peeling for the last few decades, probably since the widow's husband failed to return from Europe. The stairs leading up to the porch were dilapidated. All in all, it wasn't a scene that inspired visions of prosperity. I tried to remember my hopefulness regarding the clerk's story of Mrs. Cahill's payments in cash for her supplies and, reinforced by the scene that spread itself in front of me, the obvious need of some help.

Unless I just wanted to give up without trying and walk back down the mountain, there was nothing to do but go announce myself and the reason for my visit. As I made my way up the gravel walkway toward the stairs to the porch, I could hear loud barking from inside the house. Based on the volume and seeming ferocity of the barking, it sounded like a large dog, quite possibly a very large, very aggressive dog. At least I wasn't going to have to knock on the door and wait around, trying to decide if someone heard me or not. My presence had already been announced. As soon as I stepped onto the porch, the inside door opened to reveal a woman restraining a very animated German Shepherd by the collar. However, my attention was not on the dog.

Through the rickety screen door, I found myself speechlessly staring at Mrs. Cahill's maid. She was one of the most striking women I have ever seen. As the clerk at the hotel had said, she was obviously an Indian, given her cinnamon-colored skin and angular features. She was not a great beauty, but she was certainly very compelling to look at. She wore her jet-black hair in a long braid that hung down her back to her waist. She was wearing a white blouse and a light blue skirt that reached down to her ankles. A somewhat threadbare white apron was tied around her waist. Her brown moccasins were unadorned. Both hands were covered in what I took to be flour, which I took as a sign that I had obviously interrupted her baking something in the kitchen.

I stood there, transfixed, for several seconds without saying anything. She must have decided that she would be required to start the conversation; otherwise, the two of us might have stood there in a little tableau for the rest of the day.

"Yes, can I help you? Major! Down! Quiet!" The last part of this was obviously directed at the dog, who at least had the manners to cease his barking and his attempts at leaping through the screen door to get to me. I hadn't yet decided whether this was Major's way of showing his excitement at seeing a newcomer or represented a heartfelt urge to tear out my throat.

"Uh, yes. Hello. My name is Sean Gallagher. I am here about your advertisement in the Seattle newspaper for a gardener and handyman?" I held up my folded newspaper as evidence. "I hope the position is still open?" I was barely able to keep from stammering out of my concern regarding the potential hostility of the dog and from being totally flummoxed at the intensity of her gaze. "I certainly could use the job. Ma'am," I added to fill the bit of silence that occurred after my initial introduction. If I had a hat, I probably would have been wringing it in my hands at that point.

"Yes. The job is still available. We haven't had anyone interested in months. I told the Missus we should stop paying for that ad in Seattle. No one is going to come from the big city to come out here to work out here in the mountains. All the men are going off to the war." She stopped and examined me closely through the screen door. "Are you certain you are interested in this job? It is difficult work, especially in the winter." She seemed dubious — with a hint of hostility that was possibly just my imagination. However, she hadn't said anything about my scars yet, which was a hopeful sign.

"Oh, yes. You see, I was working down in Seattle when I... I quit because of some personal reasons, I suppose you would say. My boss didn't like me much. He was always on me for not doing the job in the way he thought it should be done." I thought I better get this out of the way immediately because everything else would be a waste of time if this turned out to be an issue. "You see, I was in the Navy, stationed at Pearl Harbor and was injured when my ship was hit. Torpedoed. I... Uh. I have some injuries that making moving my right leg and wrist a little difficult, and I am sure you have noticed this scar here. I think my boss didn't much care for me because of that. So, I decided to take my leave. I wanted to get out of the city. I have had my fill of people lately."

She gave a little snort at this. Whether she found this genuinely funny or from the irony of my declaration while standing in a clearing surrounded by a huge forest and looming mountains, I wasn't sure. "Yes, this would be the place to do that." She continued to gaze at me through the screen door. However, the hostility seemed to have dissipated. She didn't ask if I could do the work with the injuries that I had just described, which I thought a bit unusual given the circumstances.

I decided it was now my turn to restart the conversation. "Ma'am, do you think I could come in and talk with Mrs. Cahill about the job? And I would certainly like to sit down for a bit. That was quite a walk up from town."

She regarded me with some distrust. "The Missus is taking her nap. She usually takes her nap after lunch and she is not to be disturbed while she is napping."

That sounded final and not at all hopeful. This conversation was not going at all the way I had envisioned on my walk up from Skykomish. As yet, I hadn't actually been asked any questions about my qualifications. As a matter of fact, what the job would actually require hadn't been mentioned at all. However, she finally acquiesced as she had determined that I was going to stand on her porch until something happened. I wasn't likely to turn around and go away on my own. "Yes, please come in. You may sit in the kitchen. I am baking some bread. There are some leftovers from Missus' lunch, if you are hungry."

That was enough of an inducement all by itself. Once in the small entryway, I carefully skirted the dog. She still held Major firmly by the collar, although by this time he had apparently decided I was only of moderate interest rather than something inordinately dangerous that would attempt to harm his mistress. To the left was an open door into what looked to be the main living area. Directly in front of me was an unlit stairway to the second story, and to the right of the stairs was a hallway that led to the kitchen. I observed several places where the wallpaper was coming loose, the edges curling into small cones up near the ceiling. The dark wainscoting contributed to the gloom of the passageway.

The kitchen proved to be much brighter and more cheerful than the rest of the house. Bright sunlight filtered in through white lace curtains that hung in several small windows, the largest of which was in the door leading out to the back of the house. It was quite warm from her baking. It was altogether a domestic scene. After dishing up a plate of beans from the pot sitting on the oven, with several pieces of homemade bread on the side, she opened the iron door on the oven with a big mitt on her hand and began feeding a few more logs into the fire. That interested me, as I hadn't seen a wood fire oven in operation before this.

As lunches go, the food itself was rather nondescript. However, as there was quite a bit of it, I was not going to complain. It was certainly more palatable than some of the Navy fare I had been subjected to. As I ate, I examined the kitchen. There weren't any electric lights, switches or anything else that might indicate that the house was electrified. All the cooking was obviously done with a wood fire, as evidenced by the small stack of lengths next to the oven. I saw a few candles on the shelves along with several old fashioned oil-burning lamps weren't obviously weren't just for decoration. This was a bit of a surprise to me. All of the homes and businesses back in Cowlitz County had been electrified for decades. The United States Navy certainly took the existence of electricity for granted. The lack of electric power on the farm put a new wrinkle in my idea of what this job was going to be about. I foresaw many hard hours chopping up alder trees for firewood. Fortunately, it didn't look like I would have to travel far to find them, as there was a large stand of alders very near the rear of the house. There was no way I was going to attempt to chop down a Douglas fur or hemlock. At least it appeared the house was equipped with running water. I was also relieved that I hadn't seen anything resembling an outhouse anywhere. I hoped that indicated the house had indoor plumbing. Running outside in the middle of a cold winter night to relieve myself did not appeal to me in the slightest.

The woman continued to go about her kitchen duties as if I didn't exist. She was of medium height, just a few inches shorter than I was. She moved about the kitchen gracefully and with an economy of effort, no motions wasted. I watched her knead a huge lump of dough with her bare knuckles. Her hands were small and I could see they were used to manual labor. Her current task obviously entailed more than just baking one or two loaves for the next day. Given the amount of effort she was putting into the endeavor, I decided this was a week's worth of bread that was being produced. It would certainly make sense to bake enough bread and whatever else the household needed for the coming week.

As I was finishing up my second helping that she had handed to me without speaking, I considered how I might go about starting a conversation. I have never been much of a conversationalist, especially with striking women who didn't seem particularly interested in my presence. But if she and I were going to inhabit the same living quarters as the domestic help for the household, I thought being able to have a conversation would be better than ignoring each other for weeks on end. I decided to go with the obvious beginning. "Uh, I never caught your name."

"That is because I didn't give it to you." She spoke as she continued with her task of cutting and shaping the large blob of dough into loaves ready to put into the oven when the current batch was ready to come out. "However, as you asked, my English name is Willa. We do not give our real names to strangers."

As it happened, I knew a little about the tribes around the Pacific Northwest, as I used to have a school classmate who was an Indian. I dug around in my memory. "Are you from one of the local tribes? Perhaps Makah or Salish?"

She did turn to look at me with that. Her gaze was inscrutable. Was she interested in my knowledge of local tribes or astonished that someone would be so forward as to actually ask a question like that?

"No, I am not of a local tribe. If you must know, my family is from British Columbia in Canada, close to the border with Alberta. I am of the Dena'ina people. White men sometimes refer to us as the Beaver clan. Do you always go around asking strangers about their personal history?" Perhaps there was a glint of amusement behind her face. At least her response didn't sound hostile.

"Well, I just haven't met many Indians. And I…"

"We refer to ourselves as the First People, " she interrupted. "You white people gave us the name of 'Indians.' Your Christ-o-pher Co-lum-bus got lost in his ships while crossing the Atlantic Ocean and stupidly thought that he had landed in India, giving us that very insulting and incorrect name."

This conversation wasn't going the way I had intended. "My apologies! I am sorry for my lack of knowledge. And rudeness!" I added quickly as her eyebrows furrowed. "That was rude of me. Please forgive me!" She waved her hand at me in a way I had not seen before but I took to mean something along the lines of 'All right, I forgive you. But don't do it again.' I made a mental note to myself, *No more use of the word 'Indian.'* It was also obvious that Willa was not particularly fond of nosy questions. I would need to watch that. My mouth tended to run on unchecked when I was nervous or upset.

"So, do you think that Mrs. Cahill will be up soon? The sun's going to start going down soon and it's a long walk back to town. I don't fancy the walk through the forest on that bad road in the dark."

With that, Willa looked at me with some renewed interest. She narrowed her eyes and said, "You may call her Martha. That is her name," she added somewhat unnecessarily. "Yes, you are correct. Forests are not a place to be walking around in the dark. Especially these forests. Twilight can be a very perilous time." She did not elaborate on what that might mean. She gave me a long gaze. I assumed I was being appraised. "Missus gave me the discretion to hire the help for the house. She… Sometimes, she does not know where she is or who she is talking to. This is not often but she is having one of her days today. It is not bad yet with her, this old person's sickness of the mind. I saw it take two elders of my clan when I was a young child and it is not a pleasant thing to watch. My time is taken up with caring for the Missus and doing the chores around the house and the cooking. There are many things that I cannot do and I certainly need help. We are running out of firewood, which we will need during the coming autumn and winter. Once a week, the cistern up the hill needs to be filled from the well using the hand pump." That answered my question about how there was running water in a house that had no electricity, a gravity fed line from the cistern. "There are many other things that need fixing before winter. It is too much for me to keep up with."

She again examined me with her frank, dark brown eyes. "I will hire you for one month to see if we are both agreeable to continuing the arrangement. You may stay here tonight and you shall start work tomorrow. Is that acceptable to you?"

Given that this was largest number of sentences Willa had strung together since I had arrived at the house, I felt buoyed. Another positive sign was that Major seemed to have concluded I am not a threat, as he was sitting on the kitchen floor next to Willa, his pointed ears erect, gazing at me with obvious interest. "Yes, certainly, that is acceptable to me. Thank you very much. I am sure that I can help you out! I just need the chance to show you. Uh, all my belongings are down at the hotel in town. How shall I get those if I am not going to return there? And I paid for my room tonight as well. They required payment in advance."

She thought a moment before answering. "Tomorrow is my day to go to town to buy supplies. You may go with me and we will pick up your belongings and your money. Is that acceptable to you?"

She kept asking me if this was acceptable to me. That was a bit odd but was certainly better than other things that I have heard in the Navy. I replied that yes, everything was quite acceptable and, with that, the deal was done. I had a job, at least for the coming month. Given how much work that needed to be done — obvious even with my cursory inspection before I came inside — and the fact they had been looking for help for the last six months, it seemed likely that I would have a job here for as long as I wanted to stay. We hadn't settled on actual wages yet, but I assumed that would come in due time. As long as room and board were provided, I could subsist on supplying labor for a long time. All in all, it suited my needs quite nicely. My scars and obvious limp hadn't even come up in our conversation.

Willa motioned for me to follow her. We went back out to the hallway and up the dark, narrow stairway. I was suddenly distracted from my visual explorations of the wooden banister and antique wallpaper by the sight of Willa's swaying hips in front of me as we ascended the stairway. I felt an immediate rush of embarrassment and quickly dropped my eyes to where I could see my feet climbing up the worn wooden stairs. It wasn't as if I didn't appreciate the finer aspects of the female form — and Willa's seemed to be very fine indeed. It just seemed to me to be an intrusion into her privacy, especially given her cool reception downstairs. My gaze seemed too intimate for the cramped, dark stairway, even though there was no way she could have seen me.

When we reached the top of the stairs, she pointed down the short hallway. "You may have the room on the right. My room is at the end. You may wash up here." She pointed to the door on the left. "I must return to my baking. You may look around the house and the grounds if you want. There are many tasks that will need immediate attention, as you will soon see. We can discuss which ones should be done first later." With that, she turned to descend the cramped stairway. As I was still gazing at her receding back, she turned on her way down the stairs and added, "I keep my room locked when I am not there." She then turned her back to me and descended.

I wasn't certain what to make of her last pronouncement. Did that reflect some personal judgment regarding my character? Just based on our fifteen minutes together, did she expect me to go rummaging around her belongings at my first chance? Or was that just a general statement reflecting her distrust of strangers, any stranger? I shrugged my shoulders. I supposed it didn't matter one way or the other. If I were to work and live here with Willa as my close and, in fact, only co-worker, it was obvious I would need to be on my best behavior. It wouldn't do to upset her, even accidentally.

My room, as I had anticipated, was spartan. There was a narrow bed along the wall to my right. It had an iron pipe headboard that had been painted white some time ago, but was now pocked by patches of rust. In the middle of the wall opposite the bed, there was a small, dusty-smelling closet with a few clothes hangers on the wooden dowel. Next to the closet door was a small nightstand with a metal washbasin, a ceramic pitcher that was currently empty and another oil lamp complete with a book of matches. A dingy mirror hung on the wall next to the nightstand. The wallpaper was decorated with vertical lines alternating with columns of small pink roses but over the decades, the colors had faded to ghostly pastels. The floor was bare wood with a dark varnish. A small window poked out of a dormer on the sloped ceiling that was the underside of the exterior roof. A small pot-bellied stove in the corner was the obvious source of heat during the winter. Cheerful, it was not. However, it wasn't a hospital ward and it wasn't a cramped metal bunk inside the bowels a ship shoved up underneath some equipment racks. It was clean, warm and provided lots of privacy. It would certainly suffice. I would go back into town soon and get a few books from the library and perhaps buy a picture to hang on the wall. To me, walls without framed pictures seemed barren. *Something lighthearted,* I thought. *A family on a picnic, maybe.* I also made a mental note to myself that I should visit the local bar to see what they might have that might tide a weary worker through some cold nights.

As I didn't have any luggage to unpack, I decided to venture outside in order to evaluate my future job. I examined the garden, such as it was. It seemed to me that there was not much to do there for the remainder of this summer other than pull a few lingering weeds and harvest the remaining potatoes and squash. The corn was already gone from the forty or so desiccated cornstalks that were still standing.

On my earlier walk up to the house, I had missed the fact that, in the rear, there was a dilapidated barn sheltering what appeared to be a dark green 1935 Ford four-door. It had a number of rusty spots around the fenders and running boards but looked to be serviceable enough to make the drive back and forth between the house and town. There was a small wooden split-rail pen that abutted the side of the barn, containing four medium-sized goats. There was a small shed-like structure in the back of the pen where they could get out of the weather. I supposed these to be a source of milk for the household, not that I knew much about goats or milking. One corner of the pen was in dire need of shoring up, as it appeared to be have collapsed on the corner furthest from the house. There was a small woodpile stacked next to the rear stairs that led to the kitchen. The rest of the dwindling firewood was stacked just inside the barn door. It was obvious the firewood situation was going to need some immediate attention. I spent about a quarter of an hour putting the fence in a little better shape that would at least keep the goats from escaping. I would make more permanent repairs the next day. Goats certainly couldn't be easy to come by in this neck of the woods.

I strolled back around to the front of the house, picking up four brownish-colored eggs the wandering hens had deposited in several locations. I noted the stairs and railing leading up to the porch were in need of repair and the entire property could do with a general cleanup. *All in all, not too bad,* I thought. *I can manage this!*

When I returned inside, Mrs. Cahill was in the kitchen with Willa. Handing Willa the eggs with both hands, I introduced myself but let Willa explain that she had hired me, on a temporary basis, as a handyman and gardener. Martha looked to be around five and a half feet tall and walked stooped over, as some older people do. I guessed that she might be sixty-five, possibly seventy years old. She wore her grey hair pulled into a bun on the back of her head. Several skeins of hair had been pulled loose from the knot on the back of her head during her nap. She seemed to be aware of her surroundings and completely lucid as she inspected me. Perhaps she wasn't under the shadow of the old person's sickness after all.

"Yes, I believe that you will do nicely, young man. May I ask you a question?" I steeled myself for the expected questions about my scars. When I nodded my consent, she asked, "Why are you not in the Army? Do you not know that we are at war? The Army could use a soldier like you." The way she asked me these questions made me consider carefully before I answered. She hadn't asked in a casual manner. Her voice quivered slightly when she spoke. If you lose your one and only husband in a gigantic war in Europe fighting against Germany, I imagined that it would be difficult to forget how our country had just entered into another one that looked as bad or worse than the one that had claimed her husband.

"Yes, ma'am. I do know we are at war. I was in the Navy. I was onboard a ship that was sunk in the Japanese attack at Pearl Harbor. I.... I was injured, quite badly. Burns. I was in the hospital for seven months and I was discharged from the Navy because of my injuries. I have a Purple Heart." I reluctantly turned my head to the left to let her see the scarlet and pink mottling on the side of my neck and jaw, then the scar tissue on my right hand.

She gave a little gasp and put her hand to her mouth. The clarity that had been in her eyes seconds before seemed to waver and her posture became a little more stooped than it had been. "Yes. Of course. There are always the injured as well as the dead in war. It is a terrible thing. I feel for you, young man. It must have been terrible. I feel very tired. I believe I will sit down in the front room. Willa, will you bring me my tea? Thank you."

With that rapid change of subjects, I assumed I had been dismissed. I did not know whether I met with her approval as her new hired hand or not, so I just stood there, watching, as Willa helped Martha out to the living area in the front of the house. When Willa returned, I gestured an unspoken query. She returned my question with a steady gaze that offered nothing in the way of information. When the silence continued, I asked, "Do you think she approves of me? I am still hired?"

"Yes, of course. Nothing has changed. She approves of you. You were injured in the war." She then mentioned my proposed monthly salary for my work. I was astonished. This was double the amount as I might have optimistically expected, given the state of the house and grounds. I wasn't going to protest, of course. I could save quite a bit of my salary for whatever I might decide that I was going to do next, as there certainly wasn't much of anything here or the small town of Skykomish to spend money on. I assumed Martha was not only a little bit eccentric but was also likely offering more money than she knew the job was worth in order to keep someone. She apparently could afford it, which gave credence to the rumors about her hidden hoard. And perhaps the connection with her dead husband through my war injuries made me into a sympathetic person for her. Although that type of attitude from people usually offends me, in this case I was not going to argue. Things, I thought, might finally be looking up for me.

3

I awoke sometime that night, trembling and my mouth bone dry. I swallowed a few times to try to get that awful taste out of my mouth. I was very disoriented and had no idea what time it might be. It took me a good minute or two to calm down, rid myself of the debris of the nightmare and to actually remember where I was. *I am in the widow's house in my second floor bedroom.* It came back to me gradually. *It's okay! Calm down!* The bright moonlight was streaming in the window, illuminating a narrow rectangle of the floor at the foot of my bed with a silvery light. I was breathing very hard and the sheets on the bed were damp from perspiration.

My nightmares didn't happen every night, but they were coming often enough that I was never quite comfortable with the idea of going to sleep when it was time to retire for the night. Many times, including at my aunt's place in Greenlake, I had resorted to several snorts of bourbon to quiet whatever part of my brain that kept coming up with these god-awful images that left me a quivering mess. But, as my luck would have it, my bottle was in my luggage back at the hotel in town. I would have it back the next day, thanks to Willa, but that did me absolutely no good at that moment. To make matters worse, I could never remember much about my nightmares after I woke up. All that was left was the residual terror. I could recall small flashes about the *West Virginia* taking several torpedoes. Explosions… Flames… People screaming… But my father was in my nightmare as well, who had obviously been nowhere near Pearl at that time or at any other for that matter. Shouting… Something about a half empty bottle lying on the ground. I usually never remembered the details; the emotions clamoring for attention were the only residue left.

One of the doctors I had spent time with at the military hospital in Oakland was a psychiatrist by the name of Dr. Farmer. I thought that was a pretty humorous name for a doctor, which illustrates the maturity level I inhabited at the age of twenty-three years and some months. He spent his days talking to all the injured and traumatized survivors from Pearl that were in the ward. If the patients were too injured to walk or be pushed into his office, he would pull a chair very close to your bed and conduct his interview in a very soft voice. I very much wanted to punch him. I supposed that he was a nice enough person and likely a competent doctor, as shrinks go. However, I found it somehow very disturbing to be asked questions regarding how I felt about being a survivor, did I have any guilt about my shipmates who had died in the attack and how I felt about going back into society with my injuries. Frankly, at the time, I hadn't believed that this was anyone's business but my own.

He was very persistent with his questions and I finally broke down and told him a little about my nightmares and waking up with night sweats. He put on his best 'bedside doctor' persona and delivered a little monologue he likely pulled out at least several times a week. "Soldiers and sailors who have seen violent action sometimes exhibit a delayed emotional reaction to that violence. Many times, that reaction can be quite severe and debilitating. In the Great War, scores of Americans returned from Europe with severe tics and overreactions to small noises." Etc., etc. Yes, Doctor, I had heard all about that. Yes, you are probably right about that. When will the nightmares go away? He was unsure, saying that each case is different and therefore difficult to diagnose with complete accuracy. He seemed very surprised when I hit him with one detail I had left out before, just to see what his reaction would be. I told him that I had been having these nightmares and waking up in a panic for several years before Pearl Harbor. There was nothing particularly traumatic about lazing around Honolulu when we had shore leave, or scrubbing down decks and repainting large grey swathes of the battleship. He wasn't certain what that meant but he would give it his full consideration and we would talk later.

Recalling all this information didn't help me at all while I attempted to regain control of my breathing. I was hyperventilating and it was an effort to do anything beyond concentrating on not passing out until I was able to get hold of myself.

I knew from experience that I would get very little sleep the rest of the night. I had no idea what time it might be. My room wasn't equipped with a clock and I had never worn a watch. Getting out of the bed, I stepped over to the nightstand. I

32

poured cold water into the basin from the pitcher and splashed some in my face in an attempt to focus my attention and rid myself of the last remnants of the nightmare that I couldn't recall. I then padded over to the window in my bare feet.

The night was very clear and the bright moonlight bathed the stark landscape in a cold light. There was no color to be seen; everything looked to be in black and white. I stared out the window at the bleak and alien landscape for several minutes, trying to get my breathing under control. I gradually became aware of a small fluttering movement past the small plot of denuded corn stalks near the back of the house. I needed to crane my head around in order to get a better view of what I was seeing. When I did, I was startled to see Willa standing there, very still. She appeared to be staring out into the woods. Other than the light breeze that rippled her long white nightgown and dark hair, she stood motionless, looking across the clearing into the woods on the other side. In the moonlight, she looked like a ghost.

I stayed there at my window watching her for several minutes. She remained motionless. I was baffled, as it seemed that if you are going to get up in the middle of the night to go outside, you likely have a pretty good reason. Willa didn't seem like someone who would go outside just to enjoy the moonlight. I wondered if this was something to do with her Beaver clan upbringing. Perhaps it was a ritual of some sort, although I would have imagined rituals actually involved movement, dancing or prayers. This was just... standing there. After watching her for several minutes, I eventually decided that I had no idea what Willa was doing — and that it was none of my business.

I went across the hallway to the small bathroom to relieve myself. Idly, I wondered if Willa had locked her door before she went outside. Again, that wasn't any of my business. My task completed, I quietly walked back to my room. I had no idea how light a sleeper that Mrs. Cahill was, but I didn't want to take the chance of waking her on my first night there. When I looked out the window before I climbed back into my narrow bed, I saw that Willa was no longer there. I scanned the entire area that I could see from the window, but I didn't see any trace of her long unbound hair or fluttering nightgown. I fell asleep without hearing her climb the stairs and return to her room.

*   *   *   *

The next morning during breakfast, I made another attempt at conversation. This was going to be a very long autumn and winter if she continued to treat me as someone that ranked below Major.

"This is very good, Willa. Thank you! It's the best meal I have had in quite some time. My aunt in Seattle wasn't really all that enthusiastic about cooking. She liked playing cards with friends." She glanced in my direction from her cleaning up but didn't say anything. I continued to have difficulty when attempting to read her facial expressions, as Native Americans were apparently far more stoic than your average Navy sailor. *She would make a very good poker player if she cared to try,* I thought.

Trying again, I asked about a subject that I knew she would have to answer. "Willa, I was wondering about what task you thought I might tackle first. I know that we need much more firewood. I plan to work on that every day. I was thinking, however, maybe I might split my day between firewood and other tasks. Yesterday when I was out looking around, I tried to fix that corner of the goat pen. I assume you don't want any of your goats wandering around. I'll do a better job of it after we get back from town."

That did seem to catch her attention, as she turned to stare at me. "The pen was damaged? It was fine the evening before you came when I milked the goats. Are you certain?"

"Yes, very certain. It looked like some animal had pushed the fence down, actually. Some of the poles ended up inside the pen, so it looked a bit deliberate to me. I didn't see any tracks, however."

I now had her undivided attention. "How many goats were in the pen? Do you remember how many?"

"Four."

34

I caught the immediate dismay in her eyes. This expression was one that I didn't have much trouble reading. "Four! We have seven goats! Seven, not four! Are you sure the others weren't hiding in the shelter?"

"I was out there for quite a while, working on the fence. If they were in there, they never came out to see what I was doing. I don't think I ever saw more than four. Maybe the other three must have climbed out over the poles. Although they may have come back by now." I added that last part because of her obvious distress.

I followed her outside as she rushed to inspect the enclosure. There were still only four goats, just as I had observed the previous day. I showed her the area that I had repaired and the fact that I didn't see any tracks. At the very least, I concluded that a bear couldn't have snatched them. That would have been my first suspicion out here in the mountains. However, a bear, no matter how heavy or light, would have left some sort of sign of the activity required to snatch three goats. Willa didn't say anything. She opened the small gate to get a closer look at the remaining herd.

When Willa had seen enough and exited the goat pen, I was surprised to see she had been crying. Her eyes were shiny with tears. I quickly turned away to examine the fence again, as I thought that she probably wouldn't want me to see her being emotional about her goats. I assumed they were pets as well as providers of milk.

Without turning around, I stared out toward the woods behind the house. "Look, maybe they just climbed out over the poles. They're probably roaming out around the woods right now. Why don't I go look around and see if I can find them? I'll take some rope and collar them if I find them. Why don't you go back inside and finish cleaning up? I'll see what I can do."

Willa looked at me thoughtfully, the bright tracks of her tears drying on her face. "Thank you. That is very thoughtful of you. Yes. Perhaps they might still be near. I am wondering why the fence was down. It didn't fall down by itself."

I had to admit that I didn't have an answer for that one. The fence had been constructed using split rails laid in a zigzag pattern that allowed them to be supported without using fence posts. It was an easy type of fence to build, but it did have the disadvantage of not being terribly sturdy. However, unless the rails were rotten, I didn't see any reason a fence should just fall over by itself and it didn't seem reasonable to think that three goats knocked it down themselves. Without further information to go on, I put that consideration out of my mind. I was more focused on going out and either finding the goats or making a very visible good-faith effort to do so. This seemed a likely opening into at least getting on friendlier terms with Willa.

With that, I went out to rummage around inside the barn where I hoped to find some rope suitable for rounding up stray goats. After a few minutes poking around dusty corners and shelves, I concluded that there wasn't any rope, but I did come across a large ball of coarse twine that, unless they turned out to be very aggressive goats, I thought would suffice. I also took a walking stick I found leaning against the rear wall. Thus armed, I proceeded up the shallow slope from the house to the woods behind.

Although I didn't admit this to Willa, I felt there was not much hope of finding a single goat, much less all three. Even if I did find one, I wasn't exactly certain how I was going to convince a goat to stay in one place long enough so that I could slip a loop of twine around its neck. I was also concerned what even a short hike might do to my leg after my walk from town the day before. But I had a goal to achieve and I was going to give it my best shot. I thought I would walk around the area close to the house, looking for clues. I could also take advantage of this sojourn to scope out the lay of the land that surrounded the house.

As I pushed deeper into the forest, I was suddenly aware of a large rustle of undergrowth behind me. As noise grew louder, it became obvious to me, whatever it was, it wasn't a goat. A frightening thought flashed into my mind that it might be a cougar or some other form of wildlife that might want to mess with a human being foolishly stumbling into its domain. I was painfully aware of the fact that I didn't have anything with which I could defend myself. I certainly wasn't up to fending off an angry cougar with a walking stick. I was therefore more than a little relieved when the dark form that crashed from the underbrush revealed itself to be Major. I blew a little puff of relief. I was still a bit wary of the dog, but dealing with him, I felt, was going to be much easier than with a hungry predator. When he saw me, he bounced over to me with an expectant look on his face.

"Well damn it all, Major. You scared the beejesus out of me. You decided to come with me? And you decided that I'm not a bad person after all, huh? Well, that's great. We're going to be great buddies, you and me. I can see that now. I don't suppose you happen to know what goats smell like and could you maybe pick up a trail or two? I have no idea what I'm looking for out here."

In response, Major promptly sat down on his haunches. He stared at me intently, ears erect. "Yeah, I suppose not. Well then, let's go see what we can find." With that, I set off back up the slope with Major following closely behind.

The forest was peaceful but not silent. I became aware of the myriad of bird sounds that surrounded me. I could hear the whisper of the light wind rustling the branches of the trees. You don't get that kind of quiet in a city like Seattle or even in a small town like Kalama. Something is always going on there, cars whizzing by on the road, a neighbor banging on something in his backyard with a hammer, someone mowing his lawn. Noisy kids on bikes or skipping rope. After years of acclimation to the background commotion, it all begins to seem like silence. Everyday noises eventually fade out of your consciousness. This was different. This was the quiet of the wilderness. Other than my boots clumping noisily along the ground, there was a complete lack of any man-made sound. I could hear the gurgling sound of running water from somewhere to the left of me. I reasoned this was likely the brook that tumbled down near the side of the house. I stopped walking and listened intently. There were a number of individual sounds that I could pick out, but none of them sounded like lost goats.

Even just before midday, the thick trees allowed very little light to penetrate to the floor of the forest. Shafts of light pierced the canopy here and there to eventually find their way to the ground, but for the most part, we were in shadows. I had to crane my neck up to be able to view the tops of some of the largest trees. There were trees that looked to be eight to ten feet in diameter. I wouldn't have been able to make my arms reach even halfway around them. The sweat I had worked up during the climb evaporated from my shirt and exposed skin and I realized I was getting cold. I began to wish I had brought my jacket. The giant trees towered over us and I felt very small.

With Major bounding out in front of me, I continued the shallow climb up the side of the hill. I hiked for what seemed like another half an hour when we finally broke into a large clearing where the exposed grey granite rocks made it impossible for large trees to gain a foothold. The bright rays of sunlight illuminated a large, jagged mountain ridge several miles in the distance. I shaded my eyes with my hands. I had been in the shadows of the forest for some time and my eyes hadn't had time to adjust to the bright sunlit landscape.

It was an imposing landscape, raw and unforgiving. Hard. It was beautiful, of course. But it was beyond my puny definition of beauty. It was what it was — regardless of what I might think about it — and it would continue to be so long after I was gone. I shivered slightly. I did not like to contemplate mortality — mine or anyone else's — especially after the attack at Pearl. I had seen enough death to last me for a long while.

I suddenly decided that I had enough of wandering around the side of a mountain out in the middle of nowhere, looking for three goats that were not likely to be within miles of my present position and were probably not even alive anymore. Nature has a harsh way of dealing with the innocent and the unprepared. All I wanted was to be out of there. I could go back to the house and inform Willa that, after several hours of searching, Major and I neither saw nor sniffed any trace of the errant goats. Even without the missing goats, I thought that I might still get some appreciation from Willa. Not that I was expecting to be worshipped as a hero or anything, but it would be nice to get a little gratitude and be able to have an extended conversation. We could converse about the loss of our three goats in particular and the silliness of goats in general, and then we would move on to other topics such as... well, I supposed I would cross that bridge if and when I ever got to it.

"Major, I don't see any sign of 'em up here. What say we head back down the hill? I could use some lunch. I wonder what Willa is making up? Chili, perhaps. And cornbread! That would be a nice lunch. Do you suppose Indians from Canada know how to make chili?"

Major likely missed the finer points of my musings regarding lunch, but he turned and bounded back down the hill nevertheless. Major was turning out to be a rather good companion. He didn't talk or complain. He didn't accuse me of things that I didn't do. That's the way of dogs, I guess. If you treat them nicely and see to their needs, they will be your friend forever regardless of whether or not you were good-looking or maybe had a limp and some scars.

We left the clearing and were back in the forest again. Although I had grown up in Washington, home to old-growth forests, mountains and water in all its incarnations, I felt distinctly uncomfortable. This was nothing like what I had been used to while growing up near the Columbia River, and the terrain here was about as far away from the beaches and palm trees of Hawaii as you can get without going to Mars. It had been warm in Hawaii, with soft evening breezes and starry nights. Hawaiian girls... Sometimes they danced the hula. There were pretty nurses, although those were few and far between and usually very much off limits to anyone below the rank of ensign. Loads of exotic scented flowers and palm trees. Loud bars filled with sailors with too much time on their hands and as much booze as they could pay for. I began to miss Honolulu — the pre-Japanese sneak attack Honolulu — with an unexpected fierceness. *What in the world am I doing here*, I thought to myself, *wandering around the Cascade Mountains looking for some stupid goats that are probably not even among the living anymore? They're bear food, more than likely.* I shook my head, trying to clear it from the onslaught of memories that had suddenly appeared.

"Damn. This place is getting to me, and it's getting dark." This was more than an excuse. The massive mountains of stone and soaring trees combined to make it seem like dusk was approaching even though it couldn't have been more than about two o'clock. The burning sensation in my hip and leg informed me that I had better be getting along. I found that going down the slope was much easier than it had been on the way up, but I was still limping heavily.

As we proceeded down the slope, I realized that I didn't recognize anything we might have passed on the way up to the clearing. It all looked like huge trees to me and I certainly hadn't marked my trail with breadcrumbs. I wasn't really concerned about losing my way. I knew all I needed to do was continue to walk down the slope and I would eventually hit the large clearing where the house is located, or if I didn't manage to find the house first, I might at least stumble upon the road. As a last resort, I could always just turn to my right. I could walk in that direction until I came across the little mountain stream again. I could then just follow it down the hill and it would lead me directly to the house. I shivered again, even though it was still August. After the relative warmth of the clearing, the deep gloom of the forest made the change in temperature seem more pronounced. The sound of my footsteps had a peculiar booming, echoing quality, as if the forest floor was actually hollow. They didn't sound like ordinary footsteps.

"Stop it, Sean! You're driving yourself buggy!" I whacked myself lightly on the forehead, hoping to drive out unwanted thoughts. As I walked, I suddenly realized that Major was no longer with me. I had been so wrapped up with my internal conversations that I had no idea how long he had been gone. One minute, it seemed as if he had been right in front of me, dancing around and investigating things that might be of interest to a dog, and the next minute, he wasn't there. I had hoped that he would just lead me back to the house and all that would be required of me was to follow him. Now it seemed as if that option had been taken away. I shook my head in frustration and continued on.

Anxiety started to blossom in the emotional side of my mind. Along with not being certain where I was, I began to become aware of a peculiar sensation. Somehow, I felt certain that I was being watched. That, of course, was ridiculous. As far as I knew, the only people closer than town were the two women back at the house I was trying to find, and I was pretty certain they weren't out here with me in the forest. I remembered reading a detective story where one of the characters said something like, "I could swear that someone was watching me!" I had never experienced the feeling myself, so I had been of the opinion this was just some cheap literary device to make a dull story seem more suspenseful. I chided myself again for being silly. I was letting my imagination get the better of me.

I walked for another fifteen minutes before I heard the bubbling of the little stream that I had heard on my way up. I breathed a sigh of relief and limped in the direction of the running water. The unease I was feeling, though, continued to grow with each step. I scanned my surroundings as I walked, although I was certain there couldn't be anyone there. I tried to write off my strange sense of being under observation to my near-exhaustion and being lost in unfamiliar surroundings

I came across the stream just a few minutes' walk to the right of the track that I had been following. I trekked down the shallow incline for another ten minutes, letting gravity do most of the work for me, when I popped through the tree line behind the barn. I saw Major observing me from the landing at the top of the steps to the kitchen door. He was gazing at me as if he were saying, 'Where have you been? I have been waiting here for you for hours!' I gave him a sour look as I mounted the stairs: "Thanks a lot, buddy. No table scraps for you tonight."

Willa looked up as I entered the kitchen. She was stirring something in the big pot that smelled very good but likely wasn't chili. "Did you find anything?" she asked hopefully. I gave her a little shake of my head, trying to look disappointed that I had to be the bearer of this bad news. However, what I was really trying to do was attempting to dispel the remnants of that unnerving feeling that I had been under observation.

Frowning, Willa said, "I just can't imagine what could have happened to them." She handed me a plate of what turned out to be beef stew with a big slice of newly baked bread. I nodded appreciatively. "And I don't understand how the fence was damaged. You are certain you didn't see any footprints?"

"Nope, not that I saw," I replied as I spoke through a mouthful of stew. "I might have missed some little marks, but I am certain I would have seen prints or a bear or a cougar, something big enough to carry away three goats."

"Did you see any goat prints leading away from the pen?"

That gave me a little pause in my chewing. I had to admit that I had not. As with many animal pens, the area inside the fence and immediately outside was wet and muddy. It was not ankle-deep muddy, but it was soft enough that it should have shown something. "I'll go out and check again when I finish this. Thank you very much for this stew! It's fantastic!"

She threw me a little distrustful glance, as if I were a bit of a dunce to not have checked out that little detail to begin with and I was now attempting to change the subject. I supposed I should have made a better inspection my first time by the enclosure, except that I hadn't actually been expecting to be dealing with missing goats and therefore had no reason to be looking for their prints. The second time out, Willa was with me and she could have easily looked for herself. However, I left that unsaid. There's some old saying about 'discretion' and 'valor.' I opted for discretion.

When I went outside to inspect the pen and surrounding area, the scene was as I had remembered from our inspection earlier in the day. The muddy areas were so tracked up and disturbed by my efforts in repairing the fence, there wasn't much there to be able to examine. Whatever might have been there had been wiped away. The ground leading off toward the trees, however, was firm and dry. It exhibited no footprints, even mine.

I stood up from my inspection of the mud puddle, brushing off the dirt and mud from my clothes. I was sorry that Willa was upset about missing almost half of her small herd of goats, but I felt that it really wasn't my problem. After all, I reasoned, they had disappeared before I was actually on the job. It wasn't as if Willa had actually blamed me for anything, but I was wary of being criticized for things that I didn't feel were my fault. I still remembered my aunt's accusing look when I told her I had lost my job at Boeing. Yes, it was curious that the side of pen had been knocked down but, really, it didn't seem as if there was much I could do about it.

I climbed back up the step to the kitchen to make my report to Willa. She had finished her work there, as I found sitting in the living area in the front of the house, sewing on something I couldn't make out.

"Nope, no goat tracks. But really, Willa, that isn't all that unusual. The ground was really messed up around that area from when I was repairing the pen, and the ground away from the pen is hard enough that it's not going to show much of anything. It's too bad they're gone, but I don't think there are any clues out there. " I considered the mystery of the missing goats further. "When you go outside at night, do you ever see or hear anything? Anything that might be a bear or a cougar?"

She looked at me, baffled. "What do you mean, 'when I go outside at night?' I hardly ever go out at night."

I was as confused as she seemed to be. "I am sorry if I am prying. I didn't mean to intrude. I just happened to wake up last night, I am not sure what time but it must have been after midnight, and when I looked out the window, you were in the back of the house, standing there, looking up at the woods. I guess I wasn't supposed to see you. I wasn't spying, really, I wasn't. I was just wondering...."

Willa interrupted me hotly, "I was not standing outside last night! I do not go outside the house at night and certainly not after midnight!" She glared at me, her sewing now lying forgotten in her lap, apparently waiting for me to challenge her. I was taken aback, as she was reacting as if I had accused her of some wrongdoing. I thought fast or at least as fast as I was able to think. I presumed that I had stumbled upon something of a ritual nature related to her Dena'ina heritage she didn't want to discuss. Willa had certainly shown in our few conversations she was sensitive about certain topics related to her heritage. I had just committed some tactless white man foot-in-mouth blunder. I reflected that I was certainly doing a stupendous job of not getting on her better side.

"I'm sorry, Willa! I didn't mean to upset you! Really. I know that I wasn't supposed to watch you, as you were obviously..."

She threw her sewing aside and stood up from her rocking chair. "I do not go outside at night!" With that, she turned and angrily strode back into the kitchen. If the kitchen had a door, I was certain she would have slammed it.

I stood there in the living room, a little shell-shocked about how quickly our conversation had descended from a speculation about missing goats into something quite passionate and totally confusing to me. I slowly walked over to Willa's sewing on the floor and put it back over the arm of the rocker. I saw it was an old flannel nightgown with floppy lace around the neck and sleeves, likely belonging to Mrs. Cahill. *Something like that just wouldn't look right on Willa,* I thought a bit numbly. My next thought was that I was glad that I just had lunch because there was a very good chance I wouldn't get anything to eat if I were to ask right now. It was an even bet that I probably wouldn't get anything for dinner.

I sighed to myself, contemplating the confusion that is the female of my species. Whenever I had conversations with women, I never quite seemed to understand what was going on. The women in the bars in Honolulu were much easier to talk to. They knew what they were about and they knew that you knew it. It was all a matter of small talk and deciding where the two of you might want to go after you finished your drink. The Navy nurses were easy to talk to as well, although they were usually quite strict about the nature of their conversations with enlisted men. If it wasn't something about your queasy stomach or the nasty scrape on your elbow from falling off the retaining wall when you had less than your full faculties, they weren't really interested in having a conversation. Whatever had just occurred with Willa, it seemed beyond my understanding.

Shrugging my shoulders, I decided that I wouldn't worry about it right then. I was still of the opinion that I had observed something I wasn't supposed to see, but was at a loss to know what I was going to do about it other than stop asking Willa questions. I turned and shuffled out of the living room, back out to the woodpile to work on some firewood for the coming autumn and winter.

The next few days were spent getting accustomed to my new routine at the farm. I discovered Martha spent much of her waking hours in either her own room or sitting in the living room. We spoke occasionally and she was usually quite polite, asking about how my work was going, did I like it there and wasn't Willa's cooking just wonderful? Our conversations were short but mostly lucid. I had seen little evidence of the old person's sickness Willa had attributed to her.

Willa and I took the Ford to make her weekly shopping trip to Skykomish that had been postponed due to search for the missing goats. She pointed out a few of the establishments around town that I had seen upon my arrival. We also stopped by the hotel to pick up my valise and suitcase, and I asked for and got a refund for the night I had paid for but didn't use. The clerk, however, insisted on a small payment for keeping my bags safe for me. I thought that was unreasonable but I didn't argue. I was just thankful to have my luggage with me, as I could change into actual work clothes and have the clothes I had been wearing for the last couple of days laundered. My bag also contained the bottle of bourbon I used to suppress whatever it was in my head that produced my recurrent nightmares. Sometimes it worked, sometimes it didn't. But having the bottle with me comforted me in a way that I found difficult to explain, even to myself.

Other than chopping and stacking firewood, my job was not physically demanding. I had been concerned, due to my injuries, I would have difficulty keeping up with my assigned tasks. Swinging the ax was somewhat painful for my affected shoulder and wrist, but the pain was not unbearable. In fact, I ended up having quite a bit of time on my hands. There wasn't a lot of gardening that needed doing in the late summer heading into autumn and, unless Willa had a very specific task in mind, the handyman part of the job seemed to be very sporadic. I cleaned out the garden area, pulling up all the dried corn stalks and getting it ready for planting the next spring. I considered trying to do something about the dilapidated barn, but

I didn't have a lot of spare lumber to replace the damaged boards. I found some old tools in the barn in an ancient wooden tool case, several cans of rusty nails and some other odds and ends. I did the best I could with what I was able to scrounge up. No one could blame me for not doing more than that. I also came across some very old work gloves that would certainly be helpful when cutting firewood. I had started to get blisters already from swinging the ax.

As jobs go, this was turning out to be just what the doctor ordered. It looked as if the three of us — four if you counted Major — were getting settled in and the issue of Willa's month-long trial period hadn't come up. As there certainly wasn't much up here in this mountain valley to spend my money on, I was going to be able to save a good nest egg for myself. I wasn't going to have to worry myself about where I was going to live or having to cook for myself. Except when I went into town — which Willa had informed me I was going to do at least once as week, as I would be taking over her weekly shopping trip — I wasn't going to have to put up with strangers staring at my scars. There was no angry boss scrutinizing my every movement, just aching for an excuse to fire me. My biggest concern seemed to be boredom. I had always done pretty well on my own for extended periods of time, so I wasn't worried about that. I planned a side trip to the little library in Skykomish during my next sojourn into town, so I should always have a ready supply of reading material on hand. Yes, I could imagine a number of less comfortable possibilities, several of which involved the spare bedroom in Aunt Irene's house.

My only source of discontent during that time was that I continued to experience night terrors nearly every night. Even a stiff jolt or two before going to bed didn't seem to do much in alleviating the nightmares. I would wake up in a panic, the bedding damp with sweat, breathing heavily and frightened out of my wits, yet unable to remember much of anything about the dream except a few sketchy fragments that somehow involved fire, explosions and glimpses of my father's angry face. Dr. Farmer — the shrink that wanted me to tell him all about myself — had explained the current theories about how dreams were the brain's way of sorting through all the information it had stored up, putting it all in the correct places. Apparently Carl Jung — whose theories I knew about as much as I

46

did about the theories of Karl Marx — believed that dreams could be understood as symbols. Our brain "talked" to us using symbols, which seemed to me to be a pretty silly way to go about it. There was also something about the relationship between a person's ego and id, which I had a difficult time understanding — and frankly hadn't been all that interested in while confined to the Navy hospital burn ward. None of that psychology business helped me understand my nightmares or how to stop them from happening. I wondered if I should revisit that subject now that I was out on my own. I doubted the tiny library in town had any books by Jung or on the analysis of nightmares, but perhaps I could order something. Otherwise, I would just deal with them as they came.

It was after one of these after midnight episodes, perhaps ten days after I arrived at Mrs. Cahill's, yet again not being able to go back to sleep. When I looked out the window, I again saw that Willa was out back, just like that first night when I had seen her. Except for the fluttering of her nightgown and her loose hair in the night breeze, she was standing motionless, gazing out into the forest. I knew that she was very secretive about her nighttime sojourns and I wasn't likely to learn anything further from direct questioning. However, I was still very curious. It seemed to be a natural thing, my curiosity. I had never come across anyone who would stand outside in the middle of one night and deny it the next day. I wasn't really keen on the idea of spying on Willa, who really was my only human contact in the valley and hopefully, somebody who'd become a friend — perhaps even more than a friend. But I was still curious. What was she doing there and why did she feel she had to hide it? The old adage of curious cats and what usually happens to them popped unbidden into my mind. However, I was reasonably certain I could make it so that she wouldn't see me if I did a little investigating. I also reasoned that if I were able to figure out what was going on and what she was doing, I would be better able to navigate any tricky conversation that might come up in the future, as I would know what subject to avoid. My motives, if not exactly pure, were at least honorable.

I quietly slipped on my jeans, shirt and boots and crept down the stairs. Martha, it turned out, was a heavy sleeper. I could hear her snoring from behind her door on the first floor as I made my way out the door. Unfortunately for me at that moment, Major also appeared to be having some sleeping issues, as he was right on my heels as I opened the door. Maybe he needed to go outside to take care of his doggie business or maybe he was just bored and was wondering what was up with all the humans messing around in the dark.

"No, Major. You have to stay inside. Good boy!" He whimpered slightly at my admonishment and attempted to nose past me as I closed the door. I gave him a little push to get him back inside the house, concerned about the noise we were making. I was finally able to convince him I really didn't want him to accompany me. Major joyfully pouncing on Willa as she contemplated the trees would have been a dead giveaway that something was up. While I was not exactly ashamed of my spying, I just wasn't keen on the idea of Willa finding out about it.

I crept as quietly as I could around the side of the house by the newly cleared cornfield. From my vantage point, I was able to peer around the back corner to where Willa was standing. I was fortunate to be between where Willa was standing and the half moon illuminating the scene. I recalled this tactic from my basic training. During any nighttime surveillance, the moon should be behind you so that the moonlight would not illuminate you to any enemy you were attempting to spy on, but you could see them very well indeed. The moonlight would be shining into their eyes and not yours. In this particular instance, it was more by fortune than intention, but I was willing to accept any good luck that I had been dealt.

I crouched down as best I could to keep my watch. As it turned out, however, there wasn't much to see. Willa made no discernable movements during her ritual, vigil or whatever it was she was doing. I could see absolutely nothing in the dark of the woods that might be the object of her attention. Nothing moved in my field of vision besides the wispy, scuttering clouds in the moonlight and the ruffling of her hair and nightgown. After about fifteen minutes of this decided lack of activity, I felt silly and slightly embarrassed. I concluded that the night was too chilly to be crouching outside at night without a coat, waiting for something to happen.

It was just at that moment Willa made a sudden pivot and started walking toward the house. However, rather than go the quickest way through the kitchen door in the rear of the house or go around the house using the pathway by the goat pen, she strode directly toward the side of the house where I had concealed myself.

I panicked. There was absolutely no place for me to hide and it was going to be impossible for me to run around to the front of the house before Willa came around the corner and saw me. I pressed up against the side of the house as best I could while attempting to formulate some excuse that might lessen the guilt of admitting I had been spying on her. I had just come to the realization that I was caught and had probably ruined whatever chance I might have had of becoming friends with Willa when she made the turn around the corner of the house. The beginnings of an apology died in my throat when, to my astonishment, Willa walked steadily past me without so much as a glance in my direction and continued toward the front of the house. I heard the screen door creak open and then slam.

I was as confused as I was surprised. There really was no way that she could have missed seeing me, given she had passed within three feet. It wasn't all that dark and the moonlight was illuminating that side of the house. There just weren't any shadows in which to hide. But Willa hadn't even turned her head in my direction as she passed by.

The idea she was sleepwalking had not occurred to me before then. It would certainly explain why she did not confront me immediately when she discovered me spying on her. It would also explain her earlier protestations about not going outside during the night. I had heard about people walking in their sleep, of course, but I had never actually encountered anyone who suffered from the affliction. In fact, I knew very little about the topic except that you are not supposed to waken someone in the middle of a sleepwalking episode. I had no idea why that might be, but as I had heard this several times since I was a child, I assumed it must be true.

I mulled over this unexpected revelation as I retreated slowly toward the now-silent house. Major was there to greet me as I entered the dark living room. As dogs are wont to do, he acted as if he had not seen me in two days rather than the fifteen minutes I had been outside. I quietly attempted to shush him, although there no longer seemed to be much danger in waking Martha. Among the three of us in the house, she was the one that seemed most likely to sleep through a hurricane. I

49

wasn't certain about Willa, but I reasoned if she could take a stroll around the grounds and not wake up, nighttime dog noises would probably not arouse her. Major likely made these kinds of noises all the time such that they just became part of the nightly routine. I ruffled his fur around his neck and assured him that Major was indeed a good dog and he should now go lie down like all good dogs do at God knows whatever time it was. I mounted the stairs wearily. I decided that I was ready to go back to bed. I would consider this latest revelation in the morning.

* * * *

The next morning, I decided to try another go at having a friendly conversation with Willa. It was going to be a long, rather boring autumn and winter if we never talked to each other about anything other than chores and goats. But I also knew that I was going to have to be very careful about unintentionally offending her or letting her know I suspected she might be walking in her sleep.

While she had begun to prepare breakfast, I sat down at the kitchen table and tried to consider my opening gambit carefully before I said anything. "Willa, I was wondering how you came to be out here in the mountains in Washington if your home is in Canada. What about your family? Did they come with you?"

She turned her head to examine me before replying. There was a hint of suspicion in her look. "You seem to want to know about me. Why is that?"

"I'm just trying to be friendly." That was a true enough statement. "I thought we might get to know each other a little better if we are going to spend the winter together in this house. You seem like a very nice person. I don't see the harm in wanting to be friends."

"Oh, I see," she responded. She turned back to the stove. "You want to be friends and you want to know more about me. And what makes you believe that I desire to be friends with you?"

That didn't seem an entirely promising beginning. However, her voice didn't seem overtly hostile, although I couldn't really be certain with her back turned toward me. "Yes, I agree that is an assumption on my part. I apologize for being forward. But I really am a rather nice person when you do get to know me."

That last bit was said with what I hoped was a "lonely puppy dog" look on my face. I had never been any good at small talk, especially with women. After I was released from the hospitals, I had been very self-conscious about my scars and limp, so any thought I might have of such an attempt was very much a non-starter. However, given the situation we found ourselves in and the fact that, even though the ice had not really been fully broken, it was showing some distinct signs of cracking, I plowed ahead. Learning to speak to each other seemed to me to be necessary for surviving the next six months without going completely batty.

She gave a little laugh and shook her head at my transparent attempt at being likeable. "I see. You are a nice person and you want to be friends with me. I have heard that scoundrels say such things, trying to be one thing on the outside but are something much different on the inside. Are you a scoundrel? Are you one thing inside and another thing outside?" She said this as she turned to face me, wiping her hands on her apron.

She's teasing me, I realized in surprise. I was going to have to be very careful if our conversation turned into a game of words. I knew that I didn't know all the unwritten and unstated rules and protocol regarding conversations between the men and women from my own culture, much less hers. I was momentarily at a loss for an adequate response.

"I... Uh... Well, no. I don't think so. That would be pretty pointless in our situation. I'm certainly not trying to get anything out of you. I'm not hiding anything, if that is what you mean," I said in what I hoped was a very sincere voice. At the same time, I was thinking that it really wasn't true in my case, and it probably was never the case in any conversation that had ever occurred between two human beings beyond the age of seven. All of us are hiding things that we do not want others to know.

"I see. If you aren't trying to get anything from me, shall I give your breakfast to the goats then?" She held up the tin plate in the air. Small crinkles showed around her eyes appeared, which I took to be her way of smiling.

This is getting a little ridiculous, I thought. I started this conversation by asking her about her family and it had somehow turned into trying to convince her that I was not a scoundrel. "No, please don't! It smells wonderful!" It did smell wonderful and I was getting more than a little hungry as the conversation progressed.

She gave me another appraising glance and apparently came to some sort of decision. "All right. If you are so determined to know something about me and to be my friend, I will make this proposal. You shall tell something to me about yourself and, if I believe you are telling me the truth, I shall tell you something about me. We shall continue this so long as I am convinced you are not a scoundrel. You will go first." With that, she turned her back and started to dish out the hash and scrambled eggs onto three plates. Apparently we were going to have breakfast together. That was another very good sign.

When she returned to the kitchen after taking the third plate into Martha's room, she took the chair opposite mine. I began, "Well... Let me think. I have never been very good about talking about myself."

She responded quickly. "Oh, now that is your first lie that you have told me. I shall be keeping track. If you tell me too many lies, I will be forced to discontinue this game. Men are always very happy to talk about themselves in front of women. The men in our clan loved to tell stories about how many deer they killed and skinned or how brave they were when faced with danger. I very much doubt that white men are different from the men in our clan when it comes to talking about themselves. You should start over or else I shall take my breakfast in the other room and you and Major can sit here in the kitchen by yourselves."

She was doing an excellent job in keeping me off balance. I had no doubt this was deliberate. Even more disconcerting, she seemed to be enjoying herself. She had me at a disadvantage and she knew it. I was embarrassed but realized I was also enjoying myself. I had never had a conversation like this before with a woman.

"Yes. I see your point. I was just talking in order to figure out what I was going to say. No harm intended." I had no idea how much detail she was expecting me to provide and whether we were supposed to get really personal or as something as trivial as what my favorite color is. I thought I would go for the middle ground and see how she responded before the next round of this "game."

While we ate our breakfast, I told her about growing up in Kalama and what my mother and father were like. I didn't go say much about my father, given that we were never on very friendly terms and he was dead anyway. I did go into some detail about my mother, what she was like, what she wore, how she made foods that I really liked as a child and how she used to take me on walks down along the Columbia River and explain to me that the opposite bank was in Oregon. We would sit and watch the boats plow up and down the river. Even the big boats seemed very small against the huge river.

After I had talked for about five minutes, I looked at her expectantly. It was her turn. I hoped that she would follow my example and tell me something about her background and family.

Willa turned her head to gaze out the window. She seemed to be gathering her thoughts, perhaps trying to decide what she would say to me and what she would keep to herself. The sunlight streamed in the little window in the back door and illuminated her raven hair with a fuzzy yellow halo. The effect was dazzling. I studied her profile. She was indeed quite beautiful. I was amazed I hadn't recognized that before.

"I told you that I am from Canada. The name of our village is not important. It wouldn't increase your knowledge. It is near the *Saaghii Naachii* River in eastern British Columbia. The white man's name for this is the Peace River. The people in our village speak the Beaver language, which is what your anthropologists refer to as an Athabascan language. Several of our people also knew English or French. The winters are very hard there. It is very cold and food must be stored up during the summer months in order to survive the winter."

She stopped speaking momentarily. I thought that she might be done with her part of this round of the game, but she continued speaking while staring out the window at the trees in the distance. "I was the youngest child of three. I was the only girl." I noted the past tense. She frowned a bit. "My father was... harsh with his wife and children. He loved us, as all fathers love their family, but he did not show it outwardly. You may not understand this." She turned her head to give me a look as to see how I might take this statement. I gave a non-committal shrug of my shoulders, hopefully signifying that I might understand a bit more than she might imagine.

Willa continued. "One very cruel winter, my father and two brothers went out to forage for more firewood and to see if they could find any game or fish they might take for food. Our stockpile was growing small and would likely not last through winter to the spring. I was probably seven years old by this time. My mother and I spent the time inside sitting by the fire. She was mending one of my brother's heavy leather moccasins. I was playing with my little doll she made me from cloth, cornhusks and a doll's head made from carved wood. The day became dark and the snow started to fall heavily. My father and brothers had not returned. My mother was concerned, I could see, but she smiled at me and started to get supper ready for the family when they did return. We waited all night but no one came. The next morning..." She stopped and took a little swipe at her eyes with the heel of her hand. "The next morning, the men of the village went out to look for them. They found nothing. The snowfall had covered any tracks that they might have made which would have shown which direction they went. The men searched the regular places that they go to fish and look for game. They found nothing.

"My mother became frantic. They had not returned by the next evening. We went to the other side of the village to stay with my mother's elder sister. My two cousins were older than I was, but the younger boy was close to my age and we played together on many occasions. I was scared, mostly because my mother was obviously frightened and my aunt was trying to calm her. The search was called off when the sun started going down, which is quite early during the winter. I tried to go to sleep but I couldn't. I listened to my mother crying to herself. They had still not returned the next morning. They never returned."

Willa stopped speaking. She seemed overcome with her emotions and was having difficulty continuing. Having me see her cry was likely embarrassing to her. She sniffled a bit and wiped her eyes again. I got the impression that she hadn't meant to discuss this with me.

Willa cleared her throat. "I believe that is enough for this morning. I need to check on the Missus and clean up after breakfast. I should take her outside for a walk a bit. She gets so little exercise just sitting around the house all day. And I believe that you have your chores to get done."

That sounded like very much like I was being dismissed. I was disappointed, as I found Willa's story fascinating. I was curious to hear the ending, if there was indeed an ending. I wondered if her father and brothers were ever found. I also realized that her story, compelling as it was, did not explain how she ended up here in Washington all the way from eastern British Columbia. However, it was obvious that Willa was done talking, as she had turned her back on me and was cleaning off the breakfast plates that were stacked in the chipped enamel sink. I went outside to continue my assault on the alder trees.

That night, I awoke to find myself on the bedroom floor with my sheet and blanket balled up around my legs. In my dream, I clearly remembered I had been screaming. I was hyperventilating and it felt as if the walls of the room were spinning around me. I felt as if I might throw up. I rested my forehead on the cool wood of the floor while I tried to force myself to breathe normally. After a few minutes, I had regained at least partial control of my composure. As I scrabbled back onto the narrow bed, I felt my embarrassment rising. I didn't think I had been screaming out loud, but I realized I couldn't be absolutely certain. I listened carefully for twenty or thirty seconds but heard no noises in the house. I was relieved I hadn't disturbed anyone.

Knowing that I wasn't going to get back to sleep for quite some time, I got up and shuffled over to the washbasin where I splashed some water in my face. I was thankful there wasn't much light in the room so that I didn't have to see my face in the mirror. I opened the small door on the nightstand below the washbasin and removed the bottle of bourbon that was now only a quarter full. I took a large mouthful and swallowed quickly. I knew in the rational side of my mind that it wasn't normal to drink in the middle of the night, but these were very special circumstances. My nightmares seemed to be spiraling out of control. What was especially infuriating to me — aside from waking up not knowing whether I was screaming out loud or not — was the fact I couldn't remember much of anything about them. I had no idea what had scared me to the point of screaming. I could only assume that my brain was playing around with all the debris floating around in my subconscious about the Japanese attack. It didn't seem unreasonable that a close brush with death from being burned alive and drowning while many of my shipmates didn't make it out alive provided sufficient fodder for whatever mechanism in the brain that produced my nightmares.

I took a final mouthful from the bottle. The burning sensation in my throat and stomach was a welcome relief. Wearily, I thought to myself that I wasn't sure how many more nights of this I could take. It was definitely starting to take a toll. For one thing, after I did finally manage to make it to morning, I was having headaches. Horrible headaches. I hadn't had headaches in quite a long time, at least since before I signed up for the Navy. I hoped that this wasn't turning into a nightly occurrence, but I was afraid it might be.

I stowed the bottle away underneath the cabinet and stumbled over to the window. I wondered if I would see Willa outside. Was she sleepwalking again? I searched the area visible from the window, but she was not there. A slight sense of disappointment welled up. I certainly didn't intend to go outside and follow her again, now that I knew more about what was going on. However, I was still curious. I pondered how I might find out more without asking her directly, which would, no doubt, cause her defenses to immediately spring into action. I knew that I wasn't going to get anywhere by a frontal assault, that was for certain. Only later did I understand the irony of thinking about my developing relationship with Willa using military terminology.

A dry little chuckle escaped from my throat, not that I found anything particularly humorous in the situation. It seemed that both Willa and I were experiencing some serious issues with getting a good night's sleep. The only person able to sleep well was Martha.

I went back to the nightstand and opened the door. *One more swig before I go to bed just to help me get to sleep,* I told myself. I picked up the bedding that was still balled up on the floor and straightened it out to put on the bed again. I felt like a wet towel wrung out by a washerwoman. It was not a good feeling. I threw myself back on the narrow bed and hoped that I could get some sleep before the sunlight started streaming in through the window.

* * * *

The next morning, I awoke with an angry, pounding headache and an ugly taste in my mouth. I had no idea what time it might be, but based on the angle of the sunlight filtering into my room through the narrow window, it appeared to be later than my normal time to wrench myself out of bed. After my morning ministrations in the small washroom across the hall, I dressed for the coming day and eased myself down the stairs, carefully gripping the handrail as I went. I found Willa cleaning up in the kitchen. She looked at me as I came in and sat down at the table. The wariness in her gaze had returned.

"You're late. I saved you a plate of breakfast." She nodded in the direction of the counter to her left. "You look terrible," she added as she turned back to the sink.

"Thanks, but I think I will pass on breakfast today. I have a headache." This was an understatement on my part. It felt like a malicious dwarf was inside my skull, kicking and punching the back of my eyeballs. I rubbed my temples with both hands. "I don't suppose you have any coffee around this place, do you? I sure could use a cup or seven."

"No, no coffee. The Missus doesn't like coffee. She has tea with her breakfast." Through my interlaced fingers I had covering my eyes and face, I could see she was examining me. "You have a headache, do you? I believe you are suffering from what is called a 'hangover.' You have been drinking in your room. I can still smell it on your breath. Did you even brush your teeth this morning?"

My protest died immediately when I saw the angry frown on Willa's face. She was facing me with her right hand on the counter and a large spoon in her left. She looked angry. "And don't even try to tell me that you haven't been drinking. I heard your whiskey bottle sloshing around in your bag when we came back from town that day. I have seen what people look like the morning after they have been drinking and that is exactly what you look like. Do not even try to lie to me. Lying to me, especially about drinking, is not allowed. You are still on probation for the first month working here, remember?" She turned sharply back to the sink.

"Yes, I admit that I had a drink last night." She scowled at me over her shoulder. "Okay, several drinks. Look, I have been having a real difficult time sleeping lately. I can't go to sleep and then when I do, I have been having these horrible nightmares that wake me up in the middle of the night. Last night, I woke up and I was on the floor! I really can't go to sleep without having a drink first!"

Willa pierced me with her glare. "Have you tried?"

"Uh, tried what?"

"Going to sleep without getting drunk first. Drinking doesn't seem to helping you very much right now. You said you had a nightmare last night?" she asked me rather pointedly.

"Yeah, a doozy! I told you that I woke up on the floor last night. I couldn't control my breathing and I felt like I was going to be sick!"

She countered my argument. "Well then, it doesn't sound like drinking is helping you, now is it?" She waggled the spoon at me. "Drinking is a crutch for people with weak spirits. I have seen what drinking can do to people. My father drank. It was horrible how he changed when he had been drinking!"

I had to concede that point to her. I also had first-hand experience of what drinking can do to people. In addition to having a bastard of a headache, I was also annoyed that Willa was upset with me. I massaged my temples again. *Way to go, Sean,* I berated myself silently. *Now you have her mad at you.*

Not knowing what to say, I mumbled, "I'll go brush my teeth. You can give my breakfast to the goats." I got out of my chair, pushing Major out of the way. He was probably calling dibs on anything left on the table.

I went back up the stairs with slow, measured steps, stumbling once when my toes caught on the lip of the stair. My internal dialog was ricocheting all over the place. *Willa really has absolutely no right to complain about my drinking before bed,* I thought angrily. *She didn't have any right! And I really do need it*! My thoughts raced around and were gone almost before they had registered in my consciousness. I found myself surprised Willa even knew what the word 'probation' actually meant. *Wherever the hell she got her education in Canada, her command of the English language is certainly very good. She probably speaks French as well,* I thought sourly. *Besides, I wasn't bothering anyone. It wasn't like I was busting up that bar in Honolulu.*

I stopped abruptly at the top of the stairs. I suddenly recalled how that particular escapade turned out. The MPs had crashed through the doors of the Trade

Winds bar during the fight. They ended up thumping several people over the head with their truncheons before arresting all the participants and a few other bystanders that probably just looked like they might be guilty. A couple of my shipmates and I ended up spending the night in the military jail for that one. Our CO had to come and get us out the next day. There was a hearing later that month. I got busted down from a Petty Officer 2nd Class to 3rd Class for that one. I had told myself that I had learned my lesson after that. Hadn't I? I didn't remember. I seemed to remember a few drinks after that, but nothing serious. I hadn't had much of an opportunity, for one thing. It had only been a few more weeks after the hearing that Japanese Zeros transformed the *West Virginia* — along with the *Arizona, Oklahoma, California* and numerous other ships — into fiery, watery tombs. I certainly hadn't had much chance to get lit during my enforced stay in the various hospitals.

I shuffled down the hall and turned left into the washroom. I found my toothbrush and the toothpaste. When I glanced up, I found myself staring at my own haggard face in the mirror. She was right; I did look like hell. My eyes were bloodshot and I was in dire need of a shave. The face that looked back at me looked like someone in the early 40s, not in his mid-twenties. I was angry. I was angry with myself, I was angry with Willa for accusing me. Yeah okay, she happened to be right in this case. I had been drinking but still, I didn't like people accusing me of things. I hated it, as a matter of fact. It seemed like people had been accusing me of something all of my life. I began seething at memories of long past injustices.

I finished brushing my teeth. I glanced at myself in the mirror again and decided to hell with shaving. *Irishmen don't have heavy facial hair in the first place and maybe I will just grow a beard. That would show Willa.* That thought made me feel marginally better, but not for very long as I realized I was being childish. I continued back to my room where I changed into my work clothes.

As I was heading toward the front door, I heard Willa call out after me. "Sean, would you please look at the shingles on the roof above my room? I think there is a leak somewhere. I don't want to be staying in room with a leak when the weather turns bad. I think there is a pile of old shingles somewhere in the barn."

I thought to myself, *Well, maybe I will. Maybe I won't. I'll see when I can get around to it. I have other stuff to do around here, you know.* But I also wanted her to not be mad at me anymore. I realized that I was fixating on her and her opinion of me mattered. She was obviously the only thing of real interest around the house. I certainly didn't want the only interesting person within miles to be upset with me. That would defeat the entire purpose of getting to know her. There I was, being angry with her for asking me to take a look at her roof so her room wouldn't get wet during the coming winter. That was my job, wasn't it? That's what I was being paid to do, be a "handyman." If I wanted to continue to have the job — and I did — I concluded that I should do as Willa asked and that I should probably be nicer to her while doing it.

*   *   *   *

Shading my eyes from the glare of the mid-morning sun, I looked up at the roof above Willa's room on the second floor. The roofs on many houses from the late 1800s were constructed using a very steep pitch. I supposed the owners believed that this made their house resemble a castle. Steep roofs and some turrets. Grandiose houses from that period seemed to always be equipped with a good turret or two in order to attract the attention of the neighbors. Nothing declares, "I'm rich!" better than matching turrets. The pitch of the roof of Martha's house wasn't as steep as some I had seen but, from my vantage point on the ground, it seemed steep enough. I was still wobbly in the legs, but being outside in the sunlight helped. The light breeze on my face was invigorating.

I eventually found a pile of shingles hiding in the corner of the barn behind the Ford. The ladder was lying in the weeds along the wall of the barn opposite the goat pen. I examined it with suspicion. It appeared to be ancient. The rough wooden rungs were heavily weathered with large gaps showing along the grain in the wood, but they appeared to be solid. I certainly didn't want one of them to snap in half while I was twenty feet in the air.

After I had successfully maneuvered the ladder around to the back of the house and propped it up against the eaves next to the dormer of Willa's room, I bounced up and down on the lowest rung several times. It wouldn't do to have one leg sink into the ground while I was up there and suddenly find myself hurtling toward Mother Earth as the ladder tipped over sideways. The ground beneath the ladder's feet seemed stable enough and the rung didn't seem to be in danger of breaking. Of course, that one was the one closest to the ground. That didn't mean beans about its brother twenty feet in the air where I would be standing. I found myself wishing I could have a drink, just a small one, before I began my climb. However, I was reasonably certainly that wouldn't have gone over well with Willa. I might also end up breaking my neck if I wasn't very careful.

Gritting my teeth, I slowly ascended the ladder to where I could examine the roof for the leak. When I got to the top, I could see that there were indeed a number of wooden shingles where the dormer met the face of the roof that appeared to be darker than the others. *That might be some wood rot*, I thought. *It was too bad that original owner didn't spring for slate shingles. I wouldn't have to be way up here in the air if he hadn't been so stingy in his construction.*

I fervently hoped I could replace all the rotten shingles from my position on the ladder. Otherwise, I was going to have to come up with some method of working directly on the pitched surface of the roof without sliding off. I climbed carefully down the ladder rung by rung, right leg first with a minimum of bending of the knee and hip, followed slowly by the left leg. After having survived the most horrendous attack on the U.S. in history, falling off a ladder would have been a pretty stupid way to die.

With some effort, I managed to manhandle a bundle of the shingles up the ladder, along with a claw hammer and a pocket full of the least-rusted nails I could find. I tossed the new shingles out of the working area but where I could still reach them. I tried to work carefully but quickly, as I really wanted to get the task finished so I could get down. I was definitely not comfortable on a perch more suitable for a pigeon than someone who had an issue with heights.

After removing all the water-damaged shingles, I paused to wipe the perspiration off my forehead with my sleeve. Sweat was running down my forehead into the corners of my eyes. As I blinked furiously, I glanced over to my left where I could see the beginnings of the trees. From this height, the forest looked darkly ominous. I could see the forest canopy as it climbed up the slope of the hill toward the summit of the mountain ridge. A small chill ran down my spine as I remembered the feeling of being watched while I stumbled around up on the hill. I scolded myself for continuing to let my imagination affect me this badly.

As I turned around to my task, I experienced an abrupt and complete alteration of my vision. Even now, I am still not sure how I should refer to it. An illusion? A hallucination? Whatever it had been, instead of seeing the bare tarpaper on the roof of Mrs. Cahill's house that now needed to be covered with new shingles, I was suddenly presented with the sight of the burning deck of the *U.S.S. West Virginia*. Flames surrounded me and I could hear several explosions not very far away. Several Japanese torpedo bomber airplanes screamed over my head, lining themselves up for their torpedo drop. I looked around frantically while my mind buzzed. *Where was the return fire from the ground? Where are our fighter airplanes?* I was frozen in place, suffering from total confusion. I was in shock from the abrupt change of surroundings, but also from the suddenness of the attack that had appeared out of the azure blue sky that transformed an idyllic Sunday morning into a burning, exploding nightmare. I felt as if I was simultaneously experiencing two different realities that were, in fact, separated in time by nine months.

I looked down at my hands. Instead of grasping the tops rung of the wooden ladder, I was holding the top of the railing that ran around the deck of the ship. Flames surrounded me and, looking down, instead of the seedy lawn, I could see the dark water slapping against the grey hull. I could see the water was covered in a shiny fuel slick that would immediately catch fire the second it was hit with a flame. I realized that I needed to get out of there immediately or else I was going to die on board the ship. Using the force of both my arms and legs, I heaved myself up and over the railing.

The next sensation I experienced was crashing into the overgrown roses and azalea bushes growing on either side of the kitchen steps at the back of the house. Whatever air my lungs had contained was forcibly expelled by the impact of my fall. Stunned, I lay still for a few seconds as I attempted to assess what had just happened and whether I had sustained any major injuries in the fall. I groaned and tried to roll off the shrubs that had likely saved my life or, at the very least, several broken ribs. The thorny roses scratched my hands and face and tore at my shirt as I tried to extricate myself.

I heard the kitchen door crash open. Willa rushed down the stairs, followed closely by Major. "Sean! Are you all right? What happened? Please say something!"

My face and other exposed skin were covered in cuts and scrapes — some of them bleeding rather badly — but all my limbs seemed to be operating as expected without any unexpected bends or excruciating pains. "Yeah, I think I am okay. I don't feel any broken bones. Just give me a second to catch my breath, all right? Whoo!"

Major circled around me, sniffing anxiously. He seemed as concerned as Willa. He stuck his nose in my ear as I got to my hands and knees. *Good boy*, I thought dizzily. *You get a treat tonight.*

Willa, for her part, kept her wits about her admirably. While I attempted to regain my composure and figure out what the hell had just occurred, she poked and prodded in different locations. "Does this hurt?" she kept asking. I shook my head in the negative although, to be perfectly honest, my entire body hurt. However, my mind was functioning well enough to understand she was looking for major injuries. The non-life-threatening stuff could be dealt with later.

Once she was satisfied I didn't have any broken bones or obvious internal injuries, she finally let me stand up. I bent over with my hands on my knees for a bit, breathing deeply. *How about that?* I thought to myself. *Apparently, I just survived a fall from the top of the second story of the house.* The more pressing issue for me at the time, however, was the realization I had jumped off the top of the ladder, *on purpose*, while I was about twenty feet off the ground. I straightened up and raised my head to look up at the location I had occupied up until two minutes ago. The ladder was no longer perpendicular with the ground. It had started to slide sideways, but the top had caught on the side of the dormer; otherwise it would have likely also ended up on the ground. I looked around, thinking I had been extremely fortunate that I hadn't landed on the bare ground, as it was littered with the rotten shingles I had tossed down, some of them with the sharp ends of rusty nails pointing skyward. I looked back up to the roof again. *I must have tried to jump over the top of the ladder onto the roof. When I hit the roof, I immediately rolled off and fell directly on the bushes below.* I shook my head in disbelief. There were several other ways it could have turned out, almost all of them worse than what had actually happened.

Willa bent down in order to gaze up into my face. I could see she was scared but hadn't acted like it. *Very good,* I thought. *You would make a very good sailor.* "Can you walk now?" she asked me. "We should go into the kitchen so I can clean you up. You're bleeding."

She supported me by my good shoulder as we walked slowly up the stairs to the kitchen. I was pretty confident I could have made it to the kitchen without assistance, but I was grateful for her help. Her hands were warm and her shoulder supporting my left arm was soft. She guided me through the door and to the chair where I had refused breakfast not forty-five minutes earlier. I sat down heavily while she stoked up the woodstove and put on a kettle of water.

"Can you take off your shirt? Let me help you. I want to make sure that you don't have any more cuts anywhere. It certainly is lucky that you didn't get poked in the eye!"

I frowned. I was not anxious to take my shirt off in front of Willa. I had become used to seeing my scars for myself, but I wasn't exactly happy to display them to others, especially Willa. "Oh, I don't think I need to do that!" I objected. "It's just my forearms that are scratched up." I held my arms out to her to authenticate my claim. I winced at the movement, which Willa immediately noticed.

"See? I saw that. Now, stand up and take off your shirt." Her tone implied that she wouldn't accept any further objection on my part. She stood in front of me with her hands on her hips, awaiting compliance. *I take that last one back,* I thought to myself. *She would have made a good Navy nurse.*

66

I stood slowly and fumbled with the buttons. When she saw that I had accomplished that, she went around to my back and slowly pulled the shirt over my shoulders and then gently peeled the sleeves from my arms. I closed my eyes and waited for the inevitable gasp as she revealed my lumpy, multi-colored scars. However, she didn't utter a sound and continued just as if she hadn't seen anything out of the ordinary. She examined my back and then came around to my front to examine my sides and chest.

"Raise your arms, please." I complied the best I could. She slid her warm hands over my exposed skin, looking for other injuries. I bit my lower lip while she was doing this. Sweat popped out on my forehead. "See, I was right!" she exclaimed. "You have a number of very nasty scratches here. It looks like the bushes tore through your shirt. I will need to clean these off, and then I will put something on all your cuts. Please do not move."

Willa moved silently back to the woodstove where she took the kettle off the top and poured the hot water into a small pan. She grabbed a clean towel from the small pantry and returned to sit in front of me. She then dipped a corner of the towel into the hot water and gently started to clean the blood off all of my visible cuts and scratches. She made a slight "ttcchh" noise to herself occasionally as she worked, which I took to mean something along the lines of, *You idiot. You could have killed yourself out there!* I fully agreed. I could still be lying out there with a broken neck.

She continued her ministrations until she had cleaned all the blood off my face, arms and torso. I became certain she was going to ask me to remove my jeans as well, which likely would have caused me to keel over in embarrassment. However, she apparently seemed to be satisfied that my jeans and boots prevented any cuts or scrapes. After a few more minutes, Willa proclaimed, "There! That is much better. I can now see what I have to deal with. Please do not move while I get the Mercurochrome and some bandages."

She returned quickly and began dabbing the red liquid over any cut or scrape she could find. It stung like all get-out. It felt as if I was being attacked by a swarm of wasps. I winced with each new wound she addressed, tiny grunting sounds escaping my lips. I promised myself that I wasn't going to do anything else to cause myself further embarrassment. I felt her put several bandages on several of the cuts.

While she worked, she asked softly, "What happened up there? How did you fall off?"

Telling her what happened, or at least what I *thought* had happened, didn't seem like a particularly good idea at that moment. "I, ah... I actually am not sure," I stuttered. "I was standing there, pulling off the shingles and then I was falling. Maybe I just lost my balance."

She stopped her dabbing and looked at me. "You see? This is what can happen when you drink! Didn't I tell you to be careful up there?"

I didn't actually remember her telling me to be careful, but I didn't feel like I was in any sort of position to point that out to her. "Yes, Willa, I understand all about that. But listen, I really don't think it had anything to do with me having a small drink..." Her glare stopped my sentence cold. "Okay, I don't think it had anything to do with me getting drunk last night or having a hangover this morning." I stopped to consider my statement. Was I really all that certain that my hallucinations, or whatever they were, weren't somehow caused by my drinking? No, that couldn't be it. I had been drunk before — many times, as a matter of fact — and I had never had anything happen anywhere close to this experience. I even had a bit of the DTs on one occasion, after a weekend onshore party that had gotten completely out of hand. This... this had been something else entirely. It seemed to be more like a second-by-second replay, in full Technicolor, of what I had experienced last December 7th. It was as if I had a movie camera in my head then and something caused it to project the entire sequence again in my mind, overlaid on top of what my senses had been telling me was "reality," right there on the ladder way the hell up in the air. I shook my head. No, that most certainly wasn't due to drinking. What I really needed was some time to myself to figure out what it actually had been.

"Well?" Willa demanded, standing with fists on her hips. Apparently, I had been staring off into space a little bit too long for her liking.

68

"Look, I remember now. This is all very silly." I thought fast. "There was a bee, maybe a hornet, that flew into my face. I was waving my hand at it. That's when I fell. Last night had nothing to do with it."

"A hornet." She looked at me dubiously. *I am getting better at this,* I thought. *I think I can figure out what she is thinking by looking at her face.* "You fell off the top of the ladder because you were waving your hand at a hornet?"

"Yes! I remember now. There must be a nest up there under the eaves or the roof of the dormer. I must have made it really mad and it went for me."

Willa inspected me with her eyes half closed, her lips pursed. She apparently decided that either I was telling the truth or, at the moment, the truth really didn't matter much. Perhaps she had decided that I was just one of the clumsiest people on the face of the planet and I was too embarrassed to admit it. She continued to dab at my scratches and cuts with the red stinging liquid in silence.

After a few more minutes of this, she stood and put the top back on the bottle of Mercurochrome. "There," she declared as if pleased with herself. "Please do not put your shirt back on until it is all dry. You may take a bath tonight but do not rub too hard on the treated areas. I don't want you to open up those cuts again or get them infected."

Her tone softened slightly when she said, "You may take the rest of the day off from work. Falling off a ladder into sharp bushes is enough for one day. However, please do not forget that you need to replace those shingles you removed." She waggled her finger in my face in a very schoolmarm-ish way. "You cannot leave the job half done or else I should get very wet in my room during the winter!" She smiled slightly, as if to say that of course she knew that I wouldn't leave the job unfinished, but she wasn't going to let the opportunity go by to tweak me. "And please, no more drinking! I do not like men who drink." She nodded firmly, as if to indicate that she was in total agreement with herself. She then turned back to the kitchen counter to pour the pan of now pinkish water into the sink.

I grabbed my shirt and thanked her very much. I walked stiffly out the kitchen, heading for the stairway back up to my room. It wasn't until I was halfway up the stairs did I realize that Willa had not said a single word about my scars.

I was in my bedroom, lying on my stomach on the bed, reading one of the few books I had in my possession, *Robinson Crusoe*. I had read that particular tome several times when I was younger. It was an interesting story and had the distinction of being one of the few books I actually owned. My mother bought it for me one year for Christmas. As a child, I was fascinated by the story, although I found the part about the cannibals frightening. That book had launched my childish imagination in motion about distant lands that, many years later, contributed to my joining the Navy. It had been several years since I had taken the plunge back into life on the Island of Despair with Crusoe and his good companion, Friday.

I looked up when I heard a quiet tapping on the door to my room. I assumed it to be Willa, checking in to see how I was faring. I thought I would demonstrate for her my 'stiff upper lip,' bearing up through the pain of my injuries, although it occurred to me that I might make a slight embellishment here and there. I wouldn't lie to her, of course. But a bit of extra emphasis on the fact I could have easily been killed while working on the roof of her room might earn me the appreciation and sympathy that, frankly, I thought was deserved.

I was a bit surprised and more than a little disappointed when I saw it was not Willa that opened the door but Martha. She was wearing a blue checked frock embellished with little yellow flowers that pointed in all directions. I was amused by this, as it seemed to me that flowers should always be pointing up toward the sky, not lying over on their sides or standing on their heads. Willa had obviously brushed her silver hair this morning, as the bun on the back of her head showed little of the disturbance of the previous day. She shuffled into my room — her guest room — and regarded me with obvious sympathy.

"Oh please, don't get up! Especially after the fall you've taken!" Her brow furrowed in concern. "Willa told me what happened. How terrible! You had us all very worried! Are you in much pain, Sean?" I liked the sound of that. 'All' usually means everyone and not just the person speaking.

"Thank you for asking, ma'am. Yes, I was pretty frightened myself, although that only happened after I found myself in the bushes. It was all over so quickly, I wasn't even aware that I was falling. I'm very sorry I crushed your roses. They went a long way toward saving me from much worse injuries. I'll see if I can repair them or trim them back so the damage doesn't look so bad."

She waved her hand at me, indicating her flattened bushes were the least of her concerns. "How in the world did you fall off the ladder? You must have been careless. Ladders are very dangerous, young man! You must watch your feet every second you are on them!"

I considered her statement. It would be rather difficult to get any work done if all I did while up on the ladder was to look at my feet. I also wasn't going to try to explain to the widow what really happened up there, given that I still was not certain myself. What I thought I had experienced had already become very murky in my mind. How could I have experienced two different realities — one present and one past — superimposed upon each other? After a moment, I decided I should just stick with the story I had settled on with Willa, a hornet had flown into my face and I lost my balance when I waved my hand at it. It seemed to me to have the ring of truth to it while telling it the second time. A fib sounds more convincing to the ear the second time it is told.

Martha sadly shook her head at me. She started to say something and then, perhaps thinking better of it, stopped abruptly. Her mouth made some small movements that appeared to be trying to form words, but no sounds came out. She looked at me in surprise and then, in low voice, said, "Did I tell you my husband was dead? Yes, he is dead. He never came home from the Great War. He was killed by the Germans. He was so handsome. So very handsome..." Tears started to trickle their way down the creases in her cheeks. "He loved oranges. Did you know that? Of course you didn't. Why would you? Oranges. We would get a small basket of them every week in the summer. He would get out his knife and he would cut them into quarters and put a large piece of orange in his mouth and suck on it while he was working." She demonstrated his actions for me. "He would make noises with his mouth when he did it. I used to tell him that it was a nasty habit. His shirts were all

71

stained and sticky. I would scrub at those stains but they never came out all the way... " Her last sentence trailed off into a mumble.

Martha turned and stared at me, her eyes cloudier than when she entered the room just minutes earlier. She mumbled a few more words I didn't understand and turned back toward the door. As she slowly shuffled out, I said loudly to her back, "Thank you for your visit, ma'am!" I was at a loss. I had no idea as to what I should say to her about her dead husband or his fondness for citrus. I assumed I had just observed my first example of one of Martha's "bad days." I thought it would be better for both of us if we didn't have further conversations.

I punched at my pillow a few times so that it didn't resemble a saddle and rolled onto my back. I winced several times as I attempted to find a position that wasn't painful and then turned back to my reading. *No cannibals yet, only goats and a parrot,* I chuckled to myself. *He should keep watch over those goats very carefully. They might decide to get lost one of these days. Or perhaps an invisible bear might get them. Either way, he better watch out.*

>> 6 <<

Much later, I heard Willa calling me to dinner. I was pleased to hear her call, as I hadn't had breakfast that morning and hours had passed since she brought me a cup of soup and a piece of bread for lunch. It was good, as soup goes — which usually isn't very far — but I was now ready for something more substantial. I stiffly hefted myself off the bed and lumbered down the stairs. Other than a newly twisted left ankle, which made going down the stairs doubly difficult, the pains were all associated with the cuts and scrapes on my arms, back and face. No broken bones, no punctured internal organs. I shook my head, again contemplating my good fortune. My next thought had me shaking my head again, but this time as a result of my usual 'on the other hand' type of thinking. *If I would have really been fortunate*, I thought sourly to myself, *I wouldn't have jumped off the ladder in the first place.*

When I entered the kitchen, I could see Willa with Major by her side. She had changed out of her usual housework clothes and into something that suited her very well. She wore a long pleated skirt of grey wool, a white blouse with long sleeves and brown leather boots. Her glossy, black hair hung loose around her shoulders. It reached halfway down her back and swayed slightly when she walked. She was lovely.

"The Missus will not be eating with us tonight. She is... not herself right now. I helped her with her dinner earlier and put her to bed. She was very tired."

"Yeah, I think I saw some of that today when I was my room. She started talking to me about falling off the ladder but all of a sudden, she seemed very confused and starting talking about her husband and how he liked to suck on oranges."

"Oranges? I have not heard her say that before. Oranges..." She paused in thought for a brief moment before continuing. "We can have our dinner here and then perhaps, if you are not too tired, we can go into the front room and talk."

I thought that sounded like a fine idea. Hopefully, our heated discussion of the morning wouldn't come up. At the moment, she didn't seem upset with me.

Dinner was stew again with the ever-present bread. I passed on a glass of goat's milk. The bread was still mostly fresh so I wasn't really against having stew and bread again. I thought the next time I drove into town, I would try to see if I could pick up something that might provide a little more variety.

We ate without much conversation. I was concentrating on the food. I disliked trying to talk while eating. Willa, for her part, ate slowly. She finished everything that was on her plate, so I couldn't say she picked at her food. The phrase that came to mind was she ate with great deliberation. As she chewed slowly, she gazed at some fixed point on the wall over my shoulder and gave her food her undivided attention. I tried to watch her without being too obvious. Her method of eating was certainly much different from my shipmates on the *West Virginia*.

After we finished, Willa gave Major his dinner, which consisted of a mix of table scraps and something else she scooped out of a burlap sack in one of the cabinets. She then handed me a small white towel and started washing the plates in the sink. She directed me where to stack them after I dried them. By the time we completed this very domestic task, the two oil lamps and several candles were our only source of illumination. I gazed out the kitchen window as I dried the last of the silverware. The sun had long since sunk below the tops of the trees that loomed to the west. The forest that lay between the house and the steep summit of the peak had been transformed into a huge swath of darkness that began twenty yards from the rear of the barn. I frowned slightly, remembering my discomfort.

"There! Thank you for your help with the dishes," she said with finality. I smiled at her. She dried her hands on a towel hanging on a hook by the sink. "Would you please take that lamp next to you, and I will take this one. We will go sit in the front room."

I followed her down the narrow hallway and through the entryway to the open door to the living area, alternating my attention on her back and on where I was stepping. Major followed closely on my heels. I held the lamp tightly with both hands in the off-chance that he might bump into me.

Willa set her lamp on a small table by the rocking chair to the left of the hearth. She then turned her attention to stoking up the fire that had been smoldering in the stone fireplace. I put my lamp on a low table next to the worn couch to the right of the hearth. With a small groan, I eased myself down into a seated position. In the quivering light of the lamps, I watched Willa as she worked the dying fire with a metal poker. She then placed several small logs on the glowing embers. When she had a small fire burning to her satisfaction, she replaced the metal hearth screen in front of the open flame.

The fire sputtered and crackled as the new wood caught. The light in the room from the two lamps and the newly emboldened fire grew brighter. The yellow-orange flames licked at the logs, casting fantastic shadows that jumped and changed shape. Willa stepped over to the rocker and seated herself. We both watched the fire for some time. I had mixed feelings about being so close to an open fire like that. On one hand, the scene in which I found myself was one of tranquility and comfort. I found myself enjoying just sitting there with Willa, observing how the shadows flitted and capered and waiting for whatever conversation that might occur. On the other hand, I didn't want to concentrate on the flames too intently. I would forever associate fire with my burning, listing ship and the screams of injured shipmates. This fire, however, was small and safely constrained in a box made of large, round river stones. It seemed harmless enough. These flames didn't contain any of the malevolence of the conflagration that was a result of Japanese bombs and torpedoes. Even though the events of earlier of the day seemed very far away, I was wary of a reoccurrence. I had no idea what might have triggered my hallucination, but I certainly didn't want stumble over that trip wire accidently.

After a few more minutes had passed, Willa asked, "How are you feeling now? Are you in much pain?"

I quickly opted for a truthful telling without embellishments. That was part of the rules of our "game," after all. Anything else seemed unthinkable. I was also mindful of the fact that Willa wasn't likely to be very receptive to any exaggerations on my part. "Oh, I think I'm mostly all right. My ankle is swollen and it hurts to put my full weight on it when I walk. It's all purple and yellow, if you care to look at it in the morning. Some of these cuts on my arms and back hurt like the dickens. Those rose bushes had some nasty thorns on them. I need to cut them back before the winter, I guess. And having you paint that Mercurochrome on them certainly didn't help! That stung like hell! Uh, heck, I mean. Excuse my language."

She blew some quick breaths in and out of her nose, which I took to be something akin to a snicker. She smiled, giving absolutely no indication she regretted her contribution to my discomfort. "You don't want to have those cuts to become infected, do you? You should be grateful that I had that bottle in the medicine cabinet." She gazed into the fire so that I had a clear view of the profile of her face. The orange light surrounding us made her face appear softer than in direct sunlight. She continued, "I have seen pictures of the warriors of the tribes of the Great Plains, Cherokee I think, in their war paint, getting ready for a big battle with their enemies." She looked in my direction. "I think I should paint you up in war paint tomorrow while I am applying the medicine. You would look quite fierce." She snickered again.

I was not quite sure I knew how to take this. I had continually been made fun of during my school years, as kids of Irish heritage in Kalama made for an easy target for ridicule and abuse by their classmates. I hated being taunted or laughed at. However, she did not sound as if she were teasing me. My mother taught me an old saying, something about people not laughing *at* you but laughing *with* you. I never put much stock in that. I always believed it was a sneaky way of saying, "Yeah, okay, we are really are laughing at you. But if we say that we aren't, you can't accuse us of anything."

I managed a small forced chuckle, as the situation seemed to call for it. "Yeah, I suppose. Though I would probably look a lot more ridiculous than I would look fearsome."

We sat silently for a few more minutes. I really didn't want to ask my question. However, my curiosity wasn't going to let go of this one. Willa's demeanor as she sat in her chair seemed relaxed and good-natured. If I was going to ask her, this was the time.

"Uh, Willa? Can I ask you a question?"

"Do you mean, 'May I ask you a question?'"

More teasing. I took a big breath and plunged ahead. "When you were tending to my cuts and scratches, you... ah. You took off my shirt." She looked at me expectantly. "Well, you saw what I look like without my shirt on. You didn't say anything."

Her face turned somber. She asked, "You are referring to your scars?" I nodded miserably, my gaze fixed on the red and grey woolen rug that lay on the floor in front of the hearth.

She spoke softly. "Sean, I do not and cannot understand everything that you have gone through. Your injuries were terrible and I am sure they were very painful. You were in a place of war. You could not help what happened to you. You came out of it alive and for that, you should feel thankful. From what I have heard, many people did not."

She paused for a moment and then continued. "I do not understand what causes countries to make war on each other. War is stupid and cruel. Rich and powerful men on each side decide they will have a war with each other and they send out their armies and navies made up of people like you who must do as they are ordered, without question, even if they know it is likely to result in their deaths. It seems to me to be without honor. I do not know why you were in the military. You seem to be very ashamed and embarrassed by your injuries. You should not! You have gone through things that no one else around here can understand. Your country is at war. I do not believe anyone thinks they are ugly, if that is what you are thinking. I'm certainly not."

I looked back up at her. She was still gazing at me in the dancing light of the fire. Compassion, perhaps? I couldn't tell. Maybe that was just wishful thinking on my part. But she was apparently telling me she did not find my scars repulsive. I leaned back in the couch and blew out a long breath. Willa had apparently said all she was going to say on that subject. I could either continue on probing or accept what she had said at face value. I decided that I was okay with her answer and had no desire to question her any further. To blunt the very loud silence that had taken hold of the room, I changed the subject.

I asked, "Do you want to continue our truth-telling game tonight? Or is it too late for that?"

"No, it is not too late. We can continue for a while longer. You go first."

I immediately objected, as I had gone first the previous day. It should be her turn. But according to the rules of this game Willa had set down, mostly without asking for my input or agreement, she informed me that it was indeed my turn and I should go first again. It was like forever being the visiting team in a game of baseball where the home team always bats last. However, I really didn't mind. I was complaining mostly because of the principle of the thing. I would get my part out of the way first and then I could concentrate on what she was saying without worrying myself about what I was going to say after she was done.

I started talking about my childhood again. This time, I focused on my father. I felt that if my turn were about something of substance, she would likely respond in kind. My dad was the first thought that came to me.

"I told you my family is Irish. My grandfather and grandmother on my father's side came over from Dublin before the Great War, when my father was only a boy. My aunt Irene was a few years older. My mother didn't talk about her side of the family much. I actually don't know anything about my grandparents on her side.

"My father was a flat out bad-tempered, hard-drinking Irish son of a bitch. He would probably have punched me if I had said that to his face. I was always too afraid of him to talk back. Oh, every once in a while, he had his nice days. He could be pleasant and even make a joke now and again or take me out to the park. He bought me a baseball glove for my birthday when I was ten years old. I wanted one so I could play baseball with the neighborhood kids. Sometimes, he would take my Mom and me to the only movie theater in town and buy me a bag of popcorn.

"But sometimes, many times, he would come home from working in the lumber mill very tired and he was almost always in a bad mood. I mean, a really foul mood. Usually, he had stopped at the local tavern to kick back a few before he came home. I could tell what the rest of the evening was going to be like just by seeing his face when he walked in the front door in the evening. If my mother didn't have dinner ready by the time that *he* was ready to have dinner, she would catch hell.

Usually, he would just yell at her while she scurried around the kitchen, trying to get it ready. Sometimes, if he was really angry, he would slap her. Hard, right up here on the side of her face, so that the entire side of her face was pink. I saw him do that to her on a number of occasions. One time, when he was really mad, my mother was bending over, picking something off the floor that she had dropped. I don't remember what. My father put his boot right on my mother's behind and pushed her, really hard, so she went face-first into the cabinets. She was crying the rest of the evening while she was serving him his dinner. The only thing he said the entire time was that she should 'shut up and stop her sniveling.'

"I felt very sorry for my mother, that she had to put up with that, but I was mostly just scared for myself. Hell, I was terrified. I would make myself very scarce when he got that way. I would go to my room or maybe go over to my friend John's house a few blocks away. John was a good kid. He was in the class just below mine. We used to play baseball together. His parents never complained if I showed up unexpectedly at their house. I figured they knew what was going on at home and they were quite happy to give me a place to hide out if I needed to.

"I still feel terrible about leaving my mother alone to face him like that. But I didn't know what else to do. Really, I didn't. I wouldn't have stood a chance against him when he was like that."

I glanced over at Willa, who was watching me intently from her vantage point from the other side of the hearth. She gave me a small nod of encouragement but didn't say anything.

"I still remember the first time he came into my room and started hitting me while I was still asleep. None of the doors inside our house except for the bathroom had locks on them. I had absolutely no idea what was happening other than, all of a sudden, I was wide awake and cowering on my bed, scrunched up in the corner, my hands across my face so he wouldn't have a free shot at me again. He was yelling at me. I was not sure what it was about. Some imagined insult or maybe I wasn't doing well in school, I don't know. I was absolutely scared out of my mind. I had absolutely no idea why he was mad at me or why he was hitting me.

"It took me months to understand that it wasn't anything I had done. He was mad and had been drinking, just like he always did, and he just felt like beating on someone. I know my mother had been on the receiving end of his fists on many occasions. I heard them in their room down the hallway often enough. I don't know why he decided that he should start giving it to me. Maybe beating up my mother wasn't any fun anymore. I think, eventually, she would just lie there and take it, with her arms and hands over her head, not screaming or resisting. Maybe he needed a new person to terrorize. I don't know.

"Luckily, that first time it happened was in summer, so I didn't have to go to school the next day. My face was swollen and I had a big shiner of a black eye. I stayed in my room all morning. When my dad went off to the mill, my mother came in my room, put her arms around me and we both cried for a long time."

I stopped. I was not sure what else I could say that would add anything to what I said. But Willa asked, "What happened next? What did you do?"

"Nothing. I didn't do one damn thing. I put up with his drinking and beatings for the next three or four years as best I could. I tried hooking a chair underneath the doorknob of my door before I went to bed. It wouldn't stop him, I knew that, but I figured it might slow him down a little. I kept the window open halfway for a fast escape if I needed to make one. And I took it more than once, crawling out of the window to the roof over the porch and then shinning down the tree in the front yard. Sometimes, I would just hide in the back seat of the car, covered up with a blanket. He never came outside to look for me.

"A few years later, my mother got sick. Real sick. Cancer. We didn't have any money to go into Portland to get her the latest treatments; she insisted that she didn't want them. My father, goddamn his soul to whatever hell there might be, didn't object. He didn't say, 'Look, we are going to fight this, I am going to help and you are going to get better!' He just looked at her when she said she didn't want to go to the doctors anymore. After that, he started not coming home at night. I stopped going to school so that I could help her out the best I could, making her things to eat while she still was eating and washing up. She died about eight months later.

"After my dad was killed in an accident at the mill and I hit eighteen, I sold the house, packed some stuff in a suitcase and hitched a ride over to Kelso. I found the local recruiting office and joined the Navy. I never went home again."

Willa asked me in a quiet voice, "Why did you pick the Navy? Why not the Army?"

"I don't know. I suppose I had some childish dream about being able to get on a ship, sail away and see all sorts of new places. The thought seemed exciting to me at the time. After my mother and I would watch the boats on the Columbia River when I was a kid, I had this dream about being on a ship, a really big ship, going somewhere. Somewhere exotic. Somewhere mysterious. It seemed like that would be freedom. Real freedom. In my mind, it would certainly beat being in the Army, marching around a muddy field with a rifle slung over my shoulder and some bad-tempered sergeant yelling at me all the time. I saw that in a movie once. That stuck with me, I guess.

"Joining the Navy didn't really turn out the way I thought it would."

I stopped talking. I had been gazing into the fire the entire time. I got up from the couch, moved the screen away from in front of the fire, picked up the poker and jabbed at the burning logs. The fire really didn't really need my attention; it was mostly just something to concentrate on while I wasn't talking. The logs popped and threw bright orange sparks into the air as I poked at them. I tossed on a few more lengths of alder. The flames grew stronger as the new wood caught. I was still struggling with the anger and confusion that had suddenly appeared with the telling of my story. I hadn't told anyone that, ever, not even my best buddies in the Navy. I returned to my place on the sofa. Major was lying on the floor next to me. I reached down and lightly scratched his head between his ears. He didn't move but I could see his eyes looking up at me.

"Why's the dog's name Major anyway?" I asked. "That seems like a pretty silly name for a good looking dog like him."

Willa didn't respond immediately. She roused herself from her thoughts and answered, "Oh, that's because the Missus' husband was a Major in the Army. She got

81

him as a puppy a few years ago. She said his eyes reminded her of her husband and that she was going to call him Major."

I pondered that for a few seconds. I wondered why, if Martha wanted to use her dog as a living memorial to her fallen husband, she didn't just give him her husband's name instead of his rank. That seemed pretty dippy to me, but then, Martha was pretty eccentric. I realized I didn't even know her husband's name; maybe it was Horatio or some other strange name totally unsuitable for canines. I didn't know her husband's name, but I did know that he liked to suck on oranges while he worked. *How odd*, I thought. *What a strange thing to know about a person when I don't even know his name.* I decided that I really didn't care. Major was a good enough name for a dog. He certainly seemed comfortable with it. I ruffled the soft fur on the back of his neck with the tips of my fingers. That was the only place I could reach comfortably without shifting my position and I didn't feel like moving.

I wondered if Willa was going to take her turn now or whether she was tired and would keep her turn until the next time, whenever that might be. She seemed lost in thought. I was a bit uneasy, thinking that my story had been a lot more personal than she had expected and wasn't sure how she should respond. I thought maybe she was embarrassed which, in turn, made me embarrassed. I hadn't been while I was talking, as it seemed to be appropriate. But now, however, I wasn't so sure.

Willa looked up, perhaps aware that she had fallen silent and I was waiting on her to say something. She gave me a wan little smile that seemed to be more sorrowful than anything else. "Thank you for your story, Sean. That was obviously difficult for you."

She took a deep breath. "I will continue with my story from yesterday. As I was telling you, my father and two brothers had disappeared one winter day while looking for game. I told you they never came home. But several months later, the men in the village did find one of my brothers. I mean, they found his body. He was no longer among the living.

"After my father and brothers disappeared, the snow had stopped the next day but it was another three days before the deep snow had melted enough for the men to renew their search. They still found no trace. After a few more days of futility, the elders declared the men should search no more. There was much work to do to keep us alive for the rest of the winter and to get ready for the coming spring.

"Later, when spring did come, a hunting party that had been out returned to the village. The men were dragging a large bundle wrapped in several blankets on a travois that they had constructed. We soon heard they had found my elder brother's body. He was in a small valley about two days walk away. My mother demanded to see him but the elders would not let her. It would be too upsetting for her, they said. There is no reason to look, they told her. They could tell it was my brother from his clothes and his small pack and weapons. His body was... it was badly decomposed from being out in the open for so long. My mother started to wail again but she was shushed by my aunt.

"After my brother's body was properly cleansed and prepared, the clan arranged for the burial ceremony. I was very sad. My brother was ten years older than I was. He was a man when I was still a young girl. He didn't speak to me often, but I loved him anyway."

She sniffed again, although she didn't appear to be crying. I watched her carefully. She apparently wasn't through with her story yet. She seemed to be struggling with her thoughts.

"It wasn't until later that my cousin told me that he had been listening to his father talking with his mother. My uncle had been one of the men in the hunting party that found my brother. He said they didn't want my mother to see my brother's body because... he had been partially eaten. That would have been bad enough. But he said the wounds on my brother's body were very strange. They weren't like bite marks from being pecked by birds or gnawed by a wolf."

I was startled but not shocked. After all, if a body has been left exposed out in the wilderness, certainly some hungry animals would eventually come to dine on it. I waited for a further explanation. I wasn't sure what she was getting at.

I finally asked, "What do you mean, Willa? What were the wounds like, then?"

83

"My cousin told me that his father had said that it didn't look like an animal had eaten him. He didn't say what."

I was still mystified. What else besides an animal would eat a dead man out in the woods?

Willa was staring at the slowly dying flames. The room was growing dark again. The frosted glass chimneys of the oil lamps glowed yellow and projected two small yellow circles that danced on the ceiling. She didn't seem inclined to say anything else in the way of an explanation. She obviously had wanted to tell me that story. Perhaps she felt she must respond to my sordid family tale with one of her own. I got the impression she really hadn't finished saying everything she had been thinking.

I decided against asking any more questions. Perhaps she would feel like explaining herself better at some other time.

After some time, however, she did continue speaking, although I became aware that her narrative had taken a jump in time. "The next year, I was sent to the school in Fort St. John. They called it the 'Indian School.' My mother had become… lost in herself after my father and brothers disappeared. My aunt and uncle decided that my mother would move in with them. At that time, the government of Canada wanted to change all the Native children so that they would be like white children. The government had set up schools in order to 'educate' us. It was the law that all Native children had to attend one of these schools, but my village was remote so no one bothered us. My aunt and uncle apparently thought that going to a real school in a real town would be better for me than living in crowded conditions with them, my mother and my cousins. I guessed what they really meant was they didn't think it would be good for me to live with my mother who was… who was not right in her head. They seemed to be worried for me if I stayed in the village. So, that autumn, my younger cousin and I were sent away to Fort St. John.

"There were about thirty-five other Native children of all ages in the school. We were taught by an elderly white woman that wore very small glasses on her nose. Sister Edith. That was her name. I didn't like Sister Edith very much. She had a long stick that she would bang on our desks if we talked out of turn or didn't do our lessons correctly. We were taught how to speak English and a little French, the history of Canada and all about your God in the Bible. We were not allowed to talk in our own language or dress in our own clothes. They made all of us, even the girls, cut our hair short, just like white children.

"I learned my lessons well enough so that I managed to stay out of trouble with the Sisters, but I didn't believe everything that they taught us. I didn't like the way Sister Edith talked about us. She kept calling us 'savages.' I didn't like that. 'Savages.' Another word she used when talking about the children was 'heathens.' I looked that word up in the dictionary. It means someone who doesn't believe in your God of the Bible. I was thinking, of course I didn't believe. Why should I?" Willa paused briefly before resuming. "I wondered why Sister Edith wanted to teach us if she hated us that much."

"It sounds horrid. I am so sorry to hear this, Willa!"

She looked at me quizzically in the light of the lamps and the dying embers in the hearth. "What are you sorry about? You didn't have anything to do with my experiences in the school. There is nothing for you to be sorry about."

She certainly had me there. I was searching for a good way to explain to her that I felt great sympathy for what she had gone through in a way that didn't sound silly when I heard the sound an animal call outside the house somewhere. The sound was not anything I had not heard before. I had no idea what kind of nocturnal animal it might have been. It was not at all unusual to hear coyotes howl and yip in the evenings and early mornings, of course, and I had heard what I assumed to be an owl on several occasions. But I hadn't heard this particular call before. It was an odd, warbling sound that rose in pitch and volume as it went along and then trailed off until it died out. After a few seconds, the call sounded again. It didn't sound like an owl, but then it didn't sound like anything else I ever heard, either. Whatever was producing the sound, it didn't sound particularly near the house. I couldn't tell the direction it was coming from, as the sound was muffled and distorted before it reached us inside the house. *It could be coming from up in the woods*, I thought uneasily.

I turned toward Willa, intending to ask her what she thought it might be. She had been here in Deer Valley long enough to be familiar with the local animal population. My query died quickly, however. Willa was sitting ramrod straight in the rocker, eyes opened wide. Her hands gripped the armrests tightly. I could see that the knuckles on both her hands were white. She had obviously heard the call as well and seemed to be very alarmed about it. At my feet, Major had his head up with his ears erect. He whined slightly but didn't move.

I didn't know what to make of Willa's reaction. The call we heard was unusual, to be sure, but it didn't seem to be much of anything to be concerned about. I thought it likely it was just a new species of owl that had entered into the valley. Whatever it had been that produced the strange noise, I doubted it was dangerous. In any event, we were inside the house equipped with sturdy doors. Unless something was very hungry, a wild animal hardly ever broke into an occupied dwelling. Wild animals usually avoided people, they didn't seek them out. I thought that I had read that somewhere. I hoped it was true.

I bent forward in order to catch her attention and asked, "Willa? Is everything all right?"

That seemed to break whatever spell she seemed to be under. She blinked her eyes rapidly several times. "What? Oh. Yes, I am fine." She looked quickly around the darkening room, attempting to get her bearings. I didn't think she looked fine. She looked frightened.

"I am... I am just tired. I think we have had enough talking for tonight. I am going to go upstairs to my room now. Will you please put out the fire, blow out the candles and make certain that both doors and locked and all the windows are closed before you go to bed? Thank you. I enjoyed talking to you tonight. I shall see you in the morning."

With that, Willa rose from the rocker, picked up the oil lamp from the table at her side and quickly departed. I listened to her soft footsteps on the stairs as she ascended rapidly.

I turned my head to look at Major, who was still poised and alert. "What in the world was that about, do you suppose?" He turned his head to look up at me but did not move from his position on the floor next to my feet. "I guess I better do as she asked. I am not in much of a mood to sit here by myself. No offense, Major, but your conversational skills leave a lot to be desired."

I went to the front door, made sure the latch was set and the deadbolt was engaged. Holding the lamp, I walked back through the hallway to the kitchen, blew out the candles and made certain the kitchen door was also locked. I glanced out of the window in the door but couldn't see anything in the darkness.

I rubbed the back of Major's neck and scratched the top of his head. He seemed to be more relaxed than he had been a few minutes earlier. I hadn't heard the call again — if that's what it indeed had been — since Willa had gone upstairs. I went back to the living room and broke apart the remnants of the logs in the fireplace. The flames flared briefly from the scattered, blackened embers before rapidly dying down. I made certain that the metal screen fit snugly in front of the open hearth to protect against a flying cinder that might land on the woolen rug. *Never can be too careful with fire*, I thought to myself. *Got to watch the fire. Dangerous stuff, fire is.*

I slowly walked toward the stairs, the flickering light from the lamp in my hands illuminating my way up the dark, cramped stairway. After I had removed my clothes and pulled on my pajama bottoms, I found myself staring at the cabinet below the washbasin where my bottle resided. I remembered clearly what I had promised Willa, but I thought that a nip or two before I went to bed wouldn't really be drinking. I was most certainly not planning on getting drunk. I was only looking for a little reassurance that I wouldn't find myself on the floor in the middle of the night, trying to remember if I had been screaming or not. And I would make absolutely certain I brushed my teeth in the morning. Willa wouldn't ever suspect.

However, when I opened the wooden door to the cabinet, my bottle was no longer back in the rear corner. I peered stupidly into the dark interior, wondering where I might have put the bottle if it wasn't there. I knew it still contained enough bourbon for several more good snorts. As I turned toward my satchel, wondering if I had put it in there instead of my usual hiding place, the realization suddenly struck me that Willa had taken my bottle. She certainly had been angry enough at breakfast.

I slowly fell backwards from my squatting position until I felt my rear hit the floor and my legs sprawled out in front of me. *Willa had taken my bottle of booze! Right from my room!* I ran my hands through my hair several times, contemplating this surprising development. I realized I wasn't exactly angry with Willa. After all, she was the caretaker of the house and she was the person that hired me for this job. Her rules. I could quit if I didn't like them. I realized I was more frustrated than anything else. She apparently didn't fully understand that I really needed that bottle to keep the savage heebie-jeebies away from me while I tried to get some sleep.

I considered my situation carefully. I knew I wasn't going to resume that particular discussion with her. Not only had she very angry that morning but had also been very firm in her directive about drinking. I seriously doubted she was going to change her mind just because I might ask her nicely. I knew I was going to be going into town for our weekly supplies in the next day or two. I was certain the local bar in town would be able to spare a bottle or two. The one that had disappeared would have needed to be replaced soon anyway.

I eased myself back into the bed. The rusty springs squeaked in protest as I rolled over on my side, facing the wall. *Yes*, I reassured myself, *this will be okay. I can do this. I just need to hide my bottles better the next time.* With that decision made and filed away, I closed my eyes and hoped for sleep to come quickly.

7

Thankfully, no nightmares came that night. However, the following morning, I couldn't have testified that I felt particularly refreshed. Truth be told, I felt like hell. I trudged over to the closet to pull on my jeans and shirt. At least I hadn't found myself face down on the floor.

I found everyone — Willa, Martha and Major — in the kitchen. There was a large mug of tea in front of Martha. Willa turned briefly from her task at the stove. "Good morning, Sean. I hoped you slept well." I nodded, not really in agreement but more of an acknowledgment I had heard her question. I looked longingly at Martha's mug of tea. I fervently wished for a large cup of the strong black coffee that was served in the mess deck on the *West Virginia*. I made a mental note to buy a coffee pot and some coffee on my next town trip.

I sat down heavily opposite Mrs. Cahill. She peered at me over the top of her mug that she was holding with both hands. "What have you gotten yourself into, young man? You have red spots all over your arms! Were you bitten by mosquitoes?"

I glanced over at Willa. She gave a slight non-committal shrug of her shoulders. I was on my own.

"Ah, no ma'am. I got tangled up in some bushes out back and came away the loser. Willa insisted that she put some Mercurochrome on my scratches."

"That is very good! Very good indeed. You wouldn't want a cut to become infected." She smiled in satisfaction, confident of having single-handedly saved me from a prolonged and painful death due to an infected scratch.

As I had very little inclination to dwell on my incident with the ladder, I attempted to redirect the conversation with something I thought would be a little safer. "That certainly was an odd animal sound we heard last night, wasn't it, Willa? I don't remember hearing anything like that before."

Martha perked up. "You heard an animal last night? My goodness. You don't know what it was?"

I shook my head. "I suppose it might have been an owl. It didn't really sound like an owl, though. But it wasn't a coyote. I do know that for certain. I know what coyotes sound like and that wasn't it."

"Willa, did you hear anything?" Martha asked. "Do you know what it was?"

Willa paused in her dishing out the hash onto plates and looked over her shoulder at the two of us. "It was nothing. It certainly wasn't odd. It was probably just some animal that had been injured. It's nothing at all to be concerned about," she said with finality.

I looked at her in surprise, but she had turned to continue serving breakfast. The way she had reacted to the calls the previous night belied her certainty in the bright light of the morning. Willa set the plates on the table in front of us and went to get the utensils. It seemed to me that she did not want to look at us. As she sat down in her chair and started to eat, she saw me looking at her.

"What?" she asked, somewhat defiantly. "Why are you looking at me like that, Sean? I think it's very rude to stare at someone while they are trying to have breakfast. I suggest you do the same." She pointed at my plate of hash with her fork for emphasis, her dark eyebrows furrowed. "I am certain you have work to do outside today."

"Nothing at all. I just... Nothing." I finished up what was on my plate quickly. I did have work to do outside, although I didn't quite feel up to replacing the shingles on the roof yet. That would mean climbing the ladder and I certainly didn't equipped this morning for that. There was always the pile of firewood that needed enlarging. I just wanted out of the kitchen quickly without any further confusion.

* * * *

After completing the jobs I had planned for the day, I went back inside to clean up and change clothes before supper. As I was dressing, I realized I was a bit pensive about the reception that awaited me downstairs. I hadn't seen Willa since that morning and, after her odd behavior during breakfast, I had no idea if she might still be upset. Perhaps she had forgotten the incident altogether. After pausing a few moments before entering the kitchen, I decided my best approach was to act like nothing had happened and see how things developed from there.

The scene in the kitchen looked remarkably similar to the one that had occurred that morning except for Martha's vacant chair. Thinking back, I realized that I hadn't seen her in the evenings for over a week. I wondered if her condition was deteriorating or perhaps it was just that she just didn't have any energy left after a full day.

"Evening, Willa," my voice boomed out louder than I had intended. "That smells very good. I take it Martha has had her dinner already?"

"Good evening, Sean. Yes, the Missus was feeling quite tired. Here's your dinner," said as she handed me a plate of yesterday's stew and several slices of bread. As she said down, she asked, "What chores did you get accomplished today?"

"Oh, it was mostly cutting more firewood. I seem to be making good progress on the getting the stock of wood ready for winter. I spent some time working on the front steps and railing. There are some rotten boards that I wanted to replace. A person could put his foot right through one of those steps and break a leg. I found some old lumber in the barn that I cut to size. I sure could use some new nails, though. It's really hard to pound those rusty ones I found in the barn through the wood without them bending." She looked at me quizzically. "On account of the rust. The rust on the nail catches on the rough wood and it won't slide through like nice smooth nails will. When you hit a rusty nail with a hammer, it usually bends first. I don't suppose you would mind if I buy some more nails tomorrow when I go into town? I need a few other things, if you don't mind. I could sure use some new gloves. The pair I found in the barn isn't doing the job worth beans." I held up my hands to show her my new blisters. She nodded, registering her newly acquired understanding regarding the complexities of nailing one piece of wood to another.

"Yes, if you like. Get what you think you will need. I will give you some extra money when I give you the list of supplies that I need."

"Ah, and do you suppose I could get my pay for the couple of weeks I have been here too? I have a few personal things I would like to buy. If you don't mind, I thought I would buy a percolator so I can have a cup of coffee in the morning." She wrinkled her nose at the thought of coffee — Willa was obviously not a coffee person — but nodded.

We finished the meal in silence, Major waiting expectantly by my side. Occasionally, I slipped him a bit of potato, which he accepted ravenously. Willa glanced at me the second time I did this but didn't tell me to stop. Major was going to get whatever was left on the plates as the end of the meal in any event. I assumed it really didn't matter whether he got my table scraps now or a bit later.

After we were finished, she prepared Major's dinner in his bowl while I started stacking the plates in the sink. I thought, this time, I might try the washing end of the cleaning up process and let Willa dry them. Also factoring into my decision was the fact the soapy water would clean my hands and, that way, I wouldn't need to handle the clean dishes with dirty hands. I smiled to myself. *Good thinking, Sean!* While we were eating, I had seen Willa frowning at my dirty fingernails. I made yet another in my growing lists of mental notes, *clean fingernails before supper!* This wasn't something anyone who worked on greasy machinery in the Navy would normally concern himself with. In many ways, being a civilian was much more complicated than being in the Navy.

As we were finishing up, I glanced over at Willa. "Do you want to go sit in the front again tonight? We could have another round of the game."

She looked dubiously back at me. "I think not. I am rather tired tonight."

"Oh, please. Just a short one? I'll go first again." I began to think my array of faces was having very little effect on Willa. Maybe she was having as much trouble determining what white people were thinking based on non-verbal cues as I was having with her.

"All right. A short one, then."

We lit the two oil lamps and carried them into the front room as we had done the previous evening, Major following closely. I watched Willa construct a small structure of wood and kindling in the fireplace. *My god, she's so graceful*, I thought to myself as she flipped her long braid back over her shoulder so it wouldn't interfere with her fire building. I had a quick vision of Willa, a Willa of several hundred years past, preparing a fire out in the wilds of British Columbia. I again wondered what she was doing in the Cascade Mountains here in Washington. *Perhaps she will tell that part of her story tonight*, I speculated to myself. I suspected, when I heard it, it would turn out be a very interesting tale.

When the small pile of logs began to burn on their own, she placed the screen back in front of the flames and took her place in the rocking chair. She carefully arranged her long skirt so that she could sit in the hard upright chair more comfortably. She then looked up at me and said dryly, "Your turn."

I cleared my throat and thought a bit. I left off telling her about my life just before I joined the Navy. There wasn't much to talk about the four years I was in prior to the Japanese attack. I realized that was really the only thing that might be of interest left in my personal history was what happened to me during the attack and afterwards.

I cleared my throat again. "December 7th, 1941. As President Roosevelt said afterwards, 'A day that will live in infamy.' It was a nice bright Sunday morning. Everyone was aware of the war in Europe and how it was looking pretty bad for France and England. We also knew about the tensions going on between the United States and Japan, but I really didn't think it would amount to much. No one was going to want to get into it with the United States. China, Indonesia and the Philippines seemed very far away and not my concern. I had already had my mess...."

Willa interrupted, "Mess? What does this mean, please?"

I smiled. I had assumed that everyone, even non-military people, knew what that meant by then. "I'm sorry. It's military slang. It means food or a place where military people eat. What I meant was that I already had my breakfast that day. It was one of my duty days, one of the days I was officially working. I was up on the deck, trying to fix an electric winch that had jammed up. The sun was bright and the breeze was flapping the flags on the bridge of the ship. I was getting a little annoyed with the winch. Something had jammed itself into the gears and the whole thing was frozen solid. I remember banging my knuckles on one of the gears. I remember seeing the blood oozing out between my knuckles, mixing with the black grease on my hands." I paused momentarily to gaze at the knuckles of my left hand that still bore a small, white semicircular mark that stood out from the surrounding skin.

"I remember suddenly being aware of the drone of aircraft somewhere in the vicinity. This was not unusual. There were often many airplanes coming and going from Hickam Field and Wheeler, so I didn't think much about it. Maybe there were a lot more airplanes coming in than I was used to hearing, but I still didn't register anything out of the ordinary. I was swearing at the jammed winch. It wasn't until I heard sailors shouting and the explosions of the first bombs that I realized something big was going on.

"I wasn't frightened at first. The airplanes with their bombs and torpedoes just came out of nowhere. I guess I was in shock. I just stood there, watching the Zeros — that's the name of the Japanese airplanes — roar across the sky from my left to right at a very low altitude. I guess I stood there stupidly with my mouth hung open and still holding the wrench that I had used to work on the winch, watching the explosions start. I saw the first hit on the *Arizona*. I was still standing there, frozen, when the *Arizona* exploded. That knocked me backwards onto the deck and maybe woke me up out of the trance I had been in. My ship, the *West Virginia*, took a torpedo broadside, about forty feet from where I had been standing. The explosion engulfed the entire side of the ship. My clothes caught fire. I could feel my clothes and hair burning. We eventually took seven torpedoes, I learned later."

I stopped talking, as I found myself thinking back to the hallucination that I had experienced the day before while standing on the top of a tall ladder. I had seen the flames all around the ship. I had heard the people screaming. I saw the burning water far below. I glanced up to see Willa gazing silently at me. She apparently understood I was struggling with my story.

I cleared my throat again. "By this time, fire had engulfed us. There were huge flames all around. I could feel the deck of the ship starting to move and list under my feet. By then, I was starting to panic. I realized this was a life and death situation, for me and for everyone on the ship.

94

"I am ashamed now, but the very first thing I thought about was how I could save myself. It wasn't about helping my shipmates. It wasn't about trying to find a way to fight the airplanes. It was how I could save myself... I... Uh..."

Willa leaned toward me. "Sean, you don't have to continue. I understand."

"No, that's okay. I am just about finished anyway." I took a deep breath as a way of releasing the tension that had grabbed my chest. "There's not much else to say. I ended up leaping over the rail into the water. I knew I had to get away from the ship quickly, as it was beginning to sink. I think another torpedo hit it as I was swimming out away from the ship. It was bad luck for the *West Virginia* to be on the outside of the *Tennessee*, as that left us exposed to the Japanese torpedo planes. But it turned out to be very lucky for me, as I had a pretty clear opening out into the channel and away from the burning ships. I swam under the water as long as I could. I surfaced whenever I could see a spot in the water above me that wasn't on fire. Seeing the fire burning on top of the water while you are swimming underneath it is a very scary thing to see. It was beautiful in a way, I suppose, but all I could think of was the pain on the right side of my body, how terrified I was and if I was going to be able to escape.

"I was eventually picked up, along with a number of other injured sailors, by a motor launch that was circling around the burning ships. I don't remember much after that until I woke up in a hospital bed, surrounded by lots of other hospital beds occupied by all the injured sailors and soldiers."

"That's about it. I spent the next seven months in and out of a number of different hospitals. No broken bones, no internal injuries. Just a lot of burned, dead skin."

I stopped. Telling that story had turned out to be a lot more difficult than I had been expecting. I stared into the fire that was safely contained by stones and the wire mesh screen. I hadn't ever talked about my feelings of shame with anyone before, about the fact that I hadn't done anything but save myself. Nothing, absolutely nothing I did that day could be considered heroic in any way. I frowned at the flames.

Neither of us said anything for several minutes. It was just the two of us sitting inside the halo of light of the fire and the oil lamps, surrounded by the shadows of the darkened living room. I wasn't sure what Willa was thinking. Did she think I had deserted my buddies? Were my actions a dereliction of my sworn duties? The silence was getting very uncomfortable.

"Willa, can I ask you something? You may not want to answer this but I really would like to know something." She nodded her assent without looking at me, perhaps still contemplating my story.

"This morning at breakfast, you said you thought that the call or whatever it was we heard last night was nothing to be concerned about. But when we heard it last night, the way you reacted, well, you looked really spooked. It seemed as if something had really frightened you. But that's not what you said to Martha and me this morning. Do you know something about it that you weren't telling us?"

This time, I could tell from the masked expression on Willa's face that she was taken by surprise. She had likely been expecting a question about her past, maybe about her family or her schooling in Canada.

She didn't answer at first. I waited without pushing her any further. She appeared lost in thought. She started to speak but stopped, appearing to consider what she was going to say before she began hesitantly.

"You may not understand what I am about to tell you. You are a white man. White men live in a different world than the Dena'ina. I do not believe that we experience the world in the same way." I was mystified as to what she meant by her statement. There is only a single world. It seemed obvious to me that everyone must experience it in the same way. We all have the same eyes and the same ears. I didn't understand how Willa could say that different people might "experience" the world differently from each other.

She spoke softly and slowly. "When we first heard that sound, I thought it might be a *Wechuge*. I have never heard one before but I remember my aunt telling my cousin and I the story of how she had seen one when she was little. She described the sound it made. She had been terrified and hid herself in a ditch so the *Wechuge* would not see her and eat her. The sound we heard last night made me

96

think of my aunt's story." She saw the question in my eyes before I asked. "A *Wechuge* is an ancient animal spirit. I have heard the elders tell that a *Wechuge* was once a person in the world but has been taken over a giant animal spirit. Something in the person's past, perhaps breaking a taboo, has allowed the animal spirit to take possession of that person."

Willa rested her chin on the heel of her hand, her elbow propped on the armrest of the rocker, lost in thought as she gazed into the fire. At first, I assumed that she would continue, but this was apparently all that she was going to say.

"Why do you think that what we heard last night was one of these, uh... Waay-chew-gay?" I struggled with the pronunciation of the name she had given. "I don't believe in ghosts or spirits, but if one were to exist, why would it be here?"

Willa didn't answer immediately. When she did, it was not an explanation. "That is all for tonight, Sean. I am very tired. Would you please bank the fire before you go to your room?" She stood and then turned to look at me, her features again softened by the yellow light of the lamp she was carrying. "And thank you for telling your story. That must have been a terrible experience. You should not feel shame. You did what you could at the time. You survived."

With that, she turned and exited the room. Major watched her depart and then turned his head back to me, his intelligent brown eyes seemed to be asking me a question. I didn't know the answer.

I sat in front of the dying light of the fire for a long time before I went up the stairs to my threadbare room with its narrow window overlooking the forest.

8

Armed with Willa's list of supplies and a medium-sized roll of cash in my pocket, I set out for my drive into Skykomish. Before backing it out of the barn, I did a quick walk-around of the old Ford. All the tires seemed to be inflated, although I noted there was not much tread left. That would likely be a problem when driving in snow, but for now the tires seemed serviceable. Oil, check. The motor turned over several times before it finally rumbled into action. The brakes were a bit mushy; I would have to be careful about that. Otherwise, all seemed to be reasonable order. I slowly backed out of the barn and turned around before proceeding down a slight incline. I then made the sharp turn onto the dirt road in front of the house.

I assumed that the road, such as it was, had begun as nothing more than a logging road, put there to gain access to the big trees so men with saws could chop them down and haul them away to become people's houses and furniture. The builder of Martha's house, when he chose the location for his homestead, apparently just followed his men and equipment up the logging road to Deer Valley. The road paralleled the stream down from the valley until the stream converged with the South Fork of the Skykomish River. The road was full of ruts, bumps and rocks of all shapes and sizes, several as large as watermelons. These hadn't presented much in the way of obstacles on my hike up to the house, but negotiating them with a large vehicle with bald tires was another matter. In one particularly rough area, the entire roadway dipped down several feet to allow for the yearly spring runoff that comes cascading down the mountain without washing out the road. A mile down the road from the big dip, it finally hit the main highway that crosses the Cascade Mountains. From there, it was only a few hundred feet to the bridge that traversed the boulder-strewn Skykomish River into the town itself.

Main Street was only a few blocks long and ran parallel to the railroad tracks. A block north of the hotel was the local store that carried most everything a person might need. If they didn't have it, you were probably stuck making the drive west into Goldbar or Sultan. Two doors down from the store was one of the two bars in town. I smiled to myself. That would be my second stop.

I wandered through the narrow aisles, plucking items from Willa's list off the shelf as I happened upon them. I added a few items of my own as the mood struck me. On one of the lower, dusty shelves in the back, I was overjoyed to stumble upon an old battered percolator. All the parts appeared to be there, so how it looked was immaterial to me. It meant that I could have some hot coffee in the mornings to go along with Willa's eggs and hash. Things were definitely looking up. When I was finished with Willa's shopping, I loaded everything into the rear seat of the car.

That task accomplished, I sauntered down the sidewalk to the Night Owl bar. It appeared to be open, even though ten o'clock in the morning was a little early to be patronizing the local watering hole. Entering, I saw the place was indeed completely devoid of customers. However, there was a balding, grizzled-looking man behind the bar. As I walked over, he looked up from what he was working on, a crossword puzzle from the entertainment section of the newspaper.

He eyed me curiously over the top of his glasses. "Ken I help ya? What's a seven-letter word that starts with "D", fifth letter "C" an' means 'home?'"

I wasn't sure which question he wanted me to answer first. "I'm pretty sure I don't know about the word. I've never been very good at puzzles. I was just wondering if it is too early to get a drink?"

He pushed the newspaper aside. "Well now. I'm supposen that depends on the person, don' it?" I immediately recognized this from my barhopping days in Honolulu as standard banter that a barkeep uses with his patrons. No doubt standing a behind a bar half of your life would likely be very boring otherwise. "Somes peoples ken takes their lickker and somes can't. What type are ya, I wonders?" His eyes gazed at me from underneath his fuzzy eyebrows. He had more hair in his eyebrows that he had on the top of his head.

"I'm the type that could use a belt or two in the morning on occasion. Do you think you might manage to find a bit of bourbon back there?"

"I'm supposin' I might be able ta accomplish that. Jest a sec." He turned to pick up what I hoped was a clean glass from a tray.

100

Before he could pour me my drink, I said, "Why don't you break open a new bottle and just leave it with me? I'll buy the whole thing."

He peered at me again. "Ya sure about that, are ya? I don' norm'ly sells whole bottles ta strangers." He made a show of taking off his spectacles, slowly wiping them on his grubby apron and giving me the once over. "Ya be a stranger here? I don' seems ta recall ya ever comin' in here afore."

I sighed to myself. All this small talk was apparently part of the price of getting a drink in the Night Owl. "Well, if you must know, yes. I've been in town for a little over a week. I'm the new handyman out at Martha Cahill's place. May I have the bottle now?"

"Oh! So's ya be the new handyman, eh? The Widda Cahill's place... Widda Cahill, she be a right fine woman. Fine woman. Beautiful when she were younger, ya knows. I knowed her when she first moved out ta her house after she an' her husband got hitched. Her husband was keeled in the Great War, ya knows. Blowed up somewhere in France. Or was it Belgium? Let me think. Yep, it must ha' been France. The Krauts got 'im fer sure." He seemed pleased with his ability to able to recall this critical detail.

"Yeah, I knew her husband was killed in Europe. May I please have my bottle now?" I was getting a little annoyed at the old coot. His manner seemed to be more cantankerous than neighborly.

"Jest hold yer horses, mister. I be workin' on it. Here." He set a bottle down in front of me next to the glass, seal unbroken, the amber liquid glowing lightly behind the clear glass of the bottle. "Will this do good fer ya?"

I nodded in assent. "That'll do fine. Thanks."

He watched me break open the bottle and pour the drink myself; two fingers, neat. Leaning back on the counter behind the bar in order to survey me better, he continued with his small talk. "Can't sez I approve a' drinkin' afore noontimes. It does some nasty stuff ta your liver, ya know." My elbows resting on the bar, I nodded my assent. Yeah, I knew. "But ya do seems ta be a man that appreciates good likker."

I poured myself a second drink. As I took a sip, I examined the magnificent bar for the first time. It was massive. The entire thing ran three quarters of the way the length of the building. Its carved wood had darkened with age. A number of glass shelves mounted in front of a very large mirror held a vast selection of bottles of all shapes and colors. They resembled large diamonds and gems on display in a museum. Round wooden columns that would have been at home in a Roman temple stood at each side of the mirror. The whole place looked like something out of a movie, just waiting for John Wayne to come storming in and throw someone over the bar and into all those fine bottles.

The old coot saw where I was looking. "Yep, it's a good un, ain't it? This here bar were part of the original builden. 1908, it was. Built fer the railroad workers an' all the tourists that came up t' stay in the hotel. They sez that Teddy Roos-velt hisself had a drink here, prob'ly right there where ya be standin'! They built the front of the builden right around the bar! They sure couldn't have gotten it in through the front door!" He cackled lightly to himself. "That be fer sure!" I rolled my eyes when I was sure he couldn't see me and took another sip. This character could probably entertain himself for a long time without anyone else around.

Through the myriad of glittering bottles, I caught my reflection in the mirror. *Christ, I need a shave*, I thought. *I don't look too good.* A few nights of uninterrupted sleep would likely help a lot. Contemplating the events of the previous night, I suddenly had a thought.

"Hey, Pops. Mind if I ask you a question?"

"Shoore, shoore... Name's not 'Pops', though. It's Edward. Ask away."

"Edward. Good to meet you, Edward. Mine's Sean." I reluctantly shook his proffered hand. "So, do you know of anyone in town that might know about Native legends, stories and such? History?"

"Native? You mean Injuns?" I nodded reluctantly. I didn't much like that. After the last two weeks with Willa, it sounded like a nasty epithet. "Weeel, lemme think on it." Edward made a big show of frowning and putting his hand over his mouth and chin, a visual demonstration of great concentration. "There ain't many Injuns around' these parts. Hey, ya be livin' in the same house as one! Why don' ya try that maid at Widda Cahill's place? She be an Injun!" He smiled at me triumphantly.

I closed my eyes momentarily and forced myself to count to ten, as I really felt like reaching over the bar and smacking him upside his furry ear. Edward was turning out to be about as quick on the uptake as your average tree. "Yeah, I know that. We talk a lot. That's why I want to find someone who knows about Native history and legends. So I can talk to her about them better." I left it at that; this character certainly doesn't need to know any more. I had no doubt that he was going to blab about this entire conversation to his next patron regardless.

Edward looked up toward the ceiling and stroked his chin. *I bet he practices in front of that mirror when no one is around*, I thought with resignation. He suddenly came out of his trance and snapped his fingers. "Yep, I knows someone that might he'p ya. He don' live in town but ya ken drive west down the highway about five miles. There be a little tradin' post on the side of the road. It's run by an old Injun fella name-a Amos Ghost Horse. Right smart fella, Amos is. He don' hear so good anymore, though. Ya might have ta yell at him. Use his left ear. He's as deaf as a post in his right one, Amos is. He might be able t' hep ya."

"Well thanks for that, Edward. You've been a great help." I paid for my bottle, pocketed my change and turned to leave.

"Say there, Sean... Iffen ya plans on visitin' ol' Amos, ya prob'ly should takes him an offerin'."

"A what?"

"An offerin'. Ya knows, a gift. That's how them Injuns do things. Amos is what ya might call an Elder. Iffen ya wants some infermation from him, ya should brings him an offerin'. Shows respeck, I takes it. And it be a fair trade. Ya wants t' know somethin' he knows? Ya should brings him an offerin'." He nodded sagely at me.

"Okay..." I said slowly. Edward was obviously waiting on the next question. It certainly didn't appear as if he was going to volunteer this information without making me ask outright. Edward was really starting to get on my nerves. The next time I ventured into town, I was definitely going to find the other bar. "What would be an appropriate offering to take to Amos if I want to ask him some questions?"

I was expecting some more back and forth before he got around to answering my question, but this time he surprised me. "Tabakka. That's a good offerin'. Bring him a pouch of tabakka. And ya should call him 'Grandfather.' He might na' be your grandfather, but ya should call him that alls the same. Respeck, ya knows." Edward put his finger to the side of his nose and nodded at me, obviously signifying something but I had no idea what and, frankly, didn't really care. At this point, I just wanted to leave.

"Got's some right here iffen ya want ta saves yerself a trip elsewhere."

"Right. Okay, I'll take one pouch of the best you have. Thanks for the drink and the information, Edward." I picked up the pouch, the bottle and my change and then headed for the door.

"Na problem! Na problem t'all! Weel sees ya next time! We can sits an' have a good chat!"

Not if I could help it, I thought to myself as the screen door banged shut behind me.

*   *   *   *

After a drive of about ten minutes west, I came upon a small white structure on the side of the highway opposite the river. There was a small parking area that might have been able to hold five cars if they parked very carefully. A large weathered and obviously hand painted sign over the front door proclaimed, "TRADING POST! Genuine Indian Curios! Arrowheads! Jewelry! Postcards!" The spot over the door was dominated by the largest set of deer or possibly elk antlers I had ever seen. The rest of the front of the building was covered with all sorts of items that would have been right at home in the local junkyard: hub caps of all sizes and designs, a broken wagon wheel, a rusty wheelbarrow, an old wash tub with a number of large scabrous rust spots showing through what remained of the original white enamel paint, and a dented, copper spittoon, just for starters.

After coming in from outside, the interior of Amos Ghost Horse's establishment was dark; the only illumination was from the sunlight that managed to find its way inside through the open doorway and three grimy windows. Sitting on the glass counter near the back of the store was a large ornate cash register that might have once stood proudly in a Seattle area F. W. Woolworths store. Inside the dusty glass display cabinet, I could make out some bracelets and necklaces holding large pieces of polished turquoise, several old watches that may or may not actually keep the time, all types of lighters, several large shell casings and other bric-a-brac that just might conceivably be of interest to passing tourists.

Amos Ghost Horse was not behind the counter. He was sitting next to an unlit pot bellied stove in a worn easy chair, upholstered with what had once been bright red cloth. His wizened face was framed by a large black felt cowboy hat on the top and two long black braids on each side of his head. There was a single large feather — I guessed eagle — in his hatband. His forehead and the skin around his eyes were heavily creased with wrinkles that, somehow, did not make him look old. He seemed to be ageless, not aged. His dark brown eyes looked up as I opened the noisy screen door. He might have been dozing before I came in, but his dark, alert eyes showed no signs of sleepiness.

Speaking a bit more loudly than usual, I said, "Uh, good morning, Grandfather. I, uh, I brought you a gift." I walked over to where he was sitting and handed him the pouch of tobacco.

Amos received it with both hands and inspected it closely. As the brand I had purchased was the most expensive the Night Owl had in stock, I hoped it would be well received. Amos nodded at me. "This is a good brand." He tapped lightly on the brightly colored pouch with his crooked index finger for emphasis. He then held it up to a light beam coming through the window for a closer examination. "Yes, this is very good."

He returned his penetrating gaze back to me. "A white man comes into my store and gives me an offering right out of the blue, before I have a chance to say anything," he mused. "You must want something." He smiled at me, showing me his off-white teeth.

This guy doesn't beat around the bush, does he? I thought to myself. *I might as well get on with it, then.*

"Yes, Grandfather. You are correct. I was hoping you might give me some information about Native legends."

He gazed at me for a few seconds before replying. "This is a strange question from a white man. There are thousands of what you call 'legends.' What tribe do you want to know about? Each tribe has its own folklore and teachings, as different from each other as a tree is from a river or a cloud. I am Lakota. White people call us Sioux. Lakota are the Earth People because we live close to Mother Earth. Our Father is *Tunkashila*, the Creator. We use the sacred pipe, *Chanumpa*, to find our pathway to our knowledge. This is not what other tribes believe. If you were to ask the same question of someone from the Osage tribe that now live in Oklahoma, you would get a different answer than from someone belonging to the Navajo nation in New Mexico. You don't expect all white men to have the same religion, do you? I understand that Catholics believe in very different things than Buddhists." He pointed his index finger at me. "It is my belief that the teachings of all the different tribes lead to wisdom, just by a different path. So, how you asked me your question, it is a very difficult thing to answer." He closed one eye and examined me closely with the other.

I felt a little off balance. Yes, of course I knew there are many different tribes. I knew but, at the same time, really didn't realize the religious beliefs of each of the tribes would be so much different from the others. In retrospect, I didn't find that revelation very surprising. It just hadn't occurred to me before.

As my mind spun furiously about what I should say next, Amos pointed and said, "Pull up that chair from the corner and sit down. You might as well be comfortable as we talk. You seem to have a lot of questions and I don't have many customers." He leaned back in his chair and braided his fingers together, his hands over his stomach.

I dragged a wooden chair from the corner of the store by the window over to the other side of the stove. Getting the information that I was interested in suddenly seemed to be a lot further away than I had imagined. Amos, for all his knowledge, probably didn't even know anything about what I was interested in finding out. Resigned, I thought I should start at the beginning.

"I am sorry for my lack of knowledge, Grandfather. I meant no disrespect." Amos nodded as if he already understood this and had already forgiven me. "I should tell you why I am asking."

I introduced myself and explained that I had landed a job at Martha Cahill's small farm as a handyman, told him about Willa and how she was Dena'ina from British Columbia, that she was taking care of Mrs. Cahill who was having problems remembering who she is at times, about Willa's sleepwalking and about the incident with the wailing sound that seemed to upset her a great deal. I finally related the conversation I had with her when she told me her story about her aunt and her belief that the sound we heard might have been a *Wechuge*.

"It's just that I am concerned for her, Grandfather. I am worried about her sleepwalking. I don't know why she does that. I am worried she might hurt herself some night. I also have no idea what to make of her story about the *Wechuge*. She seems to be very distressed, and I know that she is very worried about Mrs. Cahill. I think Willa feels a big responsibility. Without Willa, I don't think Martha has anyone else to care for her."

After I had completed my telling, Amos leaned forward in his chair with his forearms on his knees so that he was looking at the bare wooden floor. All I could see was the top of his hat. He remained in that position for several minutes. He was obviously in deep contemplation. I wasn't going to interrupt him.

When Amos brought his head up, he refocused his eyes on me. "This is a difficult problem. I do not have all the knowledge that you require. We shall smoke the sacred pipe."

With that, he levered himself out of the chair with some difficulty and shuffled over behind the counter. From somewhere underneath the cash register, he withdrew a long thin bundle. As he walked slowly back to his chair, I observed the bundle was encased in leather and had a beautifully detailed beaded design worked into its length. The leather was dark and smooth in several places, the grain worn down from many years of handling. After Amos sat, he carefully withdrew a long cylinder made of very dark wood. It had a small bowl, made of the same wood, fixed to one end and a mouthpiece at the other. It was unadorned and gave the impression of being very old.

Amos observed my interest. "This is *Chanumpa*," he proclaimed. "I received it from my father, as he received it from his. *Chanumpa* can provide a pathway to knowledge." He stared at the pipe in his hands for a few seconds. "To do this correctly, we should have a ceremony where we are first cleansed by the smoke of sage and perform the proper chants." He pursed his lips before declaring, "I think we should begin without them. You are in need of knowledge and advice."

With that, Amos rolled his hip over to one side and pulled a worn leather pouch out of his back pocket. He began a soft chant while he loaded the small bowl of the pipe with the blackish tobacco from the pouch. I was expecting him to light it up immediately but Amos closed his eyelids and continued with his chant. It was obviously in his native language, as I didn't recognize any of the words or sounds. Several times, I heard Amos speak the name of *Tunkashila*, likely invoking his name to ask for assistance. He then held the pipe in both hands and with the bowl pointed towards his face, he ritually pointed the stem of the *Chanumpa* in four different directions, which I took to be east, south, west and lastly north. Finally, Amos took a lighter out of his shirt pocket and lit the pipe. He puffed several times to get the tobacco burning. He took several breaths with his eyes closed and slowly exhaled. When he opened his eyes, he leaned toward me, holding the pipe in both hands with the stem pointing at me.

I was surprised at this, as I hadn't expected to be included. I leaned over and carefully received the pipe with both hands. I was reluctant to smoke the pipe, even in this ritualized ceremony. I hadn't had a cigarette since I was released from the hospitals. The doctors told me there had been some tissue damage to my lungs from the fire. It was obvious, however, that this ceremony was deeply significant to Amos and, given that I was the one that came to him looking for information, I felt I should not refuse. I took a few hesitant puffs. I didn't inhale, as I didn't want to set off a fit of coughing. That would be disrespectful and would have spoiled the ritual in which I had unexpectedly found myself part of.

After I had completed my mimicry of Amos's actions, I carefully handed the pipe back to Amos. He smoked again and then bowed his head while holding the pipe up in both hands for what seemed a long time. He then opened his eyes and lifted himself out of the threadbare chair to gently place the *Chanumpa* and its leather pouch on the glass counter.

When he returned to his accustomed place, he gazed at me with a slight frown on his face. He began by saying, "I think you are right to be concerned about your friend. There are spirits at work here that are very dangerous if aroused."

I was somewhat surprised by this rather disturbing pronouncement. I had only come to see Amos for information. I only wanted to find out what a *Wechuge* might be. I wasn't prepared to hear about dangers Willa might be facing.

Amos continued, "I do not have knowledge about a *Wechuge*. However, based on what you tell me, I believe that it must be similar to the *Wendigo* of the Ojibwe. You know of the *Wendigo*?" he asked me. I shook my head in the negative. "A *Wendigo* is an supernatural being that some say used to be a human being who lost his spirit and has been overcome with greed and gluttony. The *Wendigo* is terrible and evil. It is always hungry. It is so hungry that it has eaten its own flesh from around its lips. It searches for and eats humans that fall under its spell. If a human breaks a taboo, he opens himself up to the terrible attention of the *Wendigo*. Once a *Wendigo* has eaten his victim, it begins to search for its next meal."

He frowned slightly. "A *Wendigo* is nothing to joke about. If your friend's aunt did indeed see something like that when she was a little girl, she was right to hide from it."

Amos stopped talking, took off his hat with his left hand and ran his right hand over his thinning hair. He seemed lost in thought. His gaze was fixed on, but not really seeing, the rusty red Coca-Cola cooler chest in the front corner of his store. He replaced his hat and gazed at me solemnly. "You said that the widow has difficulty remembering things and who she is." I nodded. "Have you had any problems like that? Do you have problems with your memory or vision? Have had any peculiar things happen to you while you have been there? Dreams or nightmares?"

"Me?" I recoiled a little, surprised that Amos's questions would suddenly be about me. I believed myself to be outside Willa's problems. I only wanted to help her, not to talk about me. I was also bewildered that he was so close to the actual answer without knowing anything about me at all. "Well... Yes, I suppose... Everyone has dreams. But I am sure that my issues are not related to Willa's problems. How could that be? How could the fact that I sometimes have nightmares possibly have anything to do with Willa's sleepwalking or that sound we heard? That's silly!"

Amos contemplated me silently while I struggled with the thoughts that suddenly raced through my mind. *How did he know that I was having nightmares? Is he talking about my hallucination of the other day? This is just a big coincidence! Just like some fortune-telling hack at the carnival.*

Amos was obviously expecting me to answer his question; my objections had been summarily overruled. I was very unsure of myself. I really didn't want to talk about myself with this person that I just met, no matter how wise and spiritual he might be. *He sells souvenirs to tourists on the side of the road!*

"Like what kind of things do you mean?" I asked slowly.

Amos gazed at me. "There is no need for you to be angry. You respond like I have accused you of something terrible. I think something has happened to you and you don't want to talk about it." He pointed at me with his crooked finger again. "I do not ask this to be nosy about your life. I am trying to discover the situation in the house where you and your friend live. If you do not want to talk about it, that is your business. If you want to help your friend, I think you should tell me anything you know."

As much as I felt that my nightmares were none of his business, I really couldn't argue with his logic. After a few moments of thought, I started talking.

"I have been having nightmares for some time now. They seem to have gotten worse while I have been at the house. It happens almost every night now. I don't know why that might be. I wake up in a panic, sweating. One time, I was on the floor. I think I had been screaming."

He looked at me with raised eyebrows. "What are your nightmares about? Can you remember?"

"Sometimes I remember. Mostly only little pieces, though. I never remember the entire dream. They are mostly about my experiences in the war when the Japanese torpedoed my ship. It sunk out from under me. Many of my crewmates were killed. There were flames all around. I had to jump in the burning water to save myself. I was injured. Badly. I spent a lot of time in hospitals. I only got out about three months ago." I craned my head over so that he could see the scar tissue on the side of my neck and then raised up my right arm to show him the scar on the back of my hand. I added, almost as an afterthought, "Sometimes my father shows up in my nightmares. Those are blurry and I can't remember much, other than he was in them."

Amos nodded his head at me. "This is most interesting. Nightmares are very powerful. Dreams and nightmares can be a way of the Spirit World telling you something important. You should listen to what your dreams are telling you." It occurred to me that Amos Ghost Horse sounded a bit like Dr. Farmer back at the military hospital in Oakland when he was discussing Jung. "Is that all? Just the nightmares?"

I assumed he would somehow know that nightmares weren't all and he would eventually get around to asking me about it. "No. Not all." I frowned to myself before continuing. "The other day, I jumped off the top of a tall ladder. All of a sudden, I was having a hallucination. I was seeing the exact scene I saw during the attack on Pearl Harbor. I saw the airplanes. I heard them! I could smell the gunpowder from the exploding bombs. I could feel the pain from the flames and the shock of the cold water when I jumped off my ship. It was like I was reliving the attack. It was just like I saw it when it happened. I could have been killed when I jumped off that ladder. I was very lucky that I landed in a bunch of bushes. I got off lightly with a bunch of cuts and scrapes. But I was just overwhelmed. I had no sensation that I was still about twenty feet off the ground, standing on top of the ladder. I just jumped to save myself from the fire!" As I finished my account, I realized I had been talking very loudly.

Amos nodded and pointed at me with his index finger. "You had a vision. White men don't have visions very often. If they do, they pretend it was something else. A hallucination, you said? I think it was a vision."

"But I thought visions were when you see something that's going to happen in the future, not something that already has happened." I still felt argumentative, although I wasn't sure why.

"Visions can be about anything. You never know about the Spirit World and what the spirits might be trying to tell you." I frowned at that, as I was certain that the Spirit World hadn't ever told me a damned thing, or if it had indeed been trying, it was going about it in a spectacularly miserable fashion. As far as I was concerned, spirits belonged in the Saturday morning matinees for the kids at the local movie theater or with table-tapping mediums and fortunetellers of the carnival midway.

Amos continued with a question. "Don't you think it is strange that the three people out at your house are all having problems? You say the widow is having trouble remembering things and sometimes doesn't know where she is. Your friend sleepwalks. You have dreams and nightmares. Do you believe these things are all just coincidences?" He looked at me speculatively.

Again, I was taken off guard. That hadn't occurred to me before, but then why should it have? Of course they were coincidences. How could any of our problems be related to each other? I responded to Amos with something along those lines.

Amos again pointed at me. "That is because you are thinking like a white man." I made a gesture with my hands, *Yeah, so what else is new? A white man is going to think like a white man.* I was wondering if my investment of fifteen cents in the pouch of tobacco was going to turn out to be a bad bet. *I should have bought the cheap kind*, I thought uncharitably.

"You should put aside your notions of what can be and what can't be," he continued. "We all inhabit a very big universe that we know very little about. You should stop pretending that your knowledge is superior and infallible. White people are always rushing about. You never slow down long enough for you to comprehend your place in the world and your relationship to others. You are not the only beings that reside here." He said this without any emotion or anger. Amos was just stating facts — his facts — in the same manner as I would tell someone who knows nothing about automobiles that their car needs a new transmission.

"I believe whatever evil spirit that is stalking your friend is affecting everyone who lives in that house. The *Wechuge*, if that is what it is, is making your everyday problems worse. Much worse. Your nightmares have gotten worse. You say that the widow is getting worse. I think your friend didn't sleepwalk until recently. These things are related, that much is clear. That is what is going on. I believe that your friend is in great danger. She should leave immediately. That is my belief." Amos leaned back in his chair. He was apparently finished with his pronouncement.

I stared back at Amos, my mouth wide open. This was certainly not something I had expected to hear when I walked in the door of the trading post. I was at a loss about how to respond to such as a definitive conclusion. "But, Grandfather.... Uh... I don't think she has anywhere to go! If she has any family left, they are up in Canada." Amos shrugged his shoulders. That was obviously not his problem. "Isn't there a... uh, a spell or chant or something that would, I don't know, drive away this spirit or at least make Willa believe that there isn't anything after her?"

"If there is such a thing that is effective against such a being, I do not know of one. You are seeking simple solutions where there are none." He stared back at me, his gaze implacable.

At that moment, the bell over the screen door jangled. A young couple with a little girl in tow entered the store. The woman was nicely dressed in a bright blue dress and matching jacket, her brown hair topped with a small circular hat. She looked around the store, her face showing her distaste for the dingy surroundings. The little girl, on the other hand, made a cooing noise and promptly dashed over to the display cabinet. She excitedly called out to her parents, "Look, Mommy! A necklace! It's blue! Ooo! It's pretty!"

Amos nodded to me – a silent farewell – and heaved himself out of his chair, leaving a large divot in the worn cushion. He shuffled over to the couple and began a negotiating process for the necklace that the couple had no idea they had entered.

I sat there for a few more seconds, trying to absorb what I had just heard. In many respects, what Amos told me fit very nicely with what Willa had said earlier, not only about the *Wechuge,* but also about life in general and how white people "see" things differently from how the First People do. As for Willa leaving the house, I saw that as a completely unrealistic course of action. For one thing, I didn't think she had anywhere to go. And two, I doubted very seriously that she would abandon Mrs. Cahill in her present condition. Mrs. Cahill had no alternatives, either, and even I could see that leaving her alone in her house would likely be a death sentence. As for me, I knew I could just cut and run, but that would serve no real purpose. My nightmares were going to follow me regardless of where I went and running away wouldn't help Willa. In fact, given that I seem to have taken on the role of her protector — at least in my mind — that would be about the least intelligent thing I could do.

I walked out of the trading post and left Amos to dicker with the couple over the necklace.

9

The next few weeks at the farm passed without serious incident; no goats went missing and there weren't any unnerving sounds during the night. Not all was well, however, by any stretch of the imagination. Martha's faculties continued on a slow decline, the spread of her affliction unchecked. There were many days when she didn't recognize me and she had difficulty putting a sentence together.

One very disturbing afternoon — very disturbing to me, anyway — I went into Martha's room to remove the plates and utensils from her lunch. Martha's eyes opened wide as I entered the room. She struggled into a sitting position on the bed and cried out, "Philip! You're home! You made it home! You finally made it home!" She put both of her hands to her mouth and began to cry.

My mind racing in confusion, I called out to Willa. It took me a few seconds to work out what was happening. Philip was her husband, the husband she lost back in 1917 or whenever it was. She thought that I was Philip and I had come home to her. I wasn't at all certain I could handle the situation without making things even worse. Martha, an expression of joy on her face, stretched out both arms to me. Although I had no idea what I should do next, I realized I couldn't just leave her in this state. I reluctantly went over and sat on the edge of the bed next to her. She grasped my arm and looked up into my face, tears trickling into the wrinkles of her face.

"Philip! Oh, oh! Philip. Are you all right? Why didn't you write me? I've been so lonely!" She touched my cheek with put her trembling hand, then buried her face in my side, sobbing. Awkwardly, I put my arm around her shoulder and rubbed her frail shoulder. "Willa!" I called out again. "Can you come in here, please? I need you!" I could feel the bones of Martha's shoulder and arm through her flannel nightgown. She seemed to be almost without muscles, just flesh, sinews and bones.

We sat in an awkward tableau for several more minutes, Martha's sobbing gradually becoming quieter. I heard the back door open and close. I suspected that

Martha might have fallen asleep and I didn't want to disturb her. I let Willa find us on her own.

Willa abruptly pulled up in the doorway as saw us, a surprised look on her face. I quickly held up my finger to my lips to stop her from making any sudden noise and then waved her over to the bed. She looked at me with concern on her face. Whispering, I said, "She was upset. I'll tell you later." With that, Willa helped me extricate myself and we then eased Martha back onto the pillows.

As Willa covered Martha with the quilt, I slipped out of the room as quietly as I could. I sat down heavily on the sofa. I didn't want to admit how shaken I was. While I was sitting there with Martha, I had nearly been overwhelmed by memories of when I used to sit with my mother in her bedroom during her illness. Images that I hadn't thought about for many years came rushing back: her darkened room, the sickroom smell... The cruel memory of my mother crying softly to herself from the pain of cancer pricked at my conscience. I rubbed my hands across my face in an effort to rid myself of images I didn't want to remember.

Willa appeared in the doorway of Mrs. Cahill's room. She turned and quietly pulled the door shut behind her. "Sean, what happened? What did the Missus..." She stopped short when she saw the look on my face. "Are you okay?" she asked with concern.

"Yeah, I am... Yeah. Fine. I'm fine. I was just remembering my mother, when I used to sit with her when she was sick." I shook my head to clear the memories and changed the subject. "Martha... She apparently thought I was her husband coming home from the war. She was calling me Philip and started crying. She just seemed so... happy. Happy her husband was finally home. I didn't know what else to do, so I just sat with her until she quieted down. Is she sleeping now?" I asked.

Willa nodded solemnly and came over to sit next to me on the couch. In a strange reversal of what I had just experienced in Martha's bedroom, she put her arm around my shoulder. "That was nice of you, Sean. Thank you." I thought she was going to lean over and kiss me on the cheek, but she just lifted her hand and ruffled my hair.

"If you're all right, I think I need to get back to work now." I nodded at her. She gave me one more appraising look before she got up and walked softly back into the kitchen. After a few more seconds, I forced myself off the couch. I wasn't certain what I was going to do next, but whatever it was, I needed to go do it.

*   *   *   *

I continued to be yanked out of my sleep in the middle of the night in a state of terror and confusion. My nightmares were becoming equal parts of the attack on Pearl and my father busting in my door and pummeling me while I rolled myself up into a protective ball in the corner of my bedroom. It was a horrible way to wake up in the middle of the night. I was definitely not getting enough sleep. I would barely make it through the mornings feeling as if I had been run over by a logging truck. The one bright spot was that I was now able to brew some very strong coffee to go along with breakfast. Hot, black java helped immensely.

On several of these occasions, I saw Willa standing out in her usual location, observing the forest in her sleep. Late autumn in the Pacific Northwest is known for its nasty weather. It rains frequently — sometimes quite heavily — and the rains are often accompanied with very blustery winds. It was on one of these bleak nights that I observed her out in the back, her nightgown and long black hair whipping about in the wind. When I saw her turn and start walking back toward the house, I sped down the stairs as best as I was able to ensure she made it inside safely. When she failed to materialize immediately, I cursed to myself and grabbed my coat from the peg by the front door. Dashing around the side of the house, I found her sprawled out on the ground. She was just beginning to get to her hands and knees when I reached her side.

I knelt down beside her. "Willa, all you all right? Are you hurt?"

"Sean? What? What am I doing outside?" She had to shout to make herself heard over the wind and rain. "It's pouring out here! Did you drag me outside? What are you doing!?!" This was as close to panic as anything I had ever heard out of her. There was shock and confusion on her face, but I saw that she hadn't crumbled into a state of panic. Yet. It might happen, however, if I didn't get her inside quickly. Her cotton nightgown was soaked and covered in mud. It clung tightly to her body in several places. I tried to not stare. It was obvious she was very cold; she was shivering all over and her teeth started to chatter.

"Look Willa, I can explain everything later! But right now, you need to get up and let me help you into the house! Okay? We need to get inside!" I was getting pretty wet myself. The rain stung my face and I had to squint in order to see anything.

Willa, to her great credit, didn't insist on arguing with me. I got her to her feet, which were bare, and put my arm around her waist to help her to the house. We made it up the stairs and in through the front door without great difficulty, although Willa was leaning heavily on my shoulder.

When we were standing in the dark living room, Major joined us. He circled us excitedly. All this commotion so late at night was something new to him, he was definitely going to investigate. I attempted to adopt an authoritative voice. "Willa, go upstairs right now, dry off and change into some dry clothes! I'll get a fire going in the fireplace! Please! Go! You're freezing! I'll explain later!"

I wasn't exactly sanguine about my last point regarding an explanation. I didn't know how I was going to go about that one yet. I wasn't sure how the news she had been sleepwalking for the last few months would be received. I was also very concerned that Willa could catch pneumonia or some other dreadful ailment if I didn't get her warm and dry in very short order.

Major watched me closely as I tinkered futilely with the small pile of logs and kindling in the fireplace in my attempt to get a fire to catch. The kindling generated very little in the way of flames but, in the process, I had managed to produce a generous amount of smoke. I coughed several times, waving my hand in front of my face in a vain effort to clear the air. I reached for the hand bellows hanging on the side of the mantelpiece. I was getting a little frantic by this point. Here I was, deathly afraid of fire and now I couldn't light one to save my life. In my agitated state, I hadn't heard Willa quietly pad down the stairs and come over to stand next to me.

"Here, let me do that," she said softly as she reached for the bellows. Startled at being interrupted so unexpectedly, I silently handed her the bellows and retreated from the hearth to let her take her turn in front of the recalcitrant pile of logs and kindling.

Upset and cold, I was still able to recognize that Willa had regained her composure. She still must have been very cold, but having rid herself of her soaked nightgown and now in warm clothes, she wasn't shivering anymore. Other than her damp hair that lay limply in thick strands along her shoulders and down her back, her outward appearance gave little sign anything unusual had just occurred. She was much more in control of herself than I was able to manage for myself.

Within a minute, Willa had successfully coaxed a small blaze out of the pile of firewood. She then turned to me. "Sean, you need to go upstairs now and put on some dry clothes. You are soaked to the skin." I looked down at myself. In my haste, I had not realized that I had been dripping water all over the wooden floor and woolen rug. I couldn't think of anything to say, so I just nodded at her numbly and headed up the stairs to do as she commanded.

When I returned, Willa was sitting cross-legged on the rug in front of the fire, rubbing her long hair with a towel. She had mopped up most the puddles, filled my coffee pot with water and had it heating close to the fire. Next to it were two cups with tea bags already in place. I took my place next to her, my right leg halfway bent out in front of me and my hands stretched out to the fire, seeking its warmth. Major nosed his way in between us. He gazed up at me expectantly.

Neither of us said anything immediately. Willa leaned over to grasp the handle of the battered percolator with a corner of her towel before pouring the hot water into the two mugs. I watched her fluid movements as she went about the simple task of making tea. She had changed into a grey woolen sweater, some dark slacks and, incongruously for her, fuzzy socks adorned with large, red stripes. She certainly looked much better than the bedraggled, confused woman I had helped up the porch steps less than fifteen minutes ago. The soft, flickering light of the fire illuminated her face. She looked completely in control of herself and her surroundings. Although I was slowly getting there, I was still very concerned about what had brought us to be sitting in front of the fire at one o'clock in the morning.

"We should keep our voices low. I don't want to wake up the Missus." Willa continued to gaze into the fire. I nodded in silent agreed.

Willa broke her stare at the small blaze to look over at me. "Sean, what happened? Can you tell me why we were both outside in this storm?" I saw puzzlement in her expression but no sign of panic.

I looked back at the fire, not saying anything until I could gather my thoughts. "Willa, it's… I don't know how to tell you this. I wanted to tell you for a long time, but I didn't know how. You have been sleepwalking ever since I came to the house." I heard her sharp intake of breath, but she didn't say anything. She let me continue. "When I wake up at night, I sometimes see you standing out in the back, staring up into the woods. You don't do it all the time, maybe once or twice every couple of weeks. I don't know. There may be some times when you are out there when I don't see you, so I don't know exactly how sure how often you do it. When you are out there, you don't move. You just stand there, looking out into the forest."

I fell silent and thought that I might as well go into this the entire way. No use just dipping my toes in the water, as they say, without going swimming. "One time… Well, one time, when I wasn't sure what you were doing out there at night, I went out to see what you were doing and to make sure you were all right. When you came back into the house, you walked right past me without seeing me. You went upstairs and went to bed, apparently." She let my confession that I had been spying on her go without comment. "I have seen you a number of times since then. I have been really worried about you. But this is the first time I have seen you outside with the weather like this. I was just coming outside to see if you were okay when I found you lying on the ground, all muddy. You must have tripped over a rock or a tree root or something." I sighed and made a futile gesture with my hands that really didn't signify much other than I had no idea what else to say.

Willa stared at the fire wordlessly. Slowly, she took another sip of her hot tea. I thought to myself, *She is certainly taking this well. She's not arguing with me or objecting that she can't be sleepwalking. She certainly has more poise than I would have if I found myself outside in the middle of the night, lying in the mud.*

"Thank you for telling me, Sean. This explains a number of things I have been wondering about." She paused to take another sip. "It explains why I sometimes feel so worn out in the mornings." I never thought she looked worn out, but I didn't interrupt.

Then it was her turn to surprise me. "I used to walk in my sleep when I was a child," she confessed in a low voice. "I would wake up and be outside, not knowing where I was or how I had come to be there. Sometimes I would find my way back by myself, but sometimes my mother would come and find me. I would sometimes do this at the Indian school as well. The Sisters didn't like it when they would find my bed empty. They just thought I was being a "difficult child,' trying to run away from school. After I left the school, I thought I had stopped. At least, I never woke up suddenly to find myself standing outside. I guess all that means is that I would go back to bed before I woke up."

She fell silent. Major turned slightly to lay his head in her lap. Willa idly rubbed the fur on his neck while still deep in her thoughts. Even though I still did not know what to make of all of this, I thought I should probably give her all the information I had. It might be meaningful to her.

"Um... Willa, there's more." She turned her somber gaze in my direction. "Do you know a Native named Amos Ghost Horse? He runs a little tourist shop down on the highway a few miles past town."

"I know of him. I don't believe that I have ever talked to him. Why?" she asked with some puzzlement.

"Well, on one of my trips into town, I did go talk to him. I was trying to find out more about things you had mentioned. I wondered if he might know anything about a *Wechuge*." I watched Willa's face closely as I said this. We hadn't talked about this since the first time she had mentioned it to me. She raised her eyebrows in surprise but did not say anything. "We talked for maybe fifteen minutes. He started asking me questions about the house, Martha and her condition, and also

121

about me. He was asking me if I had trouble sleeping or was experiencing dreams or nightmares."

It was my turn to take a sip of tea and to gather my thoughts. "This conversation I had with Amos didn't go the way I thought it would. He said some things about the Spirit World and what it was trying to tell me. But one of the last things that he said was that all three of us — you, me and Martha — were all experiencing some sort of problem. He said that they are all related. And that this... *Wechuge* is an evil spirit whose influence is making our problems much worse. I probably have some of that wrong. But one thing that I know that I heard correctly — he said this more than once — is that you are in danger here and that you should leave. I told him that Martha was probably not in any condition where she could lose your help and I wasn't sure if you had anywhere to go or not. Amos seemed not to care about this. He just repeated that you were in danger and needed to leave."

I stopped and wiped my sleeve across my forehead. I was getting very warm sitting so close to the fire. I scooted backwards a few feet.

When I looked up, Willa was staring at me with her mouth open. I was fervently hoping that she was not angry with me for discussing such personal matters with an outsider. As it turned out, she was.

"Sean, what gives you the right to go talking about my problems with a stranger? I don't care if he is one of the First People!" She looked at me angrily for a few seconds before she turned back to stare at the fire. "You had no right!"

Yep, she's angry all right, I thought miserably. *I guess I don't blame her. I would probably be mad as hell if someone had done this to me. So, old buddy, how are you going to get yourself out of this one? You better think quickly before she gets up to go upstairs.*

"Look, Willa..." I spread my hands out in front of me; one of my grand gestures that can mean most anything but is usually used to denote great sincerity on my part. "I know I shouldn't have done that. You are absolutely correct. I had no right to talk to Amos about you without your permission. But you know why I did it? I have been very worried. You looked frightened out of your wits the night we heard that call outside. You just about flew up the stairs after that. And I am *really* worried

122

you when you go sleepwalking. I was concerned that you might hurt yourself, just like you did tonight!" Willa still had a frown on her face but she did give me a small nod of concession with that.

I continued, "We never had any more of our story-telling game after that. You never explained to me why you thought the call we heard was one of those nasty spirit demons or whatever they are. If that is really what is bothering you and it might be a cause for your sleepwalking, I thought I better know about it. I *wanted* to know about it. I want to help you. But I have no idea how." Again, the grand gesture.

Willa continued to glare at me, light creases visible across the dark skin of her forehead and her lips pursed. I thought her expression was now something more like consternation rather than anger, but I couldn't be absolutely certain. *At least she's still sitting there,* I thought to myself.

She turned back to face the fire. "Look, I appreciate your concern. I knew you were worried about something the last few weeks but I wasn't certain what it was. Now I know why." She looked over her shoulder at me, several filaments of damp, jet-black hair trailed across her cheek. "The reason I haven't told you anything else is because I don't want you involved. This isn't your problem. It's mine. You can't help."

It was my turn to be surprised. "I am sorry to disagree with you, Willa, but I am already involved. We live in the same house and you are my friend. I don't want you to hurt yourself, like you almost did tonight. I would hate to think what might have happened if I hadn't been around!" I threw that last bit in more because it sounded good at the moment rather than a sincere belief on my part there was much validity to it. I hadn't even been able to get the damned fire going by myself. All I had managed to produce was a wet floor and lots of smoke. I had been a big help. But I wasn't going to throw away my bargaining position by admitting that to her.

Willa let out a long, exasperated breath. She looked over her shoulder at me again and asked, "So? What did you learn from Amos? What did he tell you about the *Wechuge*?"

I thought back to my conversation with Amos Ghost Horse. "Well, it's certainly not good news. He didn't know much about this specific spirit or whatever it is. He was familiar with something called a *Windigo*, from a tribe in Ohio or somewhere around there, I think. He thought they might be sort of the same thing, so he told me something about that."

Willa was resting her chin on her bent knees with her arms wrapped around her legs, gazing into the slowly dying fire. "Yes, I have heard of the *Windigo*. It sounds very fearsome. I suppose there are some similarities." She thought a few seconds before continuing. "The big difference is that the *Windigo* is a legend. A *Wechuge* has been following me, haunting me since I left my village."

I was not just startled but absolutely dumbfounded. Yes, Willa was a Native and they have their own legends and myths they have been taught since they were children. But how could anyone in the twentieth century believe that an evil spirit has been following them for almost two decades? "Willa, that's... That's crazy! I don't...."

She heatedly interrupted me. "See? This is the reason why I didn't tell you anything! You are a white man! You are never going to believe anything I might say that doesn't fit in with your religion, your Sky God in heaven with all the angels sitting around on clouds playing harps all the time! Yes, that all makes perfect sense, doesn't it?"

"Willa, we should keep our voices down. We don't want to wake up Martha." She continued to glare at me. "Look, Willa, if it makes you feel any better, I don't believe in... uh... the white man's God either. Okay? I just don't think...."

Before I could say more, Willa quickly stood up and turned to leave. I reached up and grabbed her by her sweater-covered wrist. "Willa, please don't leave! Really. I am trying. I want to know so I can help you. Look, I will shut up. I will let you tell me anything you want to tell me. Just please don't leave right now!" Major gazed up at her from his position on the floor.

Willa looked down at me, scowling. After several seconds and with some reluctance, she shook her arm loose from my grip, pivoted back toward the fireplace and took a seat in the rocker next to the hearth. I stayed in my awkward position on

124

the floor, as I was afraid of how she might react to any sudden movement on my part.

"You will hold your tongue while I am talking. If you say anything other than to ask me to clarify something for you, I will go back upstairs and go to bed. It has been a bad night for all of us. It is late and I am very tired." I nodded in acquiescence.

She turned her gaze to the dancing shadows in the corner of the room. "I think I told you that, not long after my father and brothers disappeared, my mother started to act strangely. My aunt thought my mother was losing her mind. My mother kept speaking about an evil spirit that would visit her in the deep night. It would tap on the sides of our dwelling, she said, and it would whisper to her to come outside. It had something to show her." Willa stopped and covered her mouth with one hand. "I never heard these things. I only heard my mother talk about them the next day. She said she knew she couldn't go outside. It was a *Wechuge*, she said, and it wanted to eat her, devour her. That is why she was becoming frantic. She was afraid not only for her but for me as well. If the *Wechuge* ate her, it would not stop there. It would eat me as well. That is when we moved in with my aunt and her family."

I listened in fascination. Sitting there on a rug on the floor of a dark room, illuminated only by the light of the flickering fire, I could almost believe her story. I shuddered slightly as I listened to the wind rattle the windows in their frames. The rain continued to beat its frantic pattern on the roof of the house.

"All seemed normal for a few weeks after we moved in with them. My mother seemed to be regaining her previous personality. But then, according to her, the noises and whispers started up again. She was convinced that the *Wechuge* was tormenting her, just waiting for the chance to jump on her from behind a tree and eat her right there — bones, teeth, clothes, everything. She became more and more upset and refused to leave the house. She ranted about my father and about the evil spirit that was tormenting her. Somehow, the two were related in her mind. I can guess now, but at the time, I had no idea what she meant."

Willa stopped and bit nervously at the knuckles of her right hand. I got the impression she really didn't want to continue, but had already decided she was

125

going to finish the telling of her story. "I do not know if my aunt and uncle heard these noises or if they were just becoming frightened of what my mother was saying. I think they were very concerned about the safety of my cousins and for me. That was when arrangements were made to send me, along with the youngest of my cousins, to the white man's school for Indians in Fort St. John. I didn't want to go. We were both crying the day the wagon took us away from our village.

"My cousin and I were very miserable at the school. We didn't want to be like white people. When they made us cut our hair, my cousin threatened to shoot one of the Sisters with a bow and arrow that he did not have. He eventually ran away. The school was not good for him. I do not know what happened to my cousin. I like to think that he is somewhere with a good job and a family, but I just do not know.

"It was perhaps a year later that I received a letter from my uncle. It was very short. He told me my mother was dead. He didn't provide any details so I have no idea what had happened. Again, I would like to think she passed peacefully, but I suspect that is not what happened."

Willa paused to wipe her eyes with the towel she had used to dry her hair. "It was not long after I received my uncle's letter about my mother that I begin to wake up and find myself outside the school building where the children slept. Sometimes, I was only a few feet away. I hadn't gone very far. I was able to sneak back inside before I was missed. On several occasions, I ended up several miles away from the school. I had walked all that way in my bare feet. They were always dirty and bloody. This is why I suspected I was sleepwalking now even before you told me, because my feet were dirty just like before. When I woke up in a strange place, of course I was very frightened and confused. If I was near the town, I could find the school again without any difficulty. Several times, however, I woke up to find myself out in the wilderness. I was frightened that I would not be able to find my way back. I didn't like the school, but it was all I had. I would die if I couldn't find my way back.

"I got a very bad reputation at the school because of this. The Sisters thought I was trying to run away, just like my cousin had. They wouldn't believe me when I told them that I didn't know how I ended up outside. They called me 'a little red liar' and punished me, usually not letting me have any supper that evening. Once, I got whipped by Sister Edith with her stick in front of the rest of the students."

Willa gazed into the fire, lost in her memories, her chin propped in her cupped hand. I hoped she wasn't going to stop. I was mesmerized by her tale. Willa's telling of her personal history was very far afield from anything that I, a young white man whose entire worldly knowledge came from being in the United States Navy, had ever been exposed to before.

"That was also when I began to hear noises outside the dormitory at night while I was trying to sleep. There were thumps along the wall just outside my bunk. There was a sound like an animal snuffling around. Once, I thought I heard something whispering my name. That was when I began to get really scared. I was so very frightened. I remembered what my mother had said about when she heard noises outside at night. I was convinced that whatever had happened to her was going to happen to me now she was dead. Whatever had been haunting her was now after me. I would sometimes run crying to the Sisters. They told me that I was being childish and to go back to bed.

"I had been at the school for about two years — I was ten years old, I think — when I decided to run away for real. I knew that I was taking a big risk. How was a ten-year-old Native girl going to take care of herself, without any family or friends around? This was one time in my life the gods took pity on me. Before evening fell on the day I left the school with my small bundle of possessions, I came upon a small farm. It was small and run-down but I could see there were lights on inside the little house and there was a fire going. I went up to the door and knocked. An elderly woman answered. She and her husband were about to have dinner. I remembering telling some story about being lost and that I was cold and hungry. That was absolutely true. I was very near to tears and was in a panic because night was coming, and I hadn't found a place to spend the night.

"The couple, Mr. and Mrs. Billings, took pity on me. They could see I was a Native, not a white girl, and from the school uniform, they certainly knew where I had come from, but they never said anything about it. They invited me in to sit next to the fire while Mrs. Billings finished preparing the evening meal. When it was ready, I was given a place at the table. I was so happy and grateful that I started crying. They let me spend the night in the old bedroom that had belonged to their son before he had gotten married and moved into his own house.

"Before I went to sleep that night, I gave thanks to my gods and also to the white man's God. Maybe he was real and he was listening to a little Dena'ina girl crying with gratefulness.

"I spent the next eight years with the Billings. I helped out around the house and farm where I could. I helped Mrs. Billings in the kitchen or with the housework when she needed help. Mostly, I think I was a companion for Mrs. Billings, almost like a daughter. I would sit with her as she knitted or read. We talked a lot about many different things. Mrs. Billings had been a teacher before she retired. I took the opportunity to read many books that were there in her library. She continued to help me with my English and history."

Willa paused and sniffed again. "I loved Mrs. Billings. She was the sweetest, most caring person in the entire world. I felt very safe in their house. It was a very long time before I started hearing any frightening night noises again."

Willa drained a last of her tea and looked over at me. "I think that is enough storytelling for tonight. I am very tired." She seemed very sad. "I want to thank you again, Sean, for helping me out tonight and for worrying about me. That's sweet of you. Maybe you now understand when I say there is nothing you can do for me and why I do not want you to be involved. Now, I believe it is way past time for us to be in bed. I need to be up early to help the Missus wash and dress before I make breakfast."

With that, Willa got up from her seat in the rocker. As she moved silently behind me to ascend the dark stairway, her fingertips trailed lightly through the hair on top of my head. A vibration, like a small electric shock, ran through my entire body. Goosebumps popped up on my scalp and arms. Flustered, I called out to her as she exited the room, "Goodnight, Willa! Thanks for your story!"

She turned her head without stopping and showed me a small smile over her shoulder.

After she had gone upstairs, I groaned as I heaved myself off the floor. Both my legs were very stiff and my rear end was numb. I took a few hobbled steps toward the sofa and flopped down into its deep cushions. Major followed and took his usual place on the floor next to me. I idly scratched his head between his ears, lost in thought, attempting to absorb what I had just heard. I stared at the logs in the fireplace slowly transform themselves into white ash and glowing embers. It was not long before I feel asleep.

>> 10 <<

The next week was a mixture of the familiar day-to-day life on the farm but with an undercurrent of anxiety. I had heard the old saying about "walking on eggshells" but I hadn't really fully understood that feeling until then. I had no idea what might occur next. That something would happen, however, seemed to be inevitable at this point. Things hadn't been really normal since the day I knocked on the front door of Martha Cahill's house.

Willa and I eventually came to at least one decision: If she was going to continue to sleepwalk — and I saw no reason why it was going to cease — we should take some precautions. She suggested I lock her in her room for the evening. I put the kibosh on that in short order. If some emergency were to happen, she needed to be able to get out of her room without delay. I also wasn't terribly enthusiastic about the prospect of getting up in the middle of the night if she needed to see to Martha or use the bathroom. We ended up agreeing to lock both the front and rear doors of the house. I would keep the keys in my room during the night. I hesitated, but I found that I really didn't have any valid reasons for not agreeing. It seemed very clear that none of us were going to go out after dark from that point on. It was also obvious, if there did come a time when one of us needed to be outside at night, that person would be me. Therefore, we reasoned, it made sense for me to have the keys. Although Willa and I didn't use these specific words during our discussion, I think we tacitly agreed it would be best that she be confined inside the house rather than be allowed to walk around outside in the notoriously unreliable mountain weather. That didn't even take into account the possibility of her running into any "monster spirit," real or imagined.

When things did start to occur, just like I thought they might, it was as if a dam had burst somewhere upstream. Things — bad things — started to happen in very quick succession.

* * * *

It was a Sunday mid-morning in late October. For the first time in more than a week, the sky was clear and bright blue. The slight breeze coming down from the mountains was cold but still pleasant after several days of unrelenting rain and wind. It felt good to be out of the house. Being indoors for that many days in a row was getting much too claustrophobic for me.

After chopping several more alder logs into manageable lengths, I started breaking apart one of bales of hay stacked inside the barn for the goats. I began stuffing handfuls of hay into the little wooden cage that hung on the side of the barn inside the pen. The goats were already pushing at each other in their effort to get at the hay when I was suddenly racked by another one of my "visions," as Amos Ghost Horse had called them.

Without warning, all my senses told me I was back on the deck of the *West Virginia*. The sequence of events, along with all the accompanying sounds and smells, was exactly the same as before. This time, however, when I smashed into the burning water after hurdling over the railing, I found that I was not underwater. Instead, without any transition from the one moment to the next, I was in my bedroom in the old house in Kalama. It was nighttime. I could see the hallway light streaming in through the open door of my room. I was staring up at my father's face in the semi-darkness, terror rippling through my chest. He bellowed some obscenity and then swung his ham-sized fist at me, connecting with the side of my face. I went sprawling over the side of my small bed and onto the floor. I tried to escape by crawling under my bed when I felt my father's hand grab my ankle with ferocious intensity. He began to jerk on my leg and I started sliding out from underneath the wholly inadequate refuge provided by the thin mattress and metal frame. I could see my hands scrabble and grab at one of the metal legs of the bed frame. In the dim light under the bed, I could barely make out the rusted metal of the leg terminating in a black caster-type wheel. There were several large dust-bunnies lying close by. I heard myself screaming in terror when I realized my mother had rushed into the

132

room and was yanking at my father's shoulder, begging for him to stop. I felt him release my ankle and...

I found myself lying on my back on the wet ground next to the goat pen, my fists clenched at the end of my upraised arms, fending off blows that were not going to come. When I finally realized where I was, I let my head and arms flop backwards onto the ground. I lay there, spread-eagled, for several minutes until I could gather my wits. *What the hell?!?* My panicked mind began gibbering to itself. *What the hell was that about? Am I going to have to worry for the rest of my life about blacking out and reliving every bad experience that I have ever had?* For the first time, the thought occurred to me it was possible that I had just experienced an epileptic seizure. *Was that it? Epilepsy? Was I lying here, convulsing on the ground, right next to the damn goat pen?* That was a very frightening thought. The possibility I had a debilitating disease suddenly seemed much more real and frightening than the mythical spirit monsters I had been concerned with for the past week.

With what seemed to me to be an enormous effort, I slowly sat up and took a weak swipe at my face with a dirty shirtsleeve. The goats were still tearing at the hay I had stuffed into their feeding basket. Given how much of the hay was still there, I estimated that I couldn't have been out for more than a minute or two. That was somewhat reassuring. At least I hadn't been prone on the ground for the last hour. Continuing on with my "silver lining to some pretty damn dark clouds" thinking, I supposed that I should feel grateful I hadn't jumped off the roof of the house again. *Small favors*, I thought sourly to myself.

After another minute, I managed to get myself to my knees and then my feet. Wobbling, I made my way into the dim interior of the barn. On my last visit to the Night Owl, I had changed from bourbon to whiskey. Whiskey was cheaper. I had stashed my bottle in the back corner of the barn, behind an old wooden apple crate covered in dust, spider webs and ancient chicken poop. Willa hardly ever came into the barn anymore and it was a very good bet she wouldn't find it there. I retrieved the bottle, grateful of my foresight, sat down weakly on one of the remaining bales of hay and took a large swig of the pale liquid. It felt very warm as it slid down my throat. It was a comforting kind of warmth. Feeling somewhat revived, I took another gulp from the mouth of the bottle. I felt a huge headache building behind my eyeballs and this one wasn't because of any "hangover."

I held the bottle up to eye-level where it was illuminated by light from the dirty window in the wall of the barn. I squinted to examine it more closely. The glass bottle itself was plain enough. Light brown in color, it was decorated with a very nice looking black label outlined in a bold red border with bright yellow lettering. "Since 1875," it declared proudly. *Yeah, getting people drunk on their asses since 1875*, I thought to myself. *Great deal. That's something to be really proud about.* I swirled the remaining golden liquid around the bottom of the bottle. *Only about one quarter left.* I considered. *Enough for a good time next Saturday night. A boffo good time.* I shuddered as I thought back to the vision of my father, my plastered-out-of-his-Irish-mind dad, cocking his fist back behind his head in order to get a really good swing at me while I attempted in vain to protect my head with my scrawny arms. *Maybe those old temperance biddies were right. Maybe this place would be a better place without alcohol. But then, the Eighteenth Amendment sure made a big mess of things. Prohibition, speakeasies, rumrunners, gangsters... That sure didn't help very damn much, now did it? If people wanted to get drunk, they were going to get drunk.* I guiltily thought back to the brawl in the bar in Honolulu that resulted in my shipmates and I being tossed in the clink by several very angry Military Police.

I was on the verge of hurling the bottle, along with its remaining contents, as hard as I could against the opposite wall of the barn. I was angry — angry with myself, angry at this stupid crutch in a bottle. And I was really angry, out of the blue with absolutely no explanation provided, I was experiencing nasty, unwanted hallucinations. But my arm didn't move. My hand rested limply on the hay bale, my fingers curled loosely around the bottle. Eventually, I stood up and trudged over to the dusty apple crate in the corner. I carefully replaced the bottle in its hiding place. My usually talkative internal dialog remained silent as I went back out into the sunlight to finish my morning chores.

*   *   *   *

There wasn't much conversation that evening during supper. Martha had taken to having her supper exclusively in her room, so it was just Willa and I sitting at the kitchen table. She had been unusually quiet the last few evenings. Grey clouds, heavy with moisture, had moved in during the late afternoon. By twilight, light snow began to float gently down. Within an hour, everything was covered in a thin white shawl. I hoped this wasn't the leading edge of a large storm that would dump several feet of the white stuff. We had stocked up for that eventuality, but I wasn't ready to be cut off from town just yet.

After supper, we cleaned the table and washed the dishes in silence. Afterwards, almost by habit, we picked up the lamps and moved to the front of the house where we took up our usual positions on the chair and couch. Major chose his place for the evening, this time settling down on the rug next to Willa's chair.

Staring into the fire, I decided, could be very relaxing. I realized these small flames were nothing to be afraid of, really. In fact, they had a very hypnotic quality about them. In other circumstances, I likely would have said that I was in peace, sitting there with a pretty lady that I liked in a comfortable room with the snow falling outside. However, since I had been in residence at Martha Cahill's, there had been just too a few too many odd occurrences, just too many strange things I had learned, for me to feel completely at ease.

I was seriously attempting to understand Willa's story. I found that I was of two very distinct minds about it. The overbearing side, my twentieth century rational mind, was very dismissive about Willa's history. How someone could seriously believe in evil spirits and monsters that haunted people in order to devour them was something I really couldn't grasp. Those kinds of fairy tales were for kids, not for educated adults. To believe otherwise was not only silly, it was dangerous. The United States of America had been attacked and we were at war with the Axis Powers in both the Pacific and in Europe. From what I had learned from the newspapers I picked up during my weekly trips to town, the war didn't appear to be going very well. The newspapermen reporting on the war always attempted, but were not always successful, to put a nice fine burnish on the stories that appeared underneath screaming forty point headlines. German U-boats were sinking our freighters as soon as they ventured into international waters at a clip of three or four every day. Things had not been going our way in the Pacific until the Navy finally had a big win at Midway. I was hopeful it signaled the turning of the tide with the war against Japan, but it was still very touch and go. The U.S. had suffered a huge defeat in the Philippines and it sounded like we had abandoned our troops to be killed or captured by Japan's Imperial troops. The way the Battle of Guadalcanal had been described sounded like the proverbial hell on earth. The newspaper reports tried to gloss things over, of course, but I could tell we were suffering massive causalities. Those were things we should be terrified of. Hitler and his fearsome war machine, along with his vicious Japanese allies, were the real monsters, not some mythical cannibalistic spirit scrabbling around outside, making scary noises in the bushes at night.

And yet... I could not get the uncomfortable feeling out of my head that things were happening I did not understand. I recalled my absolute conviction that I had been observed the first time I had ventured up into the forest, looking for the missing goats. The previous night, I had been spellbound by Willa's tale. It seemed as if she were telling me something that came from an alternative reality. In fact, I realized belatedly, that was precisely what it was. It was just like she had said to me: She and her people experienced the world from a much different perspective than mine. Her story about her mother and the cause of her sickness was coming directly from that alternative reality, the one which included a demon monster — possibly her father that had been transformed into some loathsome being — haunting her mother until it finally drove her insane. Sitting in the dark room that night, illuminated by the firelight, my rational mind had shut itself off long enough for me to absorb Willa's tale from her perspective. For a short while, I was able to experience firsthand the primal fear of the unknown, the unknowable, during her telling. The *Wechuge* was real, it was after her and she had no idea what to do about it.

I shook my head, chastising myself. *I am being ridiculous! There are no ghosts, monsters or things that go bump in the night! Reality is reality, period, end of story.* What did I really have to go on? What tangible evidence was there, really? Not very much. There were some missing goats and a fence that had fallen down due to some unidentified reason. No footprints. After a moment's thought, I decided I could discount my discomfort in the forest. Some vague, uncomfortable feeling was not a tangible, measurable thing. It was pure emotion, no more. I could therefore dismiss it from any further consideration. Yes, Willa had been sleepwalking. But she had told me she also did it when she was younger, so there likely wasn't anything terribly mysterious about her doing it now. Sleepwalking was something for a psychologist or other doctor to look into. Her propensity for taking midnight strolls in her bare feet, however unusual, still fell into the realm of the knowable. And my hallucinations — no matter how compelling — could probably be attributed to "battle fatigue" or something like that. I realized, of course, I hadn't been in many battles. One, to be precise, and that one lasted all of about two hours. But if I wanted to pinpoint a cause for blacking out and jumping off the top of a tall ladder, battle fatigue seemed to be an excellent candidate. That's what Dr. Farmer back in Oakland had attempted to tell me when we were discussing my nightmares during my time in the hospital there. I hadn't wanted to listen to him at that time. However, the more I considered the matter, battle fatigue seemed like a perfectly rational explanation. After all, he was a doctor. He was paid to know that kind of stuff.

I began to feel better. These things were all perfectly understandable; they weren't mysterious at all. They were known quantities that could be filed away into their correct pigeonholes. My only real problem, as I saw it at that moment, was to help Willa dispense with her superstitious notion that she was being stalked by some monstrous whatsits that had followed her from deep in the wilds of northern Canada to Skykomish, Washington, United States of America. I wasn't at all certain how I was going to accomplish that one, but at least I felt I had a defined, realistic goal to work toward. I smiled to myself. I could even begin to imagine a happy ending that involved a grateful Willa and myself, maybe on a day trip down to Seattle. We could walk along the waterfront and stop for lunch somewhere. We could take a ferry ride over to one of the islands. I smiled to myself.

My pleasant revere was interrupted by several muffled noises coming from behind the door of Martha's room. I saw Willa sit straight up in her chair, her hands

137

clenched around the armrests of the rocker. She seemed to be unsure as to whether she should go check on Martha or to let matters be. My own opinion was that Martha was likely experiencing some normal "old person" issues associated with not being able to sleep through the entire night. Perhaps Willa's cooking had unsettled her stomach.

My innocent conjecture was shattered quickly by gurgling noises from her room — as if she was having trouble breathing — followed by several gasps and then a high-pitched, feeble wail. Willa bolted from her chair and dashed toward the bedroom door, Major following on her heels. It took me several seconds to get myself off of the soft couch to bring up the rear.

I halted in the doorway, as there wasn't much space to accommodate another person in the bedroom. Major was beating a "U" shaped path around the bed while attempting to see what was going on. Martha lay prone on her bed with the sheets and blanket rumpled up around her feet. She wailed again. I went over to the side of the bed opposite of Willa. She was trying to calm Martha by rubbing her hands between her own while she made small "cooing" sounds as if she were trying to comfort a small child who had fallen and skinned her knee.

Martha was obviously agitated. Her mouth was moving, attempting to utter something, but I couldn't make out anything that sounded like a specific word. Drool trickled down the side of her chin. When she managed to free one of her hands from Willa's light grasp, she pointed her trembling hand at the window that looked out over the backyard and goat pen.

"There!" she finally gasped. "It was there!" She gurgled again. I was suddenly taken with the idea that she might be choking. I reached down, not exactly certain as to what I was going to do next. Martha's grey hair floated in small skeins and tangles around her face. Her arms seemed very thin and frail, the flesh of her face translucent.

Willa looked up at me with alarm in her eyes before turning her attention back to Mrs. Cahill, softly asking, "What's out there, Martha? What did you see?"

"Eyes! Red eyes, right there in the window! They were staring at me! Ohhhh!!!!!" Martha wailed again and covered her face with both hands. She then began to cry in real anguish. Willa sat down on the bed and put her arm around Martha's shaking shoulders.

"Sean, go out and look! See if there is anything out there. I'll stay with the Missus." The command in Willa's voice was evident, yet I hesitated. I was concerned about the well being of Martha, of course, but I was not terribly happy about the prospect of wandering around outside in the darkness. I went over to the window and glanced out. I didn't see anything unusual, other than the snow had started to come down with a little more purpose than before. I looked back skeptically at Willa.

"Sean, would you please go out and check *now*!" She glared at me, Martha's face buried in the crook of her shoulder.

"Okay, you're the boss." I shrugged my shoulders. There wasn't going to be anything out there, I could tell that already. Martha had just come out from under the influence of some bad dream and had panicked, just like I had done so many times before. *Yeah, it is really frightening when this happens to you. It takes several minutes to recover your wits. After all, I should know. She's just an old woman who woke up and thought she saw something looking in at her through her window*, I fumed to myself as I sat down on the chair next to the front door and pulled on my boots.

I removed the glass chimney on one of the oil lamps and lit the wick using the book of matches sitting on the small table by the front door. I assumed there was likely a flashlight in the house somewhere, but I wasn't going to waste a lot of time looking for it. A lamp would suffice for as long as I was planning on being outside, which wasn't going to be very long. All I wanted to do was go out there and look around to make sure everything was fine before I turned around to come back inside to reassure everyone. I pulled on my coat and grabbed the lamp. When I opened the door, Major eagerly pushed past me and dashed across the porch, down the stairs and around the corner of the house. *Great*, I thought. *That's just great.*

I took the steps slowly, one foot at a time. The damp wood of the stairs underneath the thin coating of snow was very slippery. I didn't want to have my feet go out from underneath me and end up on my back. I heard Major barking frantically from behind the house. "Okay, okay. I'm coming! Give me a minute!" I yelled furiously. I zipped up my coat and flipped up the collar to keep the snow from falling down my neck.

When I made it around to the rear of the house, there wasn't any sign of Major. I could hear him barking in the distance, seemingly in pursuit of something. But what I did see made me stop dead in my tracks. Small, evenly spaced splashes of fire traced a path across the snow of the back yard. One end of the flaming trail came from behind the corner the barn, the other end heading up towards the dark woods. In between, the smooth curve of the fiery trail diverted near the house, the bump passing directly beneath Martha's bedroom window.

Hesitantly, I walked slowly over where I could get a closer look. I placed the lamp carefully down next to me, as it was apparent that I wasn't going to need its illumination. I initially thought what I was looking at might be some sort of optical illusion, that somehow the light from the fire inside the fireplace was being reflected around through the glass windows and bouncing off the white snow. But as soon as that hypothesis entered my mind, I immediately knew it couldn't possibly be true. As I approached the flaming trail, I could see that each patch of fire was about eighteen inches long and six inches wide, with what appeared to be three or four splayed toes on one end and something that looked like a horn or spike at the other. The flames leapt up into the air about eight to ten inches from the surface of the snow. I knelt down on my hands and knees by the nearest of the patch of fire to try get a better look at what I was seeing. From that vantage point, I was able to see, underneath the flames, the surface of the snow was undisturbed. There weren't any depressions or marks that a person or animal would leave after treading through fresh snow. I looked over to my right at the deep gashes left in the snow by Major's paws as he raced up the hill. Bits of torn grass and clumps of dirt had been flung up as he ran. I looked back at what was directly in front of me. It was a large splotch of fire, burning on top of the snow, as if someone had drawn out a large, misshapen footprint with lighter fluid and then tossed a lit match on it.

Dumbfounded, unable to accept what I was seeing, I levered myself off the ground and walked slowly to the house until I was underneath Mrs. Cahill's window. I was very close to the location where I landed in the bushes not that long ago. Due to the height of the foundation of the house, the bottom of the windowsill was several inches above the top of my head. From my position, I could easily reach up with my hand and touch the glass panes of the window. However, without grabbing the bottom of the windowsill and doing a chin-up, there was no possible way I could look inside her room.

I turned around to examine the fiery trail. The flaming footprints — I couldn't come up with any other way to refer to them — by the side of the barn were guttering, on the verge of extinguishing themselves. I could easily make out the alternating "left-right-left-right" progression indicating the stride a two-footed animal. However, the distance between each print appeared to be around five feet, which again made no any sense to me. That was much longer than any normal-sized person would be able to make.

I turned my gaze up toward the dark forest, which now seemed to be fraught with the unknown. From time to time, I could still catch Major's faint bark, but he seemed to be very far away. After another minute, his barking ceased altogether. Once again, I turned to stare at the footprints. All the flames that had come around the barn and made a detour close to the house were gone. I could see no trace of anything ever having been there. The closest flame I could make out was about fifteen feet up the hill from my position underneath the window, and that was nearly gone as well.

I slowly climbed the stairs to the front porch in a state of shock. I attempted to rationalize what I had seen, or what I *thought* I had seen, into something I might be able to understand. I reasoned that a bear, walking erect on its hind legs, might have made such large prints. A hungry bear — one getting ready to hibernate for the winter — might venture close enough to the house before heading back up into the forest. That thought reassured me for less than a second before I realized that, whatever prints a bear might make, there was absolutely no way to explain why it would leave flaming ones.

In a daze, I slowly opened the door and entered the living room. I glanced around outside to see if Major had returned before I shut the door, but I saw nothing. I reluctantly secured the door against the cold air. It felt like a betrayal to

141

leave Major out there on his own. By the sound of his barking, he might have traveled a mile or more away from the house. There was no way I was going to be able to find him in the dark. I had no doubt, once morning broke, he should be able to make his way home by himself. Still, I didn't like it. I put the lamp down on the table and hung up my coat on the coat hook. I was in the process of pulling off my boots when Willa came into the room.

"I was able to calm the Missus down. I think she is sleeping now." Willa wrapped her arms around her stomach in a tight hug. "Well? Did you see anything? And where's the dog?" she asked apprehensively.

"I... I don't really know, Willa. It was dark out there. I don't know where Major went. He apparently went tearing up the hill into the forest. I could hear him barking up there. I am sure he's all right. Major can take care of himself. When he gets tired, he'll be back." I averted my eyes, concentrating on my boots, avoiding answering her first question.

"But he's never done anything like that before. He always comes inside and stays inside at night!" I just shrugged my shoulders. Dogs tend not to explain themselves to humans. She persisted. "Did you see anything? Please, you look pale. Tell me! What happened?"

"Look, I am just cold. I... I don't think I saw anything. I am not sure. We can talk tomorrow. I don't want to put you off, Willa. I am cold and wet and I am very tired. Can we talk tomorrow?"

She looked at me with a frown on her face. I could see she knew I wasn't telling her everything and was trying to decide whether to press me about it. "All right, we can talk tomorrow. You will tell me what is bothering you. I'll stay downstairs with the Missus tonight. I'll try to stay up and listen for Major and let him in if he comes back tonight."

I nodded in weary agreement. I was still coming to terms with how my carefully constructed rationale had been totally demolished by what I had just seen. Or by what I thought I had just seen.

"I'm going to bed. Thanks, Willa. You did really well with Martha. You were..." She continued to gaze at me with her brow furrowed. "Uh, I'll see you in the morning then. Good night."

"Good night," she repeated dully. I put my snow-covered boots by the door, grabbed the lamp I had taken outside and headed toward the stairs. I didn't want to admit to myself I couldn't explain what I had just seen. It was also entirely possible I had just experienced another hallucinatory episode. Or I had been talked into believing I had seen something which couldn't possibly exist. It was a case of Delirium Tremens perhaps. While I was staying at Aunt Irene's place, I had seen that new movie *Dumbo* in the theater. *Maybe that was it,* I thought. *Dumbo and his pink elephants on parade.*

I trudged up the stairs unhappily. Whatever the hell was going on, I didn't like it. But right at that moment, I wasn't able think of a single thing I could do about it other than try to get some sleep.

>> 11 <<

Sometime that night, I was jerked out of a particularly nasty dream about my father. I had been back in my bedroom in our house in Kalama. He had been drinking again and was yelling and pummeling me as I tried to make myself as small as possible. I was scared. Terrified, in fact. But in my dream, I was also very angry. He had absolutely no right to barge into my room in the middle of the night, stewed to the gills, and take out his drunken anger on me. I hadn't done anything to warrant these beatings. I kicked out with my heels, aiming for his fat stomach and crotch, screaming, "Stop it!! Get out of here, you asshole!! I hate you!! Get out!!"

My outburst resulted in a momentary pause in the rain of fists on my head, arms and back, but only momentarily. He had been shocked I had the nerve to kick him but also that I had called him an asshole. "No'ne callsh me an ashho'e!" he bellowed, redoubling his efforts to get at me. I started kicking at him again.

And then... I was awake, back in Martha's upstairs spare bedroom. "Aw shit," I moaned. My chest was heaving in an attempt to catch my breath. I rolled onto my back, putting my hands over my face. My pillow was damp with perspiration. I was attempting to will myself — with only limited success — to calm down and breathe normally. I ran my fingers through my limp hair.

Suddenly, my eyes focused on a shadowy figure next to my bed in roughly the same position my father had inhabited during my nightmare. My head jerked back involuntarily, anticipating the next inevitable swing of his meaty fist. The back of my head banged into one of the pointed decorative features that adorned the metal railing of the headboard.

"Ow! Dammit! Mmmmm!!!" My hands flew up to my head, checking for blood, the shadowy figure momentarily forgotten in the explosion of pain. After I recovered from that shock, I was then able to make out it was not my drunken father standing there, ready to lash out with clenched fists. It was Willa.

She was standing motionless at the side of my bed, her chin slightly elevated and her eyes gazing down at me dispassionately. In my confused state, still under the influence of my nightmare, she seemed to be surrounded by an aura of power and purpose. Her long white cotton nightgown glowed dimly in the faint moonlight that managed to make its way into the room from the dormer window. I couldn't see many details in the semi-darkness, but her pose made my thoughts immediately jump back to the times I observed her standing out by the barn at night, staring up into the forest.

I propped myself up on one elbow. "Willa?" I began tentatively. "What's going on? Are you okay?" The aftermath of my nightmare was pushed aside, forgotten, replaced by the dull pain where I had whacked my head coupled with the shock and confusion of discovering Willa standing in my room in the middle of the night.

She didn't respond. I could see that her body began to sway slightly, the top of her head outlining a small circle in the air. I was ready to roll my legs and feet onto the floor and sit up on the edge of the bed when she reached down with both hands and raked the twisted blankets from the bed. I had very little time to process this unexpected action before she took another step toward the bed and threw her right leg over me. She then climbed onto the thin mattress, straddling my stomach on her knees.

Once again, I was shocked, but I was also keenly aware of the intensely erotic sensation of her sitting on me. "Willa!" I managed to blurt out, a little frantically. "What are you doing?" What she was doing became crystal clear in the next few moments as she reached behind her and pushed impatiently at the waistband of my pajama bottoms. My hands reached down in an attempt to help, but they were blocked by Willa's muscular legs and hips. She then hiked her nightgown up over her knees and gathered it around her slim waist. She was not wearing anything underneath. She shoved her hands against my shoulders — effectively pinning me to the thin mattress — and began to move her pelvis against me with a determined, powerful rhythm.

I experienced a jolt of terror as I looked up at Willa's face. Her eyes were tightly closed and her lips were tightly drawn back so I could clearly see her teeth. In the dim light, her face had a feral quality. Her long hair tumbled wildly down each side of her face and shoulders, trailing across my bare chest.

146

I gasped at the intensity of the sensations that flowed through me. "Willa, wait a minute! Slow down! I... I don't think I am ready yet!" It wasn't as if I was unwilling or that she was forcing me to do something I didn't want to do. I happened to be incredibly enthusiastic about the idea of having sex with her. But I was taken aback at the suddenness and intensity of her unexpected visit. My body was apparently not ready to respond as quickly as the situation demanded. Willa changed her position slightly and slowed her gyrations. Forcing myself to relax, I laid my head back on my pillow. I ran my hands up and down her smooth, muscular legs. Gradually, I began to respond.

The thought I was having another hallucination suddenly crashed into my consciousness. What I was experiencing seemed too outlandish to actually be happening. My previous visions, however, had been events I had actually lived through. What was happening there in my small bedroom with Willa was beyond anything I had ever experienced. To be sure, I had been with a number of the girls that hung around the bars in Honolulu, waiting for sailors to take them somewhere more private. My only real experience in being with someone I really cared about had been with my on-again, off-again girlfriend Julie, back when I was in high school. This experience with Willa was so different — much more erotic and disturbing — than any of my other sexual encounters.

Later, after I had time to consider what had occurred, it seemed to me what Willa and I had done wasn't "making love." It had been something much more primitive than that, something that tapped into the basic and unthinking primal urge buried deep within our species' genetic makeup, a hunger that needed to be quelled. It wasn't as if I hadn't ever imagined coaxing Willa into bed with me, or me with her, on one of these cold winter evenings after she had helped Mrs. Cahill to sleep. Lying together on top of a soft blanket in front of the fire in the living room, that would have been very romantic. Those fantasies had come to dominate my breaks from work around the farm. But what occurred there on my hard, squeaky bed was much different from any scenario I had ever envisioned. I did my best to keep up with her, but it was almost as if my presence was a secondary consideration. My role, it seemed, had been a very limited one.

147

Very soon, it was over. We were both breathing heavily. Willa's head rested on my shoulder, my hands on her bare thighs. I could feel her warm breath on the side of my neck. I was still trying to comprehend the enormity of what had just occurred when Willa forcibly pushed herself off my chest with both hands. She pivoted awkwardly off the bed, her knee digging painfully into my scarred forearm. Facing the window, she absently smoothed out her nightgown that had been bunched up around her hips so that, once again, it fell chastely above her ankles. Without a backwards glance in my direction, she then strode across the bare floor and out the door, leaving me alone in the darkness, accompanied only by my astonishment and confusion.

* * * *

The next morning's breakfast was awkward. Given what had occurred the night before, I had no idea what to expect when I entered the kitchen. Willa was in front of the sink, washing up after serving breakfast to Martha. She turned her head toward me and gave me a small nod. "Good morning. I see you made it up on time today."

Was that a rebuke for sometimes oversleeping? Maybe it was a reference to last night? I had no idea. "Yes, I did. Good morning, Willa." I considered what I should say next. "I don't suppose Major came back, did he?" I asked, playing for time. I could see that he hadn't returned.

Willa put her palm on the counter, the other hand on her hip and turned toward me, frowning. "No, he hasn't. I am very worried about him. This isn't like him at all. He is probably very cold and hungry out there." She gazed out the window. "I hope he is all right. I would be very unhappy if he..." Her last of words trailed off without speaking the terrible conclusion that both of us were thinking.

She turned back to me and handed me a tin plate of scrambled eggs and pan-toasted bread. "Do you think you could go out looking for him this morning? Maybe he is hurt or is stuck somewhere and needs to be rescued." I saw a small ray of hope in her eyes. "Please?"

I could easily predict that any such attempt on my part would likely be in vain. There were hundreds of acres of untouched forest and undergrowth out there. There was about as much chance of coming across Major out there as I had when I was attempting to find the missing goats. However, even I could see this was not a time to express such misgivings.

"Sure, Willa. I can do that." I gave her a questioning look. "But you do realize that he has had all night to come back. If he isn't back by now, he is probably miles from here. And there's a lot of territory out there to search. I doubt it will do any good."

I could see that she had given this some thought before she asked me. "Yes, I realize that," she responded slowly. "I just keep thinking Major is still out there and maybe hurt." She bit her lower lip. "He might have a broken leg or something and he needs to be rescued right now!"

"All right, then. I think we have a plan. I'll go look for him after I have some breakfast." I saw my battered coffee maker perking merrily away on the stove. "And coffee! Thank you very much for making that! You're a life saver!"

She managed a thin, brittle smile before turning back to the sink. "Coffee stinks up my kitchen."

I walked over to the stove and poured myself some coffee. I took a sip. It was hot, although I usually had my coffee much stronger. The joe that we were served in the Navy, I had been convinced, could have doubled for the stuff we used to remove carbon deposits from engine parts.

I returned to the table with my coffee and sat down in front of the plate of breakfast. I stared at it for some time before I picked up my fork. I still hadn't decided how I was going to broach the subject of what had occurred the previous night. Then again, I wasn't even certain if I should. Maybe what had happened was meant to be something shared but not talked about. I had no idea how her people talked about sex, if they did at all.

"Willa, so... Uh... Did you sleep all right last night?" I asked in what I hoped was an innocent tone.

149

She slid into the chair at the table opposite me with her mug of tea. "Yes, mostly. I think. Since we began locking the doors at night, I haven't been waking up in the morning with dirty feet. I suppose that's a good thing." She gave a small sigh and then lifted her mug with both hands to her lips.

I decided that was about as large of an opening as I was going to get. "So, I... um... Then I don't suppose you remember being in my room last night, do you?"

Her face registered her surprise. "What? Are you saying that I was in your room last night?"

Yep, just as I suspected, I thought glumly. *She was sleepwalking again. That explains a number of things.* The conversation had just become infinitely more difficult. "Well, yes. You were. I woke up last night, I am not sure what time, and you were standing next to my bed, staring down at me."

Willa put her mug down carefully, as if she were afraid it might spill. She was obviously expecting me to say something more. When I didn't, she prompted, "And...? What happened?"

Wanting to get this over with as quickly as possible, I decided to go for the shortest possible response. "Well, you got into bed with me. And we, ah... had sex." I quickly turned my attention to my plate of scrambled eggs. I wondered if Martha had any hot sauce around, hidden in one of her cupboards somewhere. Scrambled eggs taste better with hot sauce. When I looked up again, Willa was still staring at me.

"I... No, you must have been dreaming. That isn't possible!" She started casting about for an alternative explanation. "Maybe you were having one of your nightmares, did you think of that? You said you were having hallucinations!"

This time it was my turn to sigh. "Don't you think that possibility occurred to me as well? I was surprised, to say the least. But it wasn't a nightmare. It was real. This... Well, for one thing, my nightmares scare the hell out of me. What happened last night wasn't scary. Well, mostly it wasn't scary. I was already awake when I saw you standing next to my bed and, afterwards, I never went back to sleep. I just lay there on my bed, staring at the ceiling. I didn't go to sleep for a long time." My hands gestured automatically: trust me, I am telling the truth.

Willa sat frozen in place, her mouth agape. She was obviously struggling with how to respond. She shook her head several times, her lips moving wordlessly before uttering, "No, you are wrong. I would never do that. I would never do such a thing with…" She stopped abruptly and stared at me, her eyes open very wide.

I was hit with a surge of anger and embarrassment. "What were you going to say, Willa? Why don't you finish your sentence? You were going to say 'I would never do such a thing with you, with some guy covered in ugly scars whose leg doesn't even work right! Someone who left his buddies to die while he saved himself!' That's what you were going to say, isn't it?" I flung the fork down on the table with enough force so it bounced back up and landed in my lap, spraying small flecks of scrambled egg on my shirt in the process. I couldn't even get angry with dignity.

Willa's face transformed again. She was also angry. "No! That is not what I was going to say at all! I was going to say, 'I would never do such a thing with a white man!' If that matters to you at all," she added indignantly. She glared at me, nailing me to my chair with her penetrating brown eyes. "Why do you always make everything about you? Not everything is about you! Martha is not well and I am worried sick about her. I don't know what to do. Major's run away and may be injured and you know for yourself what is out there in the woods! I am scared! Really scared!

"This isn't about you or what you experienced in the war or the fact that you have scars on your body. I don't care about things like that! I actually like you. You seem like a nice person. If I were going to criticize you about something, it would be that you continue to drink and try to hide it from me, even though I told you that I didn't want you to! Oh yes, I know all about that! Don't act so surprised! But even that is not my reason. My reason that I would not… do *that* with you is because you are not of my clan." She pushed herself away from the table and paced across the kitchen floor.

"One day, I would very much like to have a family," she continued. "I would like to live in Canada, near Peace River with my people. Right now, I cannot do that. But I very much want to someday." She turned back in my direction. "That is why

151

what you said that I did could not have happened! I just wouldn't do that. And don't think I don't see you looking me sometimes! Men are all the same. I know what you think about all the time, getting women into your bed! I believe you have been thinking about me so much that you dreamed it was true!"

"What? Willa, come on! That's really unfair!" I countered angrily, even though I immediately acknowledged to myself there was more than a little truth in her accusation. "Okay, I admit that I like you and I find you really attractive. I am sorry if I look at you in the wrong way and made you uncomfortable! I didn't mean to, really. You should have said something to me right then! You may not realize it, but I would *never* try to do anything you didn't want me to, and I am positive that I wouldn't dream up something like what happened last night. If I *were* going to imagine something between you and me, it sure as hell would have been a lot more romantic than what actually did happen!

"When I saw you standing there, next to my bed in the dark, do you want to know what I thought? I was thinking that you were probably sleepwalking again. You looked exactly like you did that time I followed you outside and you walked right past me without even seeing me. I thought maybe you were looking for the key to the front door so you could go out gallivanting out in the backyard in the middle of the night again! That's what I thought, you were sleepwalking and you wanted to go outside! Let me tell you, it sure surprised the hell out of me when you climbed into my bed right on top of me!"

My brain was having difficulty keeping pace with my mouth, which was racing full bore, completely unchecked. I gave her my best angry glare back. "You do remember that you sleepwalk, don't you? Or did I just imagine that time when I found you outside late at night, lying in the mud, and I got you up and helped you back inside. Was that just me or did that really happen? I don't know! You tell me, Willa!"

My mouth screeched to a halt when I realized what I had just said. Willa was staring at me, a stricken look on her face, her arms hung loosely at her sides. Wordlessly, she dashed out of the kitchen. I heard her moccasined feet thumping up the wooden stairs and then down the hallway to her room.

I gazed helplessly at the now empty kitchen doorway where Willa had just departed. I slapped my forehead in disgust. *Why to go, Sean! That really showed her! Very diplomatic. Keep this up and you will have her eating out of your hand in no time!*

Not knowing what else to do, I turned to the kitchen counter to make a lunch for myself. I definitely needed to get out of the house. Maybe I would find Major, probably I wouldn't. But I needed to leave.

Five minutes later, armed with a fried egg sandwich and a slightly wrinkled apple I had packed in a small mouse-nibbled Army green knapsack I had come across in the barn, I stomped noisily out the back door. After taking a few long, angry strides, I stopped momentarily and shaded my eyes so that I could peer up into the woods ahead of me. Even in the full light of the morning, they were dark and foreboding. I turned around to have a quick look at the house before I set off. I caught a glimpse of Willa's face peering down at me from her window before it was quickly replaced by swinging white lace curtains. I stared several more seconds at the window before I turned back toward the woods. Sighing, I hitched the little knapsack higher on my undamaged shoulder and set off up the hill, looking for a German Shepherd I was pretty certain I wasn't going to find.

* * * *

The sun had just started to sink over the top of the trees when I returned to the house. As winter approached, the days were getting much shorter. Here in the valley, dusk now arrived in the late afternoon. The frigid wind blew down from the craggy granite slopes of the Cascades, but I was hoping it wasn't going to be cold enough to snow. I had stayed out looking for Major as long as I thought wise, but I really couldn't avoid going back to the house any longer. I was cold and hungry, and it was going to be very dark within another thirty minutes.

I clumped noisily up the stairs to the front porch. With some reluctance, I pushed open the door that opened into the entryway. A fire blazed away in the stone fireplace in the living room, and I saw light coming through the open doorway to the kitchen at the end of the hallway. There was no sign of either Willa or Martha.

153

Hanging my coat on the hook by the door, I called out, "Hello? Willa? Is anyone here?" I knew they had to be there, as I had seen the Ford in the barn and there wasn't anywhere for either of them to go very far without the car. My shouted question had been a way to announce my presence more than anything else.

"Back here in the kitchen," Willa called out. I tried to gauge the emotion — or the lack of it — in her voice. She didn't sound angry, which seemed to me to be a good thing. She sounded... tired. I pulled off my boots before I went to meet whatever reception awaited me.

Willa was, uncharacteristically for her, sitting in one of the wooden chairs in front of the kitchen table. She was bent over at the waist, her elbows resting on the table. Several strands of her coal black hair had escaped from her long braid and stuck out from the back of her head at odd angles. The skin under her eyes looked bruised. She seemed to be exhausted.

"Willa! Are you all right? What happened?" I asked with very real concern.

She slowly leaned back in the chair and gazed at me before speaking. "I don't suppose you found Major, did you?"

"No, I didn't. I walked for hours but I didn't see any trace of him." I wasn't looking forward to this next part, but I felt I owed her the truth. "However, I did find one of the goats. What was left of it, anyway. It was sort of shoved up underneath a big boulder. I almost missed it when I walked by. I'm very sorry, Willa."

She looked at me with dull eyes. "What color was it?" she asked.

"Uh, I didn't look at it really closely. It was mostly white but I thought I saw some brown mixed in. Did you have a goat like that, white with some brown?" I winced when I saw her expression.

"Cassie. That's Cassie. She was a sweet girl." Tears begin to leak from the corners of Willa's eyes as she leaned forward to rest her forehead on the palms of her hands. "Did you see anything else? Tracks? Marks? Anything?"

"No. That was all I saw. Well, I did see some marks on some of the trees where the bark was damaged. I think that's probably just some deer rubbing the dead skin off his antlers."

154

"Deer don't do that in the winter," she explained slowly without looking up. "That only happens in the spring and early summer after their antlers stop growing. Their antlers fall off in the winter."

"Okay then, it wasn't a deer. Maybe it was a bear sharpening his claws or something like that. Or maybe those were old marks from earlier. I don't know. But that's all I saw. I didn't see any tracks or anything." Willa didn't answer, but I needed to keep her talking. I didn't like how Willa was reacting in the least. Having her angry with me would have been better. "How's Martha? Did she have anything to eat tonight?"

Willa pulled herself upright in the chair again before answering. "Yes, I managed to get her to eat something. I had to cut up her meat into very small bites and spoon them into her mouth. She doesn't chew much and I don't want her to choke. It felt like I was feeding a little baby, Sean. That's what it felt like. I don't even know if she can talk anymore. She just grunts and makes little noises like she is trying to talk but I don't understand any words!" Then she did start visibly weeping. She put her right hand to her eyes, sobbing. "I don't know what to do and I am not sure I can take much more of this!" she managed to get out between gulps.

Seeing her obvious distress, I shuffled over beside her on the chair. Kneeling down on my left knee, I put my arm loosely around her shoulder. I hadn't been certain how this was going to be received, given the loud disagreement we had earlier that morning. But she turned her head and buried it against my shoulder as she continued to cry.

We stayed in that position for several more minutes. I was getting physically very uncomfortable, as I had been walking all day. I had been hurting before I had come inside. Now, in this awkward half-kneeling position, I was experiencing shooting pains up and down my right hip and leg. I really needed to stand up and stretch, but I did not want to move before Willa was ready. I had no idea of anything I might to say to her that would provide comfort. I couldn't tell her that it was all going to be okay, because that obviously wasn't true. I couldn't tell her Major was fine and healthy, because, in all likelihood, he wasn't going to come back. I hated to think of that myself, as I had really grown attached to the old boy. In the end, I just stayed silent with my arm around Willa's shoulders, letting her cry herself out.

Willa eventually raised her head off my shoulder and I lifted my arm from around her. She sniffed several more times and then wiped at her nose with the back of her hand. "I need to go check on the Missus. I have a plate of food for you on the stove. I hope it isn't too cold." With that, she got up from her chair and walked slowly out of the kitchen and down the little hallway to the front of the house.

Groaning, I slowly maneuvered myself into an upright position with assistance from the chair that Willa had just vacated. Still leaning heavily on the chair, I winced as I flexed my right knee and hip to get the blood circulating again. I wasn't hungry anymore, but I knew I should probably eat something so that I wouldn't wake up ravenous in the middle of the night. After grabbing the plate and the nearest eating utensil I could find, I settled myself back in my chair with my intended supper in front of me. I poked unenthusiastically at the food Willa had left for me. It was frankly unappealing; clumps of white grease had congealed around the cold chunks of meat and potatoes. The fire that had been in the firebox of the oven was gone, nothing more than ash and glowing embers. I could see that my supper wasn't ever going to get any better than it was at that moment. I began to spoon the cold stew into my mouth. I finished up quickly and then grabbed a piece of crusty bread from the metal breadbox on the counter and began gnawing on it — spreading little white crumbs around on the floor in the process — in an effort to rid my mouth of the greasy residue. I then headed up to the little washroom at the top of the stairs to clean up before I hit the sack. My feet dragged along the floor, as I was completely worn out from my daylong hike in the mountains. I was also emotionally drained. There was just too much strange stuff happening.

Forlornly, I wished Major was back home. We would sit in front of the fire, getting our bodies too warm in places and too cold in others. I would rub the fur on his neck, he would put his head in my lap and we would both feel better for it. I fumbled for the wooden banister as I slowly made my way up the dark stairs.

* * * *

My lamp was still lit and I was lying on my narrow bed, staring at the ceiling, dressed in my pajama bottoms when I heard Willa's light tapping on my door. "Sean, are you awake? Can I come in?"

I called out, "Yep, I'm still up. Hold on, let me put on a shirt or something first." I reached over the side of the bed and grabbed at the cotton undershirt I had tossed on the floor. I quickly pulled it over my head and gave a futile attempt to comb my freshly washed hair using my fingers. I called out, "Okay, you come in now."

Willa opened the door slowly and peeked in before she entered. I tried to smile and gestured toward the single chair in the room. She pulled it over near the bed and sat down. She looked a little better than she had when I came back to the house several hours ago, but not by much. I felt extremely sorry for her.

"How's Martha? Is she sleeping?"

"Yes, I think she is sleeping now. She's... Well, I don't know how she is." She considered a moment before speaking again. "Sean, do you know anything about when someone has a stroke? When I lived with Mr. and Mrs. Billings, an elderly friend of Mrs. Billings fell ill. I went with her to visit her friend. It was awful. She couldn't talk, one of her eyes was closed and she couldn't move the left side of her face. I am certain she recognized Mrs. Billings when we went into her room, but she couldn't speak. She could only make noises. I was very frightened and had to go outside to wait. I couldn't stay in the room with them. Later on the way home, Mrs. Billings told me that her friend had had a stroke."

Willa looked at me intently. "I see the same things in the Missus. She isn't able to speak or feed herself. I have to lift her up out of bed to get her to the bathroom. Sometimes, she doesn't make it and I have to clean her up before I can put her back to bed." She bit at her lower lip. "Do you think she might have had a stroke?"

"Uh, that's possible, I guess. It sounds like you know more about it than I do. All I know is that it's some injury inside your brain, I think. Serious strokes can kill a person. Smaller ones can leave people without the ability to move or speak, just like you said. So yeah, I guess it's possible."

I considered the situation. "If she did have one, Willa, this isn't good. Not good at all!" I have known for some time that I have a surprising tendency to blurt out ridiculous sounding inanities just when I least expect them. It makes me sound like an idiot. "The two of us don't have the capability of caring for her in this house, especially since the snows will be hitting us hard and heavy in the next month or so. I think you're correct, we can't do this stuck out here in the mountains!" Suddenly, I realized how serious the situation was in which we found ourselves. "We need to get her into a hospital or something. Maybe a nursing home. I guess that would mean going down into Everett or Seattle. I doubt there's anything like that any closer."

Willa, for her part, looked shaken but remained calm. She clasped her hands together in her lap and was quiet for moment before speaking. "Yes, you are likely correct. I don't think we can keep her here." She turned to gaze out the window. There was a new moon that night; beyond the panes of glass was nothing but darkness. "To be perfectly honest, I don't want to stay here either."

I looked at her in surprise. She saw my expression and quickly explained. "Oh, I don't mean that I would abandon the Missus. I couldn't do that, even if she did have a stroke. She has always been very kind to me. I couldn't leave her now." Her voice trailed off, her nose and forehead wrinkled in thought. "But if we were to take her somewhere, we could leave as well. I... I think I could find someone in town that would take the goats. But I believe we need to leave this place very soon. Do you remember what you said Amos Ghost Horse told you, that I was in danger here and I should leave? Well, I believe he was right. I think all of us need to leave this place, as soon as we can manage. I hate to leave without Major, but I don't think he is coming back."

I leaned back against the wall and stared at Willa. The last time we had discussed my conversation with Amos, she had upbraided me for talking about her personal problems with a stranger. Although I knew Willa had been very worried since the episode with whatever Martha had imagined she had seen in her window, I hadn't realized she now agreed with Amos and wanted to leave. However, given the circumstances we found ourselves in, I wasn't about to disagree with her.

I took a deep breath and exhaled slowly until my lungs felt totally empty. According to Dr. Farmer, that's an unconscious but helpful stress-reliving mechanism. I was very annoyed at my brain for dragging up such useless information like that out of whatever cellar it stores such crap at a time when I really wasn't in need of it. I wished it would produce something more useful on occasion.

"Yeah, I agree. We need to talk about how we are going to do this, though. We don't want to rush off and not know what we are doing. I don't even know where a hospital or clinic might be that would take a new patient like her. I don't know how much it would cost. That kind of care for a partially disabled person can't come cheap. Does Martha have much money around? Because I think we are going to need it."

Willa waved her hand dismissively in the air. I took that to indicate money was not going to be a concern. I sincerely hoped that was the case and Martha's rumored stash was indeed a large one. We were going to be in a world of hurt if it wasn't. "Okay then. How about I drive down to Skykomish tomorrow? I can find a place with a telephone to talk to the doctor in Goldbar. If he thinks he should see her first, then I can come back here and we can turn around and take Martha to the doctor's office. But if he isn't in his office or maybe if he thinks he can't do anything for her, I can jump on the morning the train into Everett. There's a return train around five o'clock, I think. I could be back before sundown. I can find out if there is somewhere we can take her. If it all works out, I could be back tomorrow night, we could pack everything up and drive her into the city the next day. I could come back for the goats after that. How does that sound?" I knew I was omitting several very important points, such as the fact that everything would need to fall exactly in our favor for the plan I had laid out to work in such a short time frame. I had also not addressed where Willa and I were going to go if and when we ever got Martha admitted to a clinic. Willa seemed adamant that she was not going to come back to this house if Martha wasn't here. I wholly agreed with her. What exactly we *were* going to do, however, remained very murky in my mind. It would need to be one of those proverbial bridges we would cross if and when we ever got to it.

Willa seemed to sense I was leaving out a great deal, but she just nodded at me. "Yes, I suppose that is the best we can do for the time being," she said slowly, her voice devoid of emotion. She got up from the chair and pulled it back over next to the closet door where she had found it. As she turned the doorknob to open the door, she stopped and turned back toward me.

"Sean, please tell me... Did I *really* come into your room last night and we... we..." She looked at me helplessly, not knowing how to finish asking her question.

I lowered my eyes to the floor, not wanting to embarrass her any more than she already was. "Yeah. You did. And then we did." I shrugged my shoulders. "I'm very sorry, Willa. I guess I shouldn't have said anything. But if you were really sleepwalking, I thought you should probably know."

She looked at me, unhappiness etched into her face. "Yes. Thanks for telling me." She paused, looking uncomfortable, and then said, "I am sorry about the way I acted this morning. It was quite a shock, on top of everything else that has been going on. I just didn't know how to react. I didn't really believe you were lying to me. I guess I just didn't want it to be true."

About twelve different ways I could respond galloped through my head, ranging from an awkward social *faux pas* all the way to a calamity of biblical proportions. Instead, I settled for shaking my head. "Hey, don't worry about it. I'm very sorry too. It's been a tough time for all of us."

Willa nodded sadly. She then glanced at the bed where I was sitting. Pointing with her chin, she said, "That's a very small bed. We did it on that?" Her eyebrows arched quizzically.

I also looked down and gave a small laugh. "Yeah, it is pretty narrow, isn't it? It was cramped, all right. I was just hoping that we didn't fall through the springs and end up on the floor."

That produced one of her small snorts. "Yes, lucky thing, huh?" She gave me one more guarded look and then opened the door. "Goodnight, Sean. I'll get you up early so you can get ready for your trip in the morning. I think you may have a long day in front of you." With that rather unnerving prediction, she left, pulling the door closed behind her.

I listened to her feet pad down the hall to her bedroom. I punched my pillow with my fist several times to very little effect and returned to my reclining position, staring at the ceiling. *Yes,* I thought to myself, *I believe you are right. Tomorrow may be a very long day indeed.*

>> 12 <<

As it turned out, the day was much different from the one I had envisioned. I was jerked out of a deep sleep by the sound of Willa's insistent knocking on my door. My mouth tasted like rust. Rubbing my eyes blearily, I shouted at the door from my prone position. "Okay, Willa. I'm getting up. Thanks. I'll be right down."

However, my response was apparently insufficient for Willa. She pushed the door open and peered in at me, still encased in sheets and blankets. "Sean, are you awake? Have you looked outside yet?"

The fact of the matter was that I barely was and had not, as she hadn't given me much of a chance. I pulled my legs out from underneath the bedding while trying to figure out what possibly could have happened so early in the morning. The unnerving occurrences centered around Martha Cahill's house, up to then, seemed to be strictly on an evening and nighttime basis. Bad things weren't supposed to happen to people early in the morning before they've had a chance to use the toilet. I rubbed my hands over my face again, thinking I should probably shave again.

"What's up, Willa?" I said, trying to get my bearings. I craved one of those smelly cups of coffee.

She pointed at the window. "Look and see for yourself," she said simply.

I leaned over and retrieved my errant long-sleeve undershirt from the floor. I stood up and pulled my shirt over my head while padding over to the window in my bare feet. What greeted my eyes when I peered out was a uniformly colorless landscape, annotated with bumps and mounds that concealed unknown things buried beneath the thick blanket of snow. Fat snowflakes were falling heavily from a leaden sky. It didn't look like anything was going to improve any time soon.

"Well, damn. I was worried about snow. It looks like we got it. I would say there's at least two feet out there."

I turned around and studied Willa. She looked worried, but seemed to be doing much better than she had the previous evening. She had changed from her normal outfit she wore when working around the house. I was a little surprised to see she was wearing dark blue jeans with her cuffs rolled up, exposing several inches of light-colored denim around her ankles, along with a red plaid shirt tucked into her jeans. Although I was certainly not used to seeing a woman wear men's clothing, I had to admit that, on her, it looked rather fetching.

"I am sorry, Willa, but it doesn't look like we are going anywhere today, especially with Martha along. We can't chance it. I think we would need an Army Jeep to get through this. We would end upside down in the ditch or in the creek if we tried to take the car with its bald tires."

Willa didn't seem surprised. She had obviously been up and awake for some time and had sufficient time to realize, at least for today, we weren't going to be going anywhere. She just nodded at me.

"How's she doing this morning?" I asked as I sat back down on the bed to pull on my socks. "Any change?"

"No, no change. I helped her with her toilet this morning and fed her some breakfast. I think she is aware of what is going on around her and she recognizes me. But she doesn't speak and it looks like she can't control one side of her face." Willa looked down and scuffed at the floor with the tip of her moccasin. She had obviously had come to terms with the fact that Mrs. Cahill was very ill and was likely not going to get better. She looked back up and said, "I am going to walk down to town. I can find a phone and call the doctor from there. Maybe he can drive out from Goldbar. You are going to take care of Martha until I get back."

"What? No, Willa, you can't do that!" I was shocked that she would even suggest such a thing. "That's a good mile and a half hike. In this snow, it would take you over an hour, maybe two! And when you got to town, those jeans would be soaking wet. You could get hypothermia!" She looked at me questioningly. "That's when your body loses so much heat that it can't keep up and you start getting really sleepy. You can easily die from it. That's one of the first things we learned in the Navy. You don't survive very long in the cold water if you go overboard. And think

164

for a second, there may not be anything in town open! I bet everyone stayed at home today. And asking a doctor to come out from Goldbar in this weather, well... He probably doesn't even have a vehicle that could handle this kind of snow."

"Well, what would you suggest we do then, Sean? I can't ask you to go with that leg of yours. You had a difficult time walking up here in nice warm weather. I'm the only one that can make it. And I better be going soon if I am going," she said, her voice thick with determination.

"Willa, please stop and think about this," I pleaded with her. "This is *not* a good idea! Look, Martha is probably not going to get any worse than what she is right now. Whatever happened to her has already happened! We can easily hold out here for another few days until the roads are passable. We have enough food and firewood. If you go out there and something happens to you, what's going to happen here? I guess I can take care of Martha for a little while, but I'm not the one that has experience with her. And I won't be able to leave her alone! I will be stuck here until someone comes, and if you don't make it to town for some reason, there's not going to be anyone that comes out here because there is no reason anyone would know that they should come!"

I could see doubt slowly creep into Willa's eyes. I knew she desperately wanted to do something, anything, but was only beginning to understand that doing something without really considering the implications might make things worse than they were already. Much worse.

"But we can't sit here and not do anything!" she objected.

"Willa, that's about all we *can* do right now," I countered. "Look, we can catch up one some work here inside the house. I can help you with Martha. You can show me some of the things that you have to do so I can do them by myself. I can bring in more firewood from the stack outside. We'll be fine. Martha will be as comfortable as she can be."

Willa bit at her lower lip as she turned to gaze out the window. I was relieved, as I could see — although she was obviously not very happy about it — I had successfully changed her mind. She nodded her acceptance and, with a disconsolate look on her face, went downstairs. I sighed with relief and went to the little bathroom across the hallway to get myself prepared for the rest of the day.

*　*　*　*

The snow continued to fall steadily through the morning and into the afternoon. Twilight began to settle in around four o'clock. I went outside to fetch several armfuls of the firewood that I had diligently chopped and stacked for the last two months. The snow in the back of the house was at least three feet deep. I had difficulty cutting a path down the back stairs and to the stack of firewood I had piled inside the barn. The only shovel I had managed to find on the farm was of the hole digging variety and it was out in the barn.

On my third trip out, I stopped momentarily to contemplate my surroundings. The snow fell peacefully around me. The rubbing sounds my clothes made seemed amplified, conspicuously loud. The snow made a scrunching sound against the soles of my boots whenever I took a step. Being aware of such sounds as I moved was a new sensation for me. When I stood absolutely still, I could hear the slight hiss of the snowflakes as they fell onto the layer of snow already on the ground. I listened to the sound of my own breathing.

I looked up, squinting against the falling snowflakes and chill wind. I could just make out the bright patch in the dull grey sky that indicated the position of the sun behind the thick covering of clouds. Turning slightly, I gazed up the hill toward the forest. Although it was partially obscured by the several hundred feet of falling snowflakes, I could still make out the dark line of the trees. The hard granite mountains behind the belt of trees were hidden. An involuntary shiver ran down my spine. I again wondered what Willa had been looking at during her nighttime sojourns, back before we started locking the doors. Or maybe it was more of a matter of what she had been looking *for*. I couldn't decide. Even considering the question made me uneasy.

I shivered again and hurried to get my last armful of firewood. By the time I hit the bottom of the rear steps leading up to the kitchen door, I was almost running.

I kicked at the bottom of the door, which Willa opened quickly. Once inside, I was almost overwhelmed by the heat of the air in the kitchen, compared to the chill, wintery scene I had just left behind. I hurriedly dumped my load of logs in the firewood bin next to the stove.

Willa looked at me curiously. "Are you okay, Sean?"

"Yeah, I'm fine. Fine. I'm just cold, that's all." I brushed the snow off my shoulders and the top of my head before taking off the thick coat I was wearing and hanging it on the hook by the door. It had belonged to Philip Cahill long ago, before he went across the Atlantic to join in the Great War. The coat smelled musty, the leather was old and cracked in a number of places, but it was still very warm. I appreciated its fur lining and collar. I was glad Willa had dug it out of a closet somewhere. I hadn't brought any winter clothes with me that would withstand the icy cold weather held at bay by the thin kitchen door.

"Your nose and ears are red," Willa observed, stirring something in a big pot on the stove.

"Yeah, I bet they are. They sting, too." I looked over at her as I blew into my cold hands. It didn't help much. She had changed from the jeans and plaid shirt from that morning into her usual light blue full-length skirt, white long-sleeved blouse and white apron. Again, I marveled at, even in the face of all that had happened over the last few days, how composed she appeared. My entire opinion of Natives had been utterly upended during the few months I had been around her. She was nothing like what I had expected a Native — an Indian — to be.

"What? What are you looking at?" She had noticed me staring at her just a little bit longer than was called for.

"Nothing, nothing. Sorry. I was just wondering what that was you are making. It smells very good." Changing the subject seemed like a good idea.

"It's soup. There were some vegetables in the pantry that weren't going to last much longer. I also used the last of the beef you bought the last time you went into town." She grimaced. "The vegetables will be mushy. I thought the Missus might be able to eat it easier that way. She doesn't seem to be able to chew very well."

167

I nodded my approval. "Mushy vegetables are fine. You should have seen some of the stuff we were served in the Navy." I had hoped to get her to smile. She gazed solemnly back at me.

"Right. Okay, is there anything else you need me to do? I thought I might go upstairs, clean up a bit and go sit in front of the fire, maybe read my book a little."

She waved her non-stirring hand at me, freeing me from any further obligations. With that, I left the kitchen and headed up the stairs, very much looking forward to getting out of my wet clothes.

Twenty minutes later, I was back downstairs. I removed the screen on the hearth and generously tossed several new logs on the small fire. I felt it was my right, considering how many hours I had spent many hours chopping and splitting the stuff. I could burn it if I wanted to.

Satisfied, I replaced the screen and fell backwards onto the couch, my worn copy of *Robinson Crusoe* under my arm. It had been several weeks since I last cracked it open. But when I was finally able to stretch out in front of the fire, I discovered I really wasn't all that interested in Rob, his good buddy Friday or a bunch of cannibals. It now seemed pretty tame. I tossed the book over to the side of the couch and leaned back to contemplate the roaring fire. The heat felt wonderful after the chill of my wet clothes. I wriggled my toes inside my wool socks. Fires, I decided, could be very nice and cozy. At that moment, I felt totally at peace, sitting there in the living room with its large stone hearth and chimney, woolen rug on the worn wood floor and the wallpapered walls. Open spaces could be dangerous, I mused. It was much better to be inside. It was cold and snowing outside. Out there, out in the open, there might be Japanese Zeros or beasts that left flaming footprints hiding just out of your sight. They could appear, out of the blue, without warning and disrupt your entire life. Your ship could sink or the old lady in the bed might scream because she saw red eyes looking at her through the window. Yes, it was much safer to be surrounded by walls and locked doors, which would keep the bad things out... Bad things...

My eyes flew open as my chin popped up from its resting place on my chest. *Damn, I fell asleep and was dreaming!* Still somewhat dazed, I wondered what had aroused me out of my unexpected slumber. I looked around for Major until I remembered that he wasn't there anymore. A wave of sadness hit unexpectedly. I guiltily realized that I felt much worse about Major being missing than I did about Mrs. Cahill lying in her bedroom, unable to feed herself.

I pushed myself off of the couch. The fire had burned down so the middle of the blackened logs glowed orange, surrounded by low mellow flames. From that, I estimated that I had been asleep for around a half an hour, perhaps a bit longer. I didn't hear anything from the kitchen. I walked quietly over to Martha's bedroom door and opened it a several inches. From that vantage point, I could see her lying motionless on the bed, her head turned to one side. The oil lamp on the nightstand had been turned down low so that there was only a small bubble of flickering light surrounding the table and the top half of the bed. Willa was not there.

I closed the door silently and walked out to the living room and back down the short hallway to the kitchen. The pot of soup was on the stove, unattended and in danger of bubbling away until all the liquid evaporated. I was suddenly uneasy, as that seemed very unlike Willa. I grabbed at the couple of hot pads from the countertop and managed to move the pot of boiling soup from the stove onto the cutting board. I called out, "Willa, are you there? Is everything all right?"

There was no answer. I hurried back down the hall to call out in case she was upstairs. The thought occurred to me that she was in the little washroom. However, there was no response to my shouted question. When I turned around and glanced toward the front door, I could clearly see that Willa's coat was no longer on the hook at the side of the door. Her boots were missing as well. Muttering several profanities under my breath, I limped out the hallway to the front door. When I pulled it open, I could see that the heavy snow had finally tapered off. Only a few small, scattered flakes drifted down from the sky. I could also see, quite plainly, Willa's tracks in the snow where she had negotiated the thick snow on the stairs and around toward the back of the house.

My mind's internal voice started babbling away frantically. *What the hell did she think she was doing? She left supper to burn on the stove, she left Martha alone and she didn't wake me! I was right there on the couch, not ten feet from the door! And it's getting dark outside! She doesn't go out when it's dark! She can't be sleepwalking! She was in the kitchen and came out here, put on her coat and boots and went out the door! What could have possibly made her do that?*

Several possibilities occurred to me, but I couldn't really come up with any that wouldn't have involved waking me and sending me outside instead of venturing out by herself. She must have thought it was of utmost urgency for her to do all these things that seemed so out of character for her.

Standing there indecisively in the hallway at the foot of the dark stairs, I knew that I had an important decision to make and I needed to do it quickly. I could stay in the house with Martha, in case she needed help. Even a lunkhead like me knew it was never a good idea to leave an invalid alone. I recalled well the squad of nurses in the military hospitals whose job required their eyes to be glued on their injured charges at all times. I remembered sitting with my mother, her wasted body wracked with cancer, in her darkened bedroom. It would be irresponsible of me to charge out of the house and leave Martha alone for some undetermined amount of time. On the other hand, Willa was out there in the dark, floundering around through the deep snow. Who knows where she might be going? If I went after her, I shouldn't have much of a problem in following her. Yes, she had a head start, but I just needed to follow her tracks. She could have slipped and fallen into a ravine or hurt herself in a myriad of other ways. She may be in real trouble and in need of my help right away.

In the end, it was an easy decision — albeit rather a ruthless one — for me to make. Martha was old and infirm. She had lived a good life up to this point and might not ever be able to get out bed again without assistance. She could probably make it on her own for an hour or two, or how much time it turned out to be. Willa was... Willa was alive, young and had the rest of her life in front of her. The realization I was probably in love with her also played a very large part in my decision.

I spat a few out a few more of my dad's choice swear words as I lit the oil lamp and turned up the flame as far as it would go before replacing the glass chimney. I threw on my coat and boots, grabbed the lamp and flung the front door open. Easing myself down the snowy stairs, I could see I would not have a problem following Willa's tracks in the snow. I also was conscious of the fact that an oil lamp meant for indoors was a piss-poor substitute for the standard issue Navy waterproof flashlight. I would have gladly exchanged anything in my possession, which admittedly wasn't very much, for one of those flashlights.

Okay Sean, just keep your head. She can't have gone very far, I thought to myself. *This should be easy. Just don't panic. Do not panic!* I could see Willa's trail lead past the goat pen and continue up toward the forest. My emotions were jumping between blazing anger at Willa for her stupidity and paralyzing fear for her safety. When we got back to the house, I thought I might either put her over my knee and spank her soundly or hug her tightly and not let her go for a long time, even though I had serious reservations she would put up with either one from me.

Following in Willa's path that she had broken through the snow was easier than if I had to forge a new path through the new snow for myself, but it was still difficult. The depth of the snow required me to lift my feet several feet off the ground before I could make my next step. This repeated movement was already causing some significant pain in my right hip. The sound of my breathing was very loud in my ears. I hoped the snow wouldn't be anywhere as deep in the forest as it was out in the open and I could make better time. However, it could also be that, without snow on the ground, I wouldn't be able to find Willa's tracks in order to follow her.

As it turned out, I discovered that I didn't have to worry about either. I found Willa propped up with her back against the trunk of a large cedar tree just inside the tree line. She was conscious and uninjured but she appeared to be extremely cold and very groggy — not a good sign. I couldn't get much out of her. Information could wait until we got back into the house and out of the elements. At that point, I just needed to get her up and moving back down the hill.

"Willa, are you okay?" I seemed to be asking that question a lot the last few days. "Are you hurt? Can you move?"

"Y-Yes, I think I am fine. No, I am not hurt."

"All right, let me help you to your feet. We really need to get out of here and back to the house. Can you do that? I'll grab your hands and pull." With that, she

171

managed to get upright on her feet. I bit back the angry reprimand that was threatening to leap out. "Can you walk? You can lean on me as we go, but I don't think I can carry you."

"I... I can walk. You lead. I can manage. I am freezing!"

Yeah, I bet you are, you idiot, I thought. *You're from Canada! You should know better than this!*

We managed to walk, single file, me with the lamp held out in front of us and Willa with her hands on my shoulders, back down the hill toward the house without much difficulty. The path on the way down was a bit easier than it had been on my hike up to the trees. I took the longer route around the house to the front door rather than try for the door into the kitchen, however inviting the light streaming from the kitchen windows was. The stairs looked treacherous and I didn't want to have to deal with a broken arm on top of everything else. When we entered the living room, I brushed the snow off of the two of us as best I could and then helped Willa out of her coat and boots before doing the same for myself. I gestured toward her rocking chair and went to throw some fresh logs on the fire.

She objected, "I need to go to the Missus to see if she is all right first."

"You sit down. Now!" I commanded. "I'll do it. When I looked in on her fifteen minutes ago, she was sleeping peacefully."

Willa looked at me, surprised at being on the receiving end of a command from her hired hand. She sat while I limped heavily over to the bedroom to look in on Martha. She was in the same position as I had seen her previously. I thought I could hear her light snoring from the doorway.

"She's fine, no thanks to you," I said, a little more harshly than I had intended but I was cold, mad and still trying to get over my fright. "I have no idea what the hell you thought you were doing. No! Don't say anything right now. I'm going to into the kitchen and make us some tea. Stay by the fire, you hear?" As I headed toward the kitchen, my fear began to dissipate. It was being replaced with a self-righteous, burning anger at her for putting all three of us in a potentially dangerous situation. Anger felt good, I suddenly realized. It was hot. Self-righteous anger was much better than being scared.

When I made it back to the living room, I discovered Willa hadn't followed my directions to the letter. She was in her rocker in front of the fire but had first gone upstairs to change her clothes. I had to admit that was a much better idea than sitting there in her cold, wet clothes. She was now in her nightgown and a heavy cotton robe, her stocking feet stretched out toward the fire.

"Here's your tea." She nodded gratefully as she accepted it with both hands. "Now, would you mind explaining to me just what the hell you thought you were doing going outside in the dark and the snow without waking me? What do you think you were doing, you idiot?" I was almost yelling. I don't ever remember yelling at a woman before in my entire life.

"Please don't shout at me, Sean. I apologize. It was stupid, I agree." She took a sip of her tea and looked up at me from the rocker. I glared at back at her, unsatisfied by her casual apology. She continued, "I thought I heard Major barking out back. He sounded very close. I rushed out here to the living room. You were asleep on the couch. It would have taken you several minutes to wake up and then get dressed in order to go outside. I thought if I could get out there very quickly and catch hold of his collar, I could get him back inside before he ran off again."

"You heard Major barking?" I asked incredulously. She nodded at me. "Major has been out since last night. If he came back to the house, why wouldn't he come directly to one of the doors and bark, wanting to be let in? He would be want to be fed immediately. And once he was here, I doubt that he would run off again. That doesn't make a lot of sense, Willa." She shrugged her shoulders and took another sip of her tea. Considering how frightened I had been when I went out to search for her, I was getting pretty damn annoyed at the cavalier attitude she had adopted. I felt a serious show of remorse was in order. "I didn't see any of his footprints when I was out there following you. Are you sure you heard him?"

"That's what I said, Sean. I thought I heard him barking," she repeated patiently. "I rushed outside to see if I could catch him. I didn't see him in the back, but I thought I heard him barking up near the trees. I went up the hill to see if I could see him. When I got up there, I couldn't find him. I was very tired and cold, so I sat down underneath the tree where you found me."

I crossed my arms as I frowned at her. My dramatic pose was lost on her, however, as she wasn't looking at me. She had turned her attention back to the fire, placidly sipping her mug of tea. Something seemed very wrong with her explanation and I was not at all happy with her apparent lack of contrition. I had been scared out of my wits and it didn't seem to matter to her.

However, I decided I wasn't going to stand there and argue with her. "Okay, if that's what happened, fine. I am sorry you didn't find Major. I took the soup off the stove. I think the stuff on the bottom of the pot may be burned. I am going to go change into some dry clothes. I am freezing myself, you know. I hope you don't mind if I get into my pajamas. I don't think I have any dry clothes left," I said with as much sarcasm as I could muster.

"No, your pajamas are fine. I'm sorry you got wet again. When you come down, bring your wet clothes and spread them here in front of the fire. My door is open — could you please bring mine down as well? We can dry everything at the same time. Thank you." She smiled at me. I hadn't seen her smile in over a week and she chose this particular moment to honor me with a smile for bringing her wet clothes downstairs? Exasperated, I shook my head as I turned toward the stairway. I heard Willa call out to me as I mounted the stairs, "As soon as the Missus wakes up, I will give her some soup. When you get back down, we can sit here in front of the fire and have some. I hope you are hungry. I am."

Yeah, I am hungry. And I am wet and cold and mad. Soup will be just the thing! I thought blackly to myself. I didn't understand anything.

*   *   *   *

Later, after Willa had fed Martha and helped her with her nighttime routine, the two of us were sitting in our normal places around the fire, surrounded by wet clothing draped over all available surfaces. My wet jeans and shirt were lying flat on the hearth. *They should be dry for tomorrow,* I thought idly. I had no idea what might actually occur the following day, but it would likely involve the need for dry clothing. Each of us had a large mug full of Willa's soup. I tried to use my spoon but found it was easier just to drink it.

By that time, I was no longer angry. My heated emotions had diffused to the point that all that was left was a dull feeling of emptiness and confusion. I looked over at Willa. She sat in her rocking chair with her feet tucked up underneath her, gazing serenely into the fire. It was clear to me she had given me as much of an explanation for the earlier events of the evening as I was going to get. I made a decision I was not going to ask her anything else. If that's how she wanted to leave things, that was fine by me. Two could play that game. However, I felt a strong desire to break the overbearing silence. It was getting on my nerves.

"So, uh, Willa. You never finished your story. The last time we talked, you were telling me how you stayed with the… Billings?" She nodded in agreement. "The Billings. But how did you end up here in Washington? In a whole different country?" I was still very curious about this point, now that I had heard quite a lot of her personal history and what her beliefs were.

She looked at me for a moment. I got a momentary impression she resented having her quiet revere interrupted. But she looked back at the fire and started talking.

"I told you that I lived with them for eight years. I believe the Indian School knew where I was, but they never came to claim me. I think they decided that I was a bad child, just like my cousin had been, and they were more than happy to be rid of me." She took another sip from her mug. "I had a boyfriend, you know. He was one of the older boys from the school. Everyone called him Teddy. Teddy would sneak out of the boy's dormitory when he could and we would meet up in different places. We didn't want to be seen by the townspeople, as they would probably report us to the school. I didn't want to get him in trouble. We would sit and talk about what we wanted to do when we got older, where we wanted to live. We practiced our Native languages on each other, so we would not forget our heritage in the middle of a white society that did not want us to be who we were.

"Teddy was not of the Beaver clan, but his clan was also what anthropologists call Athabascan, so our languages were somewhat similar. We would play word games with each other. Eventually, we began to do the things that all young, bored teenage boys and girls do when they are alone with each other and believe they won't get caught. We were very careful, as I did not want to become with child. I didn't know if I was in love with Teddy, but I liked him very much. He was very nice, and we enjoyed our time with each other."

Willa paused in her telling, lost in her memories of more pleasant days than the ones she was currently experiencing. I felt a stab of jealousy over this young Indian boy I had never met. I told myself that was not at all rational, but raw emotions are very rarely rebuked by rational thought.

"I enjoyed those years there with the Billings, even though I missed my family — especially my mother — terribly. Of course, all things change. Mr. Billings died suddenly one autumn. I was told it was a heart attack. Mrs. Billings was heartbroken. She still talked with me, but it wasn't like before. Not long after, she decided to sell the farm and move to Saskatoon to live with her sister. She invited me to come with her, but I could tell it would have not been a good idea. I did not want to live in a big white man's city. I would have been lost."

Willa stopped again. She seemed to be gathering her courage about her. "About this time, just as the days were getting shorter and autumn was changing into winter, I began to feel that I was being watched. I became very uneasy. One evening when I had gone out of the house to meet Teddy, I seemed to feel a presence. A hateful presence."

For the first time in her narration, she looked over at me to watch for my reaction. I kept my face neutral. I told myself that this is Willa's personal story she is telling, based on her own reality. But I also knew about the feeling of being watched.

She continued, "I kept on for another half a mile or so, but I was getting very frightened. I finally reached the old barn on the outskirts of town where we usually met. Teddy would bring a lantern with him and light it. No one could see us in the barn. But this night, the barn was dark. I opened the door and peeked in, just to see if he was there. Maybe he had forgotten the lantern. I called out his name but no one answered. But I did hear a rustle in the loft above and another noise I couldn't identify. It... It sounded like an owl."

176

Her dark eyes bored into me. I nodded, showing her that I understood what she was referring to.

"It was then I saw something on the floor near the back. I couldn't make it out, but it was just a big dark shadow. There hadn't been anything there the last time we were in the barn. Suddenly, I was certain it was Teddy lying there on the floor, dead. I thought I could smell blood from there in the doorway. I was so scared that I could not move. I heard the rustle again from up in the loft. That broke the spell that had come over me. I turned and ran as quickly as I could back to the Billings' house. I ran into my room and slammed the door. I jumped in bed and pulled the covers over my head, I was so scared.

"Not long after that, I started to hear noises outside the house. They seemed to be very close to my window. I heard something like a sniffing sound, like a dog trying to get at a fox in its den. I buried my head under my blanket and held my pillow tightly around my ears so I couldn't hear anything. I was so scared. I eventually fell asleep.

"The next morning, I asked Mrs. Billings if she had heard anything during the night. She said that she didn't. She was still very sad over her husband's death. But I knew what it was. I knew the *Wechuge* had found me. It must have finally tracked me to Fort St. John after my mother died. I was terrified it had found Teddy waiting for me and killed him."

She paused again for a long time, biting at her knuckles on her right hand. I didn't want to interrupt her, as this was obviously coming from a place within her she had kept buried for a long time. "Before that nightfall, I told Mrs. Billings that I had to leave. I was sorry I couldn't go to Saskatoon with her but I had to leave, right away. She was obviously concerned, but I could see she wasn't going to try to stop me. I think she didn't have any strength left after her husband's death.

"Mrs. Billings gave me all the money as she had in the house, which wasn't a lot, but it was much more than I had ever seen at one time. I packed up as many of my belongings as I could in a suitcase and walked into town to catch the next bus. On my walk into town, I had to pass by the barn where Teddy and I were supposed

177

to meet the night before. I thought Teddy's body might be still lying on the floor. I didn't stop; I just walked past it as fast as I could. I didn't want to know.

"When I got to town, I found the next bus leaving was going to Vancouver. I didn't want to go there, but I saw that there was a stop in Kamloops. I had never been there, but it had a good sound to the name. It was a city, but not a huge city. I thought I could probably get work there. I could cook, I could take care of people, I could clean house. It felt right to me. I also thought that, if something *was* following me, it would have a very hard time finding me so far away from Fort St. John in a place with so many people. I didn't believe the *Wechuge* would leave the frozen north to follow me to a city in southern Canada.

"As it turned out, I was wrong. In the next four years, I had to move three more times. I went a little further south each time. I wound up in Everett here in Washington about two years ago, where I saw an ad for a helper here at the Missus' house. Her previous housekeeper had just had a baby, so she needed someone new. I came here to the house, much as you did, looking for a job. And I have been here ever since."

Willa looked at me with a touch of defiance, almost daring me to object to her story. I didn't say anything. I didn't know what I would have said even if I had wanted to say something.

She slapped lightly at the armrests of the rocking chair. "I am very sleepy. I will look in on the Missus before I go to bed. Would you turn all the wet clothes over and perhaps put another log or two on the fire? Hopefully, everything will be dry by tomorrow morning."

With that, Willa rose and walked silently to the doorway to Mrs. Cahill's room and went in. My mind was filled with images of shadowy beasts that hid in the bushes and a dead body huddled in a lump on a cold barn floor covered with straw. I mechanically stoked up the fire and started to rearrange our damp clothes. After flipping over a few garments so their damp side was exposed to the fire, I experienced a sudden flash of embarrassment when I realized I was holding Willa's white cotton underwear. I threw a quick glance at Martha's bedroom door to make sure I wasn't being observed. The cotton material was still damp in one or two places and warm from the fire. I lightly rubbed the soft fabric between my thumb and fingers. When I looked closer, I could see that the elastic around the waist was worn and the cotton frayed around the openings for her legs. The thoughts of grotesque monsters that had held sway in my head just seconds before vanished, replaced with remembered images of Willa and her nighttime visitation. I felt a rush of heat to face. Hurriedly, I hung the garment on the arm of the rocking chair. *Idiot*, I thought to myself. *She didn't know what she was doing. She was asleep! She didn't want you!* Still, there was no denying it been an incredibly intense and darkly mysterious sexual experience for me, one that I knew I would not be forgetting for a long time.

After I finished arranging the rest of the clothes and made certain the screen was set securely in front of the flames, I stood up and stretched the muscles in my shoulders, back and arms. After my exertions in the wet and cold, I was stiff all over. I looked around the shadowy room one more time and then shuffled off toward the stairway.

>> 13 <<

The next morning, I awoke to sunlight illuminating my small room. I lay still for a few minutes, trying to rid myself of the stale taste in my mouth. I assumed Willa had let me sleep in that morning. Unless Deer Valley had experienced a sudden heat wave during the night, we still weren't going anywhere. Eventually, the need to visit the little washroom across the hall forced me to roll out of bed. I looked around for my jeans and shirt until I remembered all my clothes were spread around the living room downstairs. Resigning myself to stumbling around in my pajamas until I could retrieve my clothes from downstairs, I found my way across the hall.

When I finally made it downstairs, I discovered Willa in Mrs. Cahill's room. She looked up with concern on her face as I knocked lightly on the doorframe.

"Hi, Willa. How's Martha doing this morning?"

"I don't know, Sean. I can't get her to respond to anything right now. Can you help me get her into the bathroom so I can get her cleaned up?"

Helping clean an elderly, non-responsive person who soiled herself overnight wasn't something I had an overwhelming desire to do. Given the circumstances, though, I knew it was necessary. Martha, even in her current state, was still my employer and Willa was my boss. I grimaced and moved around the side of the bed to help Willa lift Martha off the bed. At Willa's direction, we managed to get Martha's frail arms over each of our shoulders. From that position, we were able to lift her up with by making a cradle of our hands underneath her legs. There was not a lot of free space between the bed and her big walnut chest of drawers. I gritted my teeth as I banged my shin on the sharp corner of the small chest at the foot of the bed. Once we were in the bathroom attached to the bedroom, Willa stripped off Martha's nightgown and sleeping clothes while I held her. We then picked her up and gently placed her in the bathtub Willa had already filled with water heated on the kitchen stove. While Willa bathed Mrs. Cahill, I bundled up the clothing that was lying in a wad on the floor.

"Sean, you can just put those in the basket in bedroom. And would you strip off all the sheets off the bed? I will clean them after I get done here." As I turned to comply, I could very clearly understand why Willa had been crying when she said she didn't think she could manage caring for Mrs. Cahill in her condition. I would find it difficult to leave Willa, but if this was what my job at the farm was going to consist of for the next year, I wasn't going to be able to take it either. I absolutely felt that Mrs. Cahill deserved the best care she could afford. I just didn't believe it should be Willa and I that provided it.

I was suddenly presented with the mental image of all the military hospital beds that I had occupied after Pearl. I had been helpless for months and had required assistance with every aspect of life, including the most basic bodily functions. I remember the myriad of nurses that came by on an hourly basis to care for me, along all my hospitalized comrades-in-arms. These doctors, nurses and orderlies spend every minute of their workday caring for their patients. I felt a flush of shame at my feelings of just seconds before. *Yes, but that was their job! That's what they signed up for!* My mind scrabbled for rationalizations. *I didn't take this job to care for an invalid who can't make it to the bathroom by herself! I was going to chop firewood, fix broken down stairs and weed out the garden and plant a small plot of corn! I can't do this!*

Snow or no snow, I decided, we needed to get Mrs. Cahill into a hospital or a nursing home as soon as we could manage.

*   *   *   *

Later, sitting in Willa's normal place on the rocker in the living room, I kept watch over Martha, who we had seated on the couch. She was able to sit upright without assistance. Willa had placed Martha's hands in her lap, which had remained there since Willa had gone to clean up the soiled clothes and bedding. Martha sat there quietly by the side of the fire, her face a flaccid mask. I got up from the rocker and stooped over her to wipe a bit of drool from the corner of her mouth.

"Martha? Can you hear me?" I asked her quietly. She didn't respond. I bent down close to her face so that I could look into her eyes. They were a cloudy blue. I thought I could see some movement of her eyes but it could have been my imagination. Her gaze was unfocused. Her breathing was uneven, but at least it seemed stable.

I went to the front of the living room and pulled back the woven curtain of the window that looked out over the porch and the small front yard. The temperature seemed to be climbing. Snow still covered most everything, although I could see that the trees where shedding their patina of white. I could hear the dripping of melt water coming off the roof and striking the stairway. From my vantage point, I could barely make out the surface of the road. It looked to be still covered in snow, but I thought that I might be able to negotiate it with the Ford and its slippery tires. I wasn't sure which was the worst option, staying here for another night or two, caring for Martha and hoping she wouldn't get any worse, or venturing out in the car and trying to make it into town.

Sighing, I went back to continue my vigil from the other side of the hearth. We sat that way, each lost in our personal wilderness, for several more minutes until Willa came in from the kitchen.

"I finished up with her clothing. I hung it up in the pantry to dry. It's too cold out for me to hang them outside. I'm going to go make up her bed now."

I watched her pass through the living room and into Martha's bedroom. I noted immediately Willa seemed to have regained her usual composure. There were no outward signs of the ragged emotions she had exhibited over the last few evenings. Her posture was erect and she carried herself with the grace and fluidity that I had become familiar with over the last months. From my little knothole, it seemed to me that Willa had been able to absorb the bad news and was now "over the hump." *That was fast,* I thought to myself. *I wouldn't be able to do that.* I raised my right hand and gazed at the scar on the back of my hand and wrist. *I still haven't come to grips with this,* I thought to myself. I could easily see that Willa had much more composure and resiliency in her than I did in me. This admission did little to lighten my dark disposition.

183

My self-absorbed musings were broken by a small shriek coming from bedroom. Willa came rushing out, crying out with excitement, "I just saw Major! He's out back! If you hurry, you should be able to catch him!"

"What? Major?" I was slow to grasp what she was saying after having been fully immersed with feeling sorry for myself. I got up and, instead of grabbing my coat and boots, I walked as quickly as I was able into the bedroom and peered out the window. I couldn't see anything that looked like Major. I couldn't see even anything that moved other than the goats in the pen and a few chickens standing in the barn door.

I turned to Willa. "Are you sure you saw him? I don't see anything."

"Yes Sean, I am sure I saw him! Do you think I am lying to you? He ran across the yard from behind the barn! I could hear him barking! Listen!"

I stood still by the window for a few moments. My head jerked up when I realized that I thought I could hear a dog barking. I couldn't tell the direction the sound was coming from, as the window muffled all the noises from outside.

"Okay, then! I'll try to go round up Major." I rushed out to the front door, followed closely by Willa. "What an idiotic dog. I thought Shepherds had more sense than this," I muttered as I pulled on my boots. Willa handed me Major Cahill's coat. I pulled it over my shoulders as I went as fast as I felt able down the stairs and around the corner of the house.

"Major! Here, Major! Come, you stupid dog! You want your breakfast?" I yelled as loudly as I could as I trundled through the softening snow. I didn't see any sign of him as I rounded the back of the barn, but I was immediately heartened when I realized I could actually see his tracks. I groaned inwardly, however, when I saw they made a beeline straight toward the forest. I uttered a few more oaths regarding the intelligence of canines and their parentage in general while walking as fast as I could back up the snowy trail Willa and I had cut the night before. It took me several more minutes to make it under the trees where I found Willa the night before. I stood still very still under the green canopy and put my cupped hands behind my ears. I could hear Major's barking over to my right. That was the direction that the two of us had gone on our first journey into the woods. *Game on,* I thought. I remained there just long enough to button up the thick coat. Thrusting my hands deep into the pockets, I headed up the hill toward the cold granite outcropping, calling out Major's name whenever I thought I could spare the breath.

* * * *

It took over an hour for me to reach the rock outcropping. It looked the same as it did several months ago when Major and I made our brief visit, with the exception it was now blanketed in white. Sharp extrusions of wet, grey rock jutted through the snow. I glanced around. There was still no sign of Major, although I thought I could hear his barking in the distance from time to time. That was the only thing that kept me going. I would have turned back much earlier if not for the fact that I really believed he was somewhere close by.

I was breathing heavily, and my right leg and hip were on fire. I bent over with my hands on my knees and took several deep breaths. The white vapor drifted around my face for several seconds before wasting away in the cold air. As I stood upright, I wondered just what it was that I was doing out there. *Is this just about trying to find a lost dog,* I wondered to myself, *or did this have something to do with Willa?* I wasn't quite sure. I had missed the dog mightily the last few days, but it seemed to me at least part of my motivation was I had something to prove to her.

It was then I heard a loud *crack*, as if someone had stepped on a thick branch and snapped it in two. I turned quickly in the direction from where I thought the sound had come. I couldn't see anything except the motionless pillars of brown and green surrounding the outcropping. "Major?" I called out tentatively. *If it was Major, why wasn't he running joyfully to see his old buddy?* I asked myself. I felt a small thrill of fear run up my spine and settle in my scalp, which was suddenly covered in goose bumps. *Okay, this is getting pretty whacked out!* My fight-or-flight instincts were demanding attention. *I need to get out of here right now,* my internal voice screamed. The rational side of my mind wasn't putting up much of a fight. I experienced the same eerie feeling I had felt the first time I had come this way and thought I was being watched.

185

I had just turned to start my way back down the hill to the house when I froze in my tracks. The same warbling sound — the one Willa and I had heard while sitting in the living room weeks ago, the one I had so wanted to attribute to an owl or an injured animal — drifted out from underneath the canopy of the tall trees. It sounded very close. I attempted to shove back a rising, red-hot panic. Fearfully, I turned and looked back toward the forest. Just inside the shadows, I was horrified when I realized I could make out two glowing pinpoints of red. They appeared to be about ten feet off the ground. As I stared, a small clump of snow fell from somewhere above and hit the ground with a small *plop*, as if something had bumped the trunk of a small tree and knocked the snow off of its branches.

My mind shut down in terror. I turned and loped downhill as fast as I could, dragging my right leg behind me. I made it to the trees and did not stop running. I was making too much noise and gasping so loudly that it was impossible for me to hear if anything was coming behind me. At that point, I was beyond caring. I was running with the certainty that, if I stopped, I wasn't likely to live through what occurred next.

Eventually, though, I did have to stop. I was completely exhausted and my legs trembled from the unaccustomed exertion. I felt as if I couldn't take another step if my life depended on it. My right hip was screaming at me and I had a stitch in my side that felt as if someone had stabbed me an extra-long kitchen knife. With my hands on my knees, I tried to catch my breath as I looked wildly around. I didn't see anything out of the ordinary and I couldn't hear anything that sounded like someone or something in pursuit. I straightened up and...

Suddenly, I was back on the deck of the *U.S.S. West Virginia*, kneeling over the electric winch I had been working on. I realized I could hear the easily recognizable buzzing of airplanes approaching. *No! No, not again!* My inner voice screamed. *Not now!* The now-familiar scene I had experienced several times before once again thrust itself onto all my senses, as if a movie that I had watched several times had begun to unspool yet again. I looked up into the azure blue sky, astonished to see Japanese Zeros, large red dots on their fuselage and loaded with torpedoes, scream across the sky. I could hear explosions in the distance. I felt the familiar panic take hold in my gut, not being able to grasp what was occurring. Simultaneously, I understood that I was not actually in Hawaii and this was not December 7th, 1941. I was just experiencing some extremely vivid memories in my head. Very soon, I was going to see and feel the *U.S.S. Arizona* explode. When I launched myself over the railing, away from the explosion that rocked the *West Virginia*, I could see the flaming water rushing toward me. I was not at all surprised, however, when I found myself not underneath the water but back in my bedroom in Kalama. I was kicking at my father who was trying to get a good swing at my head. He connected and I went sprawling on the floor. I frantically attempted to find refuge underneath my bed, but felt myself being ripped out from underneath by his meaty hand around my ankle. I heard my mother rush in the door, screaming at my father, pulling at his shoulder and then...

I was sitting peacefully in the living room of the same house in Kalama. I had my copy of *Robinson Crusoe* in my lap. The binding of the book was tight and unbroken, although somehow I knew that the bound pages of my copy in Martha's spare bedroom had become detached from the front cover. Even though I realized I was reliving something from my personal history, I couldn't have said with any certainty what year it might have been. I didn't remember this.

I looked up from my reading, listening to the angry buzz of Dad's chainsaw out back. *He's finally cutting up that big branch from the cedar tree that fell last winter*, I thought idly. *It's about time he did something around here.*

I returned to my reading. I was just getting to the interesting part where Crusoe starts to salvage stuff off his wrecked ship before it sinks and all is lost forever. This was not the first time I had read the book, of course, so I knew what was going to happen next. But I liked this part.

In the midst of my reading, I suddenly became aware of the silence from the back yard. The chainsaw wasn't making any noise. I then heard my dad's hoarse yell. He sounded upset. *Well, when wasn't he upset?* I fumed to myself. *Ever since Mom died, he's always yelling at me to do this or that. He expects me to do everything all at once, and he never misses a chance to let me know when he thinks I am not keeping up with his expectations.* With a sigh of resignation, I tossed *Robinson Crusoe* over on the end table next to the sofa and got up to see what the hell he wanted now.

When I got out back, I could see my father lying on the ground next to the idling chainsaw. He was holding his leg. Startled, I started to run. When I got there, I could see a pool of deep red had formed underneath his leg and was already soaking into the brown packed dirt and weeds. He was clutching at his thigh, where I could see the blood seeping through the leg of his workpants he usually wore at the mill. As I watched, blood welled up around and through his clenched fingers. I knelt down beside him, taking in the half empty bottle of bourbon on its side a few feet away. I could smell the reek of liquor on his breath. I shook my head in disgust. *Yeah, Dad. That was really goddamn intelligent, using the chainsaw while drunk on your ass! Crap! You fucking idiot!*

"Sean, go inna house and call the doctor! Quick! I'm hurt real bad!" I could see the terror in his face. He was grasping at the jagged rip in the leg of his overalls, frantically trying to staunch the flow of blood. The wound was obviously deep, although I had no clue as to how he managed to cut himself on the inside of his thigh with a running chainsaw. I could see the flow of blood between his fingers increase with his heartbeat and then, after several seconds, slack off again. I had been a Boy Scout once, back before Mom died. I knew all about tourniquets and realized this would be a good time to try out my First Aid skills.

I slowly got to my feet and took several steps backwards. I looked around. Behind our house was a small creek and overgrown area, so that we only had neighbors on either side of us. I didn't see anyone around in either of those two houses. No one could see around to the back of the house if they drove by on the street out front. Not many did in our little cul-de-sac in the poor part of town.

I looked back at my father on the ground. "You're pathetic, you know that, Dad? You're pathetic." I crossed my arms and watched him writhe in pain and surprise.

"Sean, go call the doctor! You hear me! I'll take it out of your hide, you little shit!" He made an effort to get to his feet but his leg collapsed underneath him. He let out a yelp of pain and fell back to the ground. I saw that he was crying. "Sean, fer the love of God, go call me the damn doctor! Please!"

My father was pleading with me. He was actually pleading. The big bad ogre who thought it was just a barrel of laughs to beat up my mother as she lay, unresisting, on their bed. The monster who busted into my bedroom in the middle of the night and hammered on my face while I was still asleep. This guy who loved his booze more than he did his family. He was actually pleading for me to save him.

"Dad?" He stopped his shouting and looked at me expectantly, as if I was going to say something that would save him. "Fuck you, Dad." I turned away from his red, bleating face and walked back into the house. I thought to myself, *the more pissed off he is, the faster his heart is beating.* I let a small smile of satisfaction appear on my face, but only for a moment. I went back into the living room and picked up *Robinson Crusoe* and started to read.

* * * *

When I came to, I was on the ground. My eyes were jammed shut but I could hear something moving. It was quite close to me. I heard a snuffling sound next to my ear. The terror I had experienced earlier — before my epileptic fit or whatever the hell it was that kept happening to me — came rushing back. I remained frozen in position. Suddenly, something cold and moist poked me in my face. My eyes jerked open to the sight of the wet nose and brown eyes of Major. He whined his customary whine, likely questioning me as to what I was doing on the ground and wasn't it his suppertime yet.

"Goddammit Major! You scared the bejesus out of me! Shit! Boy, am I glad to see you!" I shook my head several times, trying to clear my mind of the fog that had moved in and made itself at home. Major, his pointed ears erect, prodded at me with his front paw. I put both my arms around his furry neck and gave him long hug. He pulled away from me and gave every indication of wanting to be away as soon as I got back on my feet.

I rolled over on my stomach and, after managing to make it to my hands and knees, hoisted myself to my feet. I blearily looked around. The surroundings were the same as they had been when I had halted my downhill rush. *No, not exactly the same*, I realized. It was almost dusk. The sun was already below the top of the trees. I realized I must have been out for a couple of hours. Suddenly remembering why I had been running, I gave a fearful look around me. I saw nothing but trees, rocks and snow.

I tried to bundle the coat closer around me. The cold ground had sucked most of the heat from my body. "Come on, Major. Let's get out of here." With that, we set off down the slope toward the house.

I was not certain how long we walked, as my mind was a jumbled mess from everything I had experienced in the last few hours. I was staggered by what I remembered from my last "hallucination." I attempted to dredge my memory of my life back in Kalama before I joined the Navy. I could come up with absolutely nothing that resembled what my vision had just handed to me. Nothing. What I remembered was that someone, I couldn't remember exactly who, had informed me that my father had been killed in an accident in the lumber mill when no one was around. I couldn't square my memory of that with what had just unfolded during my latest episode. *What the hell did that all mean?* I had no idea. I had a huge headache.

I was still wrapped up in my confusion when I realized I had been smelling smoke for the last few minutes. Major began barking furiously. He spun around to look at me expectantly and then, having decided that I was a bad bet, raced off down the hill without me. I hobbled down the slope as best I could. I couldn't fathom what might be burning at this time of the year. As I drew near the house, however, my suspicions began to transform into a gut-punch of fear. When I broke out into the clearing, I gasped in horror at the sight of Mrs. Cahill's house. Huge flames billowed out the back door and all the windows of the first floor. As I watched, the window of Willa's room above the kitchen shattered, blowing shards of glass outward over the backyard. Tiny flames began to lick at the top of her window frame.

"Willa!" I screamed as loudly as I could. I could see that there was absolutely no chance of making it inside from the kitchen door. I hobbled around the front of the house, hoping to try for the living room by the door on the porch. The flames hadn't taken hold as strongly as they had in the back of the house. I dashed up the stairs and threw open the front door. I could see through the entryway a wall of fire covered the back of the living room and the doorway to Mrs. Cahill's bedroom. I shielded my face with my arm as best I could from the smoke and searing heat. I thought I could make out a pathway through the inferno where I might just make it to the stairs, but I found that I was rooted in place. I could not will myself to make that dash to the stairway.

"Willa!" I screamed in panic. "Can you hear me? Are you up there?" I could see the wallpaper in the hallway turn black and curl itself into small cylinders of ash. All I could hear was the roar of the flames, glass breaking and the popping and snapping of ancient wood being consumed by the growing maelstrom. Horrified, I watched as flames flowed outward from where the kitchen had been, clinging to the ceiling.

I felt myself stumble backwards. My leg finally gave out and I was on my back lying on the porch. Within seconds, the entryway exploded into a mass of living flame that devoured everything it touched. Scrambling to my feet, I fled back down the stairs and ran around to the back. Frantically scanning the second story windows that I could see from the ground, I saw nothing but orange and yellow flames leaping violently from the windows. Several huge holes appeared in the roof. I saw nothing that might indicate anyone could survive if they were up there.

I realized I couldn't be certain they were inside the house when the fire began. The nascent hope that Willa had taken Martha to see a doctor was quickly shattered when I saw the rear bumper of the Ford sticking out of the barn door. Within minutes, the entire structure was a raging inferno. Both the top and bottom floors were engulfed in roaring flames. Black, acrid smoke illuminated by bright orange sparks billowed into the sky and was then taken sideways by the wind coming down from the mountains. I could hear the frenzied bleating of the goats in their pen. Major danced around me, barking loudly at nothing in particular.

I gradually sank to my knee with the sickening realization that there was absolutely nothing I could do against the raging conflagration. I had no idea how long I had been crying. I tried to scrub the grimy tears from my face with both hands. I grabbed Major by his neck and held on as tightly as I could. Sobbing, I buried my face in his soft fur. All I could hear was the thunderous roar of flames and the crashing of burning timbers as the house began to fall in on itself.

>> *Author's Notes* <<

This is a work of fiction. As such, all characters are purely a product of my imagination. However, all rivers, mountain ranges, railroads, hotels, towns, cities, states, provinces, countries and giant companies that produce airplanes are real and are used as locations in this imaginary tale. I believe I am also supposed to say something like, any resemblance to actual events, locales (other than as described above), organizations or persons, living or dead, is entirely coincidental.

The Native tribes described herein are, of course, real. I attempted to portray the Native characters in this book with dignity and respect. I do admit to taking several — hopefully minor — artistic liberties with the legends and religious ceremonies described in order to better fit the narrative. Any mistakes made are solely mine. Again, no disrespect is intended.

>> *Acknowledgements* <<

I would like to express my thanks to my family for always being there and allowing me to hog the computer almost every morning for the last nine months. I would like to give my heartfelt thanks to Cynthia Nowak for her invaluable assistance as mentor, editor and proofreader for this work. Also, a big thanks to David Bez for allowing me to use his amazing artwork on the front cover, as well as to Jamey Crow Bartley for his design of the front and rear covers and the title design. It's a wondrous thing when you discover friends and relatives who have exactly the skill set you need. And a totally gratuitous thank you to Uncle Bonsai for the beautiful, hilarious and, at times, distinctly odd music they have provided over the last four decades. They have been a constant source of inspiration and good feelings over the years.

Finally, I would like to give a huge shout-out to all current and former teachers. They do a very important and incredibly challenging job. Along with more respect, they deserve to get paid a lot more than they do.

>> *Author Bio* <<

After a thirty-seven year career in commercial aviation that involved technical writing of all sorts for many different types of audiences, this is Gregg's first work of fiction. He currently resides in Marysville, Washington with his wife, daughter and grumpy little dog.

>> *Credits* <<

Front Cover Art: *Herne*, by David Bez. Used with Permission.

>> Artist Bio <<

David studied BA (hons) Illustration at Manchester Polytechnic from 1984 to 1987. His illustration clients include Elle, G.Q., New Scientist, Rank, Xerox and E.M.I. He worked previously as a website designer and fused glass artist and is now working as a full time artist with galleries based in the United Kingdom. His paintings are in collections throughout the U.K., Europe, Australia and New Zealand.

Cover Design, Title Design and Layout: Jamey Crow Designs

>> *Bibliography* <<

Information and Inspiration

Arkowitz, Hal and Scott O. Lilienfeld (January 1, 2010). Why Science Tells Us Not to Rely on Eyewitness Accounts. *Scientific American.* Retrieved from URL https://www.scientificamerican.com/article/do-the-eyes-have-it/

Black Elk, Wallace and William S. Lyon. 1990. *Black Elk: The Sacred Ways of a Lakota.* San Francisco, California: Harper and Row.

Bruggmannn, Maximilien and Peter R. Gerber. 1989. *Indians of the Northwest Coast.* English translation. New York, New York: Facts On File Publications.

Coville, Walter J., Timothy W. Costello, Fabian L. Rouke. 1960. *Abnormal Psychology.* New York, New York: Barnes and Noble Books

Frazer, James G. Macmillan, 1890; Crown Publishers, Inc. version 1981. *The Golden Bough, The Roots of Religion and Folklore.* United States of America: Avenel Books, distributed by Crown Publishers, Inc.

Gilmore, David D. 2003. *Monsters: Evil Beings, Mythical Beasts, and All Manner of Imaginary Terrors.* Philadelphia, Pennsylvania: University of Pennsylvania Press.

Jung, Carl G. 1964. *Man and His Symbols.* London: Aldus Books Limited.

(No author noted, March 21, 2016). A History of Residential Schools in Canada. *CBC News Web Site.* Retrieved from URL http://www.cbc.ca/news/canada/a-history-of-residential-schools-in-canada-1.702280

70212698R00113

Made in the USA
San Bernardino, CA
26 February 2018